The Heart
of
Velletri

The Heart
of
Velletri

Michael J. Kannengieser

The Heart of Velletri
Copyright © 2019 Michael Kannengieser

Content Editor: Rakefet Orobona
Copy Editor: Elena Green
Cover Design: Elizabeth Dubos
Editor-in-Chief: Kristi King-Morgan
Formatting: Kristi King-Morgan
Assistant Editor: London Koffler

ISBN: 978-1-947381-17-9

Dreaming Big Publications
www.dreamingbigpublications.com

Dedicated to my father, Eugene Kannengieser. You were my father and my hero. Your memory lives on with your children and grandchildren. Your strength, courage, and wisdom are your legacy.

Prologue

Dad had few teeth, a scar on the right side of his neck, and a bullet fragment lodged near his spine. His right elbow, also shot in battle, would not extend all the way. One would not notice anything wrong with the limb unless he stood with his arms at his sides. Likewise, his hearing was diminished due to artillery barrages and gunfire – yet he never complained. As a kid, I marveled at the strength of the man who raised me. A veteran of World War II, Dad had seen combat in the unheralded Italian Campaign. The image I had of my father charging the enemy, clad in an olive drab uniform, while wielding a rifle thrilled me. My mind filled with fantasies about his bravery under fire in the face of malevolent Nazis.

My father, Eugene Koenigsmann, was a bear of a man; six feet tall with thick arms, large hands, and a barrel chest. No one called him Eugene. He hated that name. Dad insisted on being called Gene instead. The name, Eugene, had been in the family for generations. His great-uncle, Alphonse Eugene Koenigsmann, was a monsignor in the Catholic Church who lived in France. Most people heard the surname Koenigsmann and thought it was German. In fact, the name is not German but Alsatian. My father's ancestors were from the Alsace region in France. Msgr. Alphonse Koenigsmann, my father's great-uncle, wrote and published books in French. My grandfather was also named Alphonse. Yet his name was Alphonse Eugene Jean Hippolyte Koenigsmann. My grandmother liked the name Eugene and that was what my father had to endure his entire life. At the Thanksgiving table one year, my Uncle Richard from my mother's side asked him why he was given that name. Dad told him that Eugene came from his father. Afterward, I heard him exclaim, "Thank God I wasn't named Hippolyte."

My father's voice was a deep bass, and his hair was almost black, combed straight back with no part. Dad wore dark, thick-framed glasses that gave him a distinguished look, like that of a doctor or business tycoon. Yet he was a mechanic by trade. Oil burners, air conditioners, refrigerators, my father could repair nearly any motor or machine. These were some of the many skills that he had acquired while working at the Brooklyn Navy Yard and for the now-defunct Long Island State Park Commission.

From the moment I could walk, I knew that my father had been a soldier. He kept a few artifacts from his service in his closet. When no one was looking, I went in there to hold them and try them on. A helmet, canteen, ammo belt, and backpack hung from pegs at the back of the closet. I pestered him to tell me what the army was like and how he got shot my entire life. The story was not relayed to me all at once. Snippets and vignettes conveyed to me through the years. Most were relayed to me by my father, others by my grandmother. She spoke with a proud smile as she shared the painful memory of learning that her son had been injured and worrying if he would survive. That is how I recall the adventures and travails that shaped my father's service in World War II. They are a jumble of tales which play out in my mind like grainy, black and white newsreel footage with Dad leading the charge into battle as a conqueror.

Although my father shared much with me about his time spent in basic training and anecdotes about army life, he kept details about his role in combat a secret. My grandmother had heard the tale long ago from my father when he returned from overseas. Grandma provided me with various accounts of him during the war. Perhaps she was betraying a promise of confidentiality between her and her son by telling me, I thought. Dad was shot, left for dead, and revived. Where he fought, how he was wounded, and how he had survived remained a mystery for decades. To tell the story as I know it now, I need to share all that I had learned in the sequence that I heard it. My father was in the army for eighteen months. What I had discovered during my lifelong investigative quest was that the man he became, how he raised his family, worshipped God, and overcame hardship was molded by his experiences in the war.

Dad met my mother, Ann Cusick, when he was twenty eight years old. They were at her friend Marie's wedding. Dad worked with Marie's brother, Clifford. Ann had just turned twenty. He asked her to dance, and she said yes. They danced for a few songs and talked for the entire evening. Over the next month, Dad asked mom to marry him three times on three separate dates before she accepted. They married six months later. They rented an apartment near my father's childhood home in Bay Ridge, Brooklyn. It wasn't long before Ann was expecting their first child.

My sister Cynthia, or Cindy as we call her, is the oldest. My brother, Raymond, was born three years after Cindy. I am the youngest Koenigsmann, five years younger than Ray. Ray married his high school sweetheart, Linda Reynolds. They have a seventeen-year-old daughter, Jessica, and a fifteen-year-old son, Raymond junior. Cindy was married at age twenty-three to a New York City fire fighter named Daniel McMahon. Daniel died while fighting a house fire in Brooklyn at the age of twenty-nine. They had a son, Jeffrey, who is now twenty-five years old and who also became a firefighter, following in his father's footsteps. Cindy is a math teacher, and Ray works for the New York City Sanitation Department as a mechanic. My wife, Mandy, and I do not have children together. Yet I have a twenty-nine-year-old daughter, Judith, who lives in Florida. She is engaged to a highway patrolman named Henry who does nothing but talk to me about police work when they come to visit.

While I am proud to be a father, I am not proud of how I became one. In high school, I had a brief relationship with a girl named Theresa Hemmings. We were both seventeen-year-old high school seniors. Theresa and I also shared the same birthday, July 20th, and we saw that as a sign that we were supposed to be together forever. After dating for almost three months, we discovered that Theresa was pregnant. My mother and father were appalled at first, but they decided to dedicate themselves to being grandparents. Theresa's parents threw her out of the house. Mom and Dad took her in, and she stayed with us for a week. Then the Hemmings became more embarrassed by their actions than Theresa's pregnancy, and they begged her to return home.

After our daughter, Judith, was born, Theresa went to community college. I worked a string of crappy jobs while trying to figure out what to do with my life. I took the police test, never thinking I had a chance of becoming a cop. Judith lived with the Hemmings. I went there as often as I could to care for her. My mother and father bought toys and clothes and doted on their granddaughter. The Hemmings and my parents became close friends. Because of their close relationship, Judith spent a lot of time at our house. Ray and Cindy were often called upon to babysit when I worked. In the end, Theresa and I realized that we were not in love and that marriage was out of the question. I eventually dated other girls, and Theresa dated guys from college. Despite our breakup, Theresa never prevented me from seeing our daughter. When I joined the NYPD my long hours and rotating shifts made it difficult to see Judith, but I did the best that I could.

I met Mandy Thompson when Judith entered college. Mandy had just graduated Stony Brook University and had started working at a marketing firm. I was almost thirty-eight years old with eighteen years on the job. Mandy was barely over five feet tall. She had short, dark hair and fair skin. However, I learned later as we continued to date, she could get a dark tan in the summer. This was due to her Italian heritage. She played tennis in high school, and she kept herself in shape at the gym. She had brown eyes, round cheeks, and wore minimal makeup. A significant drawback early in our relationship was that Mandy is ten years younger than me. The problem was mine, not hers. I did not feel like I could ask her to fall in love with an older man. Mandy said that age did not matter to her, and she also did not mind becoming a stepmother to Judith.

I fell in love with Mandy before she loved me. Mandy and I married one year before Judith graduated with a degree in Computer Science. Soon after we returned from our honeymoon, Judith moved to Florida. Being separated from Judith, I felt ashamed. Having been raised by a dedicated father whom I idolized, I believed that I did not measure up to his ideal of how a father should behave. Dad cared for my siblings and me when we were sick, attended our school plays, and helped with our homework. My father was available when I needed advice, and he took the time to toss a baseball back and forth in the yard with me. By comparison, I was a terrible father.

Yes, my dad was a good man and raised us well. But he was not without faults. He was stubborn, he did not like strangers, and he had a temper. Dad was a man of few words, and he did not have any friends outside people he talked to at work. While he was deeply religious, a Catholic who drove us to church each Sunday in his gold Oldsmobile Vista Cruiser, he wasn't above taking things home from his job. Household goods that we needed, such as window fans or tools found their way into the back of his station wagon. He saw that as a perk of being employed and not as theft. Many from his generation did the same thing. Nearly all my friends' fathers brought home whatever they needed from work. Dad smoked, rarely drank alcohol except for an occasional beer, and he swore a blue streak when he was irritated. When I was a kid, Dad seemed to be irate quite often.

When I was ten years old, a neighbor of ours, Mr. Holt, grabbed my collar and yelled at me for cutting across his lawn at the corner to get to the other block. Later that night, my mom told my father what had happened. Dad banged on Mr. Holt's door, demanding that he come outside. My mother stood at the end of our driveway, begging him to return. I held my mom's hand and watched the scene unfold, titillated by Dad's boldness. Neighbors came out of their homes, and some of my friends stopped in front of Mr. Holt's house on their bikes to witness the confrontation.

My father's face turned beet red, and he let loose a fusillade of profanity that would make a truck driver blush. Mom covered her ears. Mr. Holt cowered indoors while shouting at my father to go away from behind a window screen. When Dad returned home, he scolded me for walking on Mr. Holt's grass. In those days, no one called the police for disputes. Those matters were settled the way my father handled it, just how he learned to do it as a kid growing up on the streets of Brooklyn. I had hoped I would grow up to be like him one day, tall, robust, and able to make men recoil in fear if they crossed me. Yet my pals, like everyone else, knew that he had a kind heart and a deep love for his family and friends.

My failure as a parent rested solely on me and my irresponsible behavior. Secretly, I wished that my father hadn't been devoted to his wife and kids. I danced along a line of admiration and resentment towards him. My treacly recollections of his parenting had as much to do with my disgust for my own behavior as my disregard for his shortcomings. Dad worked long hours and did not spend much time with us. When he came home, he was usually tired and grouchy. On weekends, he would spring chores on Raymond and I as we were walking out the door to our friends' houses. Still, he would make it up to us by giving us money or taking us fishing when he could. When I was in high school, I finally understood that he hated being so irritable and distant from his family. His sense of duty to put food on the table held a higher priority than playing catch with his kids or flying a kite in the backyard. Holding those faults against him was difficult. And again, my culpabilities as a parent were clear. I thought my father was a man whom I could measure up to.

Dad rarely showed emotion. I walked in on him after school the day after Mom had been admitted to the hospital. He was in the kitchen, sitting at the table. Mom had been ill for years, and eventually, she was diagnosed with Systemic Lupus Erythematosus. Mom was about five feet, three inches tall. Her hair was red, and she had fair skin. She kept a smile on her face, though she typically experienced pain. I have memories of her singing while she cooked dinner. Her voice rose to falsetto as she sang Ave Maria. Perry Como sang that song every Easter, and mom loved that song.

Dad saw me come in and wiped a tear from the corner of his eye. He told me to sit down. I pulled a chair out from the kitchen table and placed my textbooks down in front of me. Dad sat at the head of the table to my left. He talked about mom, her sickness, and how she would need a lot of medical attention.

"How are you feeling, Dad?" I asked.

"Me? I'm fine. I'm not worried about me," he said.

"It's just that you work so hard caring for mom all the time. I don't want you getting sick or dropping dead of a heart attack." I gulped. Dad glared at me as if I had cursed during Sunday mass. Finally, he smiled and held my forearm.

"Michael, I've almost died so many times that I'm not afraid of death. I just worry about your mother and you kids if I am gone." He grinned like he had four aces in his hand at a high-stakes card game. Then he stood and walked out of the room.

That mighty man, the comic book hero in my mind, was my idol, I thought. He had stories to tell that he would not reveal. Thinking back on it, my desire to uncover the secrets my father kept about combat had more to do with inflating his stature to the point where no one, not even me, could compare to him. That way I could convince myself that it was impossible for me to be like him. I was still a kid inside, enthralled with an army man, with a dad who faced bombs and bullets and lived to tell about it. The jumble of tales about the exploits Dad had as an eighteen-year-old kid overseas contained wide gaps. I ached to uncover more details. I needed to hear how he survived, what he feared most, and what he saw when he nearly died. The accounts of his service flicker in my head out of order. Perhaps when I heard the rest of the tale, I thought, I could bridge the gap between my ideal of him as a valiant soldier and an imperfect, yet well-meaning, father.

Chapter 1

September 1943

Basic training at Camp Wheeler, Georgia was a day in the past. Gene and his new buddies were headed by train to Newport News, Virginia to be shipped overseas. It was dusk, and the fading sun streamed through the windows and shined on the troops dozing in the car. Some chatted with each other and others gazed out the window at red barns and silos. Gene had ridden on the subway for most of his life, but he was not used to such pastoral scenery. His mind drifted as he eyed long stretches of pastures, trees, and miles of split rail fences.

None of the newly graduated privates knew whether they were headed to the Pacific theater or Europe. Killing Japanese soldiers or Germans didn't matter to Gene. While he had been caught up in the wave of patriotism that swept the country after the Japanese attack on Pearl Harbor two years earlier, by the time he was old enough to enlist, he did so more out of duty to his family than to his country.

His mother often complained that there was not enough money for food and the utilities. She worked as a secretary at American Express. This was a job that Gene's great uncle Edward recommended her for. Uncle Edward was his mother's uncle. He had worked for American Express since he was twenty years old. Gene was fascinated by the fact that his Uncle Edward rode in the Pony Express when he was seventeen. Gene loved him, and they were close. On Sundays, Uncle Edward would come by and take Gene to mass in Manhattan at Our Lady of Grace Church. After the service, Uncle Edward would take him for a slice of pie at a nearby coffee shop. Gene would sit and listen to him tell riveting tales of racing on horseback away from thieves and fording rivers while carrying the mail.

Since the end of June, after Gene had graduated high school, his mother had been hinting that he should join the army so he could send her home much needed cash. What annoyed Gene more than anything about his mother's pleading was that he had planned on enlisting anyway, despite her insistence. His father was in the army during The Great War, and it was only natural that Gene follows in his footsteps. Also, Uncle Edward had been only seventeen when he was given a six-gun and a sack of mail to deliver across hostile territory. Gene wanted to be brave just like his dad and his uncle.

Gene knew better than to believe his mother's sob story about the state of their finances. Thick envelopes filled with cash routinely found a way to their home from Mr. Molfetta. Gene worked for him also, which helped to pay for groceries and electricity. The extra money provided by Mr. Molfetta was given out of loyalty to Alphonse, who was respected even in death. One day, just before his sixteenth birthday, Gene attempted to return a bundle of bills Mr. Molfetta had delivered to their home.

"Gino, you're a big, strong man like your father. Now be more like him and take the money. Alphonse would never turn down an offering. Besides, your father earned much more for me than I have repaid to you and your mother," Mr. Molfetta said. *Gino.* Mr. and Mrs. Molfetta always called him Gino. This made Gene feel special. Gene shook his hand and left with the money in his pocket. After that, he did not feel ashamed about accepting the assistance.

A week after graduating from high school, Gene entered the recruiting station located a few blocks from his house. A sergeant dressed in a sharp uniform sat behind a desk with his head down, filling out a form. Gene waited with his arms at his sides and his legs together until the man took notice of him. The sergeant lifted his head and sized Gene up.

"How old are you, son?" The sergeant had a thick, southern drawl, maybe from Tennessee or Kentucky, Gene thought. The sergeant was in his early forties with a crew cut and a cleft chin. He stood up and walked around to the front of the desk. Gene took a step back.

"Seventeen, sergeant." Gene gulped.

"When do you turn eighteen?" The sergeant folded his arms.

"July eleventh, sergeant." Gene felt sweat dripping from the back of his head and down his neck.

"Can you see well without glasses, or are you nearly blind?" The sergeant leaned forward and examined him. Then he straightened himself.

"I see well enough, sergeant. I still need them, though." Gene's legs were so stiff that they began to tremble.

"You can't enlist until you're eighteen, son. Let me take down our name and address so I remember who you are when you return." The sergeant returned to his seat and picked up his pencil. He took a small sheet of paper from a drawer and poised himself to write.

"What's your name?"

Gene cleared his throat. "Eugene Koenigsmann."

"Koenigsmann? Are you a kraut?" The sergeant stretched the corner of his mouth.

"No, sergeant. I'm from Brooklyn." Gene shifted his weight and wiped his sweaty palms on his slacks. The sergeant laughed.

"I'm teasing you, Eugene. Now tell me where you live." The sergeant tapped his pencil on the desk and waited for

Gene's response. The sergeant's playful accusation had Gene tongue-tied. Finally, Gene told him where he lived. The sergeant jotted down the information and then set his pencil aside.

"You've done good, young man. Your mom and dad should be proud of you. Now you come back here after your birthday, you hear?"

"Yes, sergeant," Gene said. Gene raised his arm and saluted the sergeant.

"Whoa, not yet, Eugene. Though I appreciate the respect. Go on now. Get home and start running and doing pushups. I'll be here waiting for you." The sergeant smiled and sat back. Gene nodded and left the storefront.

A bright shaft of sunlight stirred Gene out of his daydream. He had been facing the window so long as he recalled his mother and the sergeant at the recruiting station that he had forgotten that he was on a train. His buddy, Louis, nudged his elbow. Gene turned to face him.

"Hey Gene, when are we gonna get there? My ass hurts from these seats."

"I dunno, Leakey, another day or so? They stop at every station. I guess the engineer is showing off the train to his friends." Gene pointed his thumb at his chest. "Hey everyone, look at me. I'm driving a train!"

Louis chuckled. "You're hilarious, Gene. I can't make anyone laugh."

"That wasn't a joke. I think these hillbillies come to the station to see trains for fun, and the engineer is delighted to step out in his cap and overalls," Gene said as he carried on with his mocking premise. "If you think that's funny, I've got a million more just like that one."

Louis Leakey was the closest person to New York Gene could find in basic training. Louis was from Newark, New Jersey and was not like the guys from the Midwest and the South. Gene and Louis were *city boys, Yankees,* or *city slickers,* as the southern boys referred to them. They didn't know how to build fires or pitch tents. But the *rednecks,* or *hicks*, as Gene and Louis called them, soon learned they knew how to fight. Not all the guys from the South disliked northerners, Gene learned. He had pals such as Edward Grimes from Alabama. Basic training was just like home to Edward, except for the marches and pushups. Edward, or Eddie, as he liked to be called, was comfortable during the long hikes when they trained in the woods. Other pals he and Louis made were Reggie Jones, Wayne Bennett, and Trevor Hartwick. Gene had hoped they would all ship out together and stay buddies throughout the war.

Gene and Louis rested on their duffels bags to get some sleep. Gene put his glasses in his shirt pocket. After a few minutes, he was sound asleep. The engine's whistle blast woke them in the morning. It was daybreak, and the train pulled into the station. A long line of buses queued up parallel to the tracks. The drivers stood next to their vehicles and watched the locomotive stop and doors open.

"Gene, this is it. We're getting off. They have buses outside for us." Louis tapped Gene's knee. The others seated near them were getting up and gathering their bags and other belongings. Gene stood up and took his glasses from his pocket. They slipped from his fingers. He bent over to pick them up.

"Lou, watch it," Gene said. It was too late. Louis had stepped on them, breaking the lenses and bending the wire frame.

"Oh damn, Gene. I'm sorry," Louis said.

"Shit, now what am I supposed to do?" Gene picked up his mangled spectacles and held them in front of Louis' face.

"Get them fixed?" Louis shrugged his shoulders.

"Get them fixed? Why that's simple enough. I never would have thought of that," Gene huffed and then put the glasses back in his shirt pocket.

"Again, I'm sorry, Gene," Louis said.

"Forget it. It was an accident. They'll issue me a new pair, I'm sure. It wouldn't be so bad if we were back at Camp Wheeler, but who the hell knows how things work here?"

They disembarked the train, each lugging their cumbersome duffel bags. Gene approached the first sergeant he saw and asked him what to do. The sergeant yelled for him to board the bus. Gene snapped a salute and obeyed his order. Louis followed Gene onto the bus. They drove for about ten minutes from the train station to their destination. Inside the camp, hundreds of troops walked in ranks, alone, or in pairs. This was their last stop before being sent out to the theater of war. Thousands of young men were processed through the base each week. Gene and Louis waited with the others for instructions. Finally, a sergeant came aboard. He ordered them to go to their barracks and told them where the barracks were located. He then told them not to get too comfortable, because they would ship out within days. The moment he concluded his speech, he instructed them to exit the bus and find their quarters.

Gene and Louis found theirs after about twenty minutes of wandering around. The building was constructed the same as their barracks in Camp Wheeler. It was a two-story structure, wood framed and painted white with the essentials for amenities. Bare light bulbs dangled from the ceiling, and a latrine was at one end of the building. The sergeant's quarters were in a room to the right of the entry door.

"I've got to find out what to do about this," Gene said as he tossed his duffel bag onto the bottom bunk of the first rack he saw. Louis chose the top bed of Gene's rack.

"Attention!" one of the privates called out.

"At ease." The same sergeant who spoke to them on the bus entered the barracks. He appeared to be in his mid-twenties. The sergeant had blond hair with a government-issued crew cut. His physique was muscular, like a football player, and he had a military bearing that matched any of the drill sergeants Gene had encountered in basic training. To Gene, he seemed more mature than some of the young hooligans who had placed bets with his father or asked for a loan. Since enlisting in the army, Gene developed new standards for judging who was tough or deserved respect. The guys who sought the services of his father or Mr. Molfetta were not model citizens, Gene realized. He now looked up to his superiors instead of the thugs on the streets of Brooklyn. The exceptions were Mr. Molfetta and those in his employ.

"My name is Sergeant Whitaker," he said. "All of you will be under my command for the next twenty-four hours or so." Sgt. Whitaker paced back and forth between the bunks as he spoke, looking each soldier in the eye. "As I stated on the bus, don't get too comfortable. I'll have your orders by ten-hundred hours tomorrow. You have five minutes to settle in here and then assemble outside. We will be heading to the mess hall. I'm sure you all have an appetite. Now, get moving." Sgt. Whitaker paused and held his hands behind his back as though he was standing at parade rest. He grinned and scanned the room. Gene and Louis looked at each other.

"He scares me. Thank God we're only here for a few days," Louis said.

"He's all right. He's got an easy detail, and he knows it. He looks tough, but he hasn't said anything bad." Gene removed his cap and tucked it into his waist with half hanging out, as was standard. Then he took his broken glasses out once more to show the sergeant. "I have to talk to him before we head out. Wish me luck," Gene said. Gene took a deep breath and approached the sergeant.

Gene approached the sergeant and stood at attention. "Excuse me, Sergeant Whitaker." Sgt. Whitaker faced him.

"What is it, private?" Sgt. Whitaker's voice boomed across the barracks. The rest of the soldiers stopped what they were doing and watched.

"My glasses are broken, sergeant. I need them fixed." Gene held them up in the palm of his hand.

"How did they break, private?" Sgt. Whitaker sneered.

"On the train, sergeant. They fell, and someone stepped on them." Gene gulped.

"Who stepped on them?" Sergeant Whitaker bent forward and eyeballed him. A bead of sweat ran down the side of Gene's cheek.

"I don't know, sergeant. There were a lot of us on the train." The other soldiers chuckled.

"I didn't hear anyone tell a joke!" The sergeant snapped his head around and glared at the others. The platoon fell silent. Then Sgt. Whitaker turned his attention back to Gene.

"Private, you will head to the medical unit after you have had some chow, and do not do anything so foolish as to drop your eyeglasses again. If you can't see the enemy, you cannot fight them. Let this be a lesson to you. Am I clear?" Sgt. Whitaker straightened up and placed his hands on his hips.

"Yes, sergeant!" Gene said.

"You're dismissed," Sgt. Whitaker said. "You're all dismissed. Get outside now and form ranks." The sergeant pointed to the exit. Outside, Louis stood next to Gene in the rear rank.

"So how did your little chat with the sergeant go? He seems like a nice guy, huh?" Louis laughed to himself.

"Ha-ha. Go sit on a tack," Gene said. "Now I have to ask another fifty people where the damn medical unit is. Do you see this place? It's a small city." Gene shook his head.

"I'll help you find it. I'll be your seeing eye dog," Louis said.

"Thanks, pal." Gene chuckled.

Sgt. Whitaker called them to attention and then led them to the mess hall. Gene was hungrier than he thought, and he piled his tray high with eggs, grits, bacon, and toast. Gene and Louis ate quickly and then set out to find the medical unit. Gene asked a corporal, a tall, lanky man who was about a year older than the two of them. He reasoned that a corporal would be less likely to deal him a tongue lashing like Sgt. Whitaker did. The corporal squinted at Gene and Louis and then blinked.

"Are you boys shitting me? It's right there," he said. The corporal pointed behind them, where Gene and Louis had just passed. Gene and Louis looked at each other and rolled their eyes.

"Thank you, corporal," Gene said. The corporal walked away without saying anything.

They went inside and told a nurse what had happened. She sat behind a small desk. Behind her was a door with a frosted pane that had the names of doctors and their ranks. The nurse was an older woman in her forties with her hair worn in a tight bun beneath her cap. She wore a white skirt and tunic with white stocking and shoes. Gene was informed that he needed an eye exam, and the new glasses would take a week to be delivered. Louis placed his hand on Gene's shoulder.

"A week? We're supposed to ship out tomorrow," Louis said.

"I'm afraid that he won't be shipping out, but you will be, private," the nurse said. Then she asked Gene to fill out a form and wait to see the optometrist. She handed him a clipboard and a pencil. Gene took them from her with the same disgust he'd have if she'd given him a dirty tissue.

"I guess I'll see you later?" Gene said. He held the clipboard in both hands.

"Yeah, sure. I'll meet you at the barracks." Louis smiled, nodded to the nurse, and then left. In under an hour, Gene was examined and sent back to Sgt. Whitaker with a note. He found Sgt. Whitaker standing outside the barracks, making small talk with another sergeant. The other sergeant was smaller than Whitaker with thick arms and puffy cheeks. Whitaker saw Gene approach.

"What is it now, private?" Sgt. Whitaker held his hand out to take the paper from Gene.

"Orders, sergeant. They're from Capt. Gibbons. He's the eye doctor." Gene stopped, stood at attention and saluted. Whitaker returned his salute. Gene then handed the sheet to Whitaker.

The sergeant mouthed the words as he read them.

"How do you pronounce your name, private?" He looked at Gene with his mouth open.

"It's pronounced Koenigsmann. The first part sounds like *cone*, like an ice cream cone," Gene said.

"CONE-igs-man? You're a a kraut, aren't you?" Sgt. Whitaker elbowed the other sergeant. They both laughed.

"No, sergeant. My relatives are from France." Gene bit his lower lip. He had been through this line of questioning before, and he wished that he had answered yes.

"That sounds like bullshit to me. Are you some sort of French-Kraut spy or something?" Whitaker was taking pleasure out of teasing Gene. Gene imagined this scene taking place back in Brooklyn. His father would have broken both of Sgt. Whitaker's legs, and then he would have lit a cigar as if nothing had happened. However, his dad was not there, and Gene was stuck dealing with the sergeant by himself.

"Alsace-Lorraine, sergeant. My family is from Alsace-Lorraine in France," Gene said in a flat tone.

"Listen, Private Koenigsmann. You and I are going to be together for a while it seems. Go make yourself scarce. You're dismissed."

"Thank you, sergeant," Gene said. He stood at attention and saluted. Sgt. Whitaker returned the gesture, and then Gene turned and walked away. He did not bother meeting Louis in the barracks as he had promised. It was Louis' fault that Gene was in that predicament in the first place. Because of Louis, he was going to be shipped out with a bunch of strangers and not the guys he had trained with. Gene felt the emotion well up within him. Hanging around the camp with Whitaker was going to be like having a root canal each day, he thought. Still, the base was big enough for him to hide from Sgt. Whitaker, and Gene would find places to lay low.

After an hour or so, he calmed down and decided to return to the barracks. He was met outside by Whitaker, who explained that Gene would be reassigned to another barrack with soldiers who were in similar situations as him.

"Get ready to peel a lot of potatoes," Whitaker said. Gene could feel his face become flush. He went inside the building, retrieved his duffle bag, and walked out. He did not see Louis and figured that he was with other guys hanging out somewhere. It was just as well, he thought. Gene was angry enough that he did not want to see him ever again.

At the new barrack, Gene met up with four other privates. They greeted each other and exchanged names. Privates Thomas Ecklund, Brent Morris, Harold Beasley, and Horace Fuller seemed like nice guys. They were the only five people quartered there. Beasley introduced himself to Gene with an enthusiastic handshake. Gene liked Harold right away.

"What's this I hear about peeling potatoes?" Gene asked as he set his duffel bag down on a bunk.

"That's horseshit. Almost nobody knows we're here. Those sergeants just like to bust chops," Ecklund said. "We get up with revelry just like everyone else, eat chow, go hide in the woods, come back for lunch, and then go into town until supper time. If you lay low, they don't give you anything to do. It's these dumbasses from the sticks who stand around with their thumbs hooked in their belt loops that drive the sergeants crazy. If they see you loafing, they'll make you clean latrines or paint fences. We've been ducking all of that." Ecklund sat down and lit a cigarette.

"What are you guys doing hanging out here then?" Gene asked with an eyebrow raised.

"Getting ready for lunch," Harry said. "We've got this routine down pat."

Gene stretched the corner of his mouth, careful not to seem too relieved. He had figured that if these GIs had it so good, they were either lucky or too dumb to see the pitfalls. He dropped his duffel bag on a nearby bunk and sat down. Gene's eyes were itchy because he had to squint to see anything close to him. He rubbed his eyes and wondered if he could endure a week without being able to see clearly.

"Ready for chow?" Harry asked. Gene shrugged his shoulders and stood. The others made haste out the door. They assembled out front and put their caps on.

"Gene, we spread out, either two at a time or alone. The sergeants become nosy when they see three or more guys together at once. We'll split up and meet in the mess hall," Ecklund said.

"Sure thing," Gene said. He nodded at him.

"I'll walk with you, Gene," Harry said. The others walked ahead of them. Harry and Gene waited for a few seconds before they followed.

"I hate the army. I can't believe I enlisted," Harry said.

"You would have been drafted anyway," Gene said.

"Yeah, but if I complained after being drafted, no one could blame me."

"I can't say that I hate the army. I just miss home," Gene said.

"Yeah, me too. I have a girlfriend. She's probably off with some other guy by now, some old man who's too old to fight and drives a big car." Harry chuckled.

"It's good that you can laugh about it," Gene said. He looked at Harry and grinned.

"What else am I going to do? I send her letters. She writes me back. But if I mention getting married, she doesn't react. The next letter I get from her, she talks about her job and her cat. I can't stand that damn cat," Harry said.

A lieutenant walked by and Gene and Harry both saluted. The lieutenant returned the gesture.

"Don't keep bringing it up. Besides, is that any way to propose to a woman? You want to get down on one knee and ask her to marry you while holding the ring in your hand." Gene looked at him and snorted.

"I guess you're right," Harry said. "Is that how you plan to ask your girlfriend to marry you?"

"When I find the right girl, yeah. Right now, I don't have a girlfriend waiting for me at home. I had girlfriends, but they never lasted."

"Why is that?" Harry asked.

They turned a corner and continued walking behind the others.

Gene shrugged. "I went to school, and I had to work. I made a lot of money, but I always gave most of it to my mom.

I just never seemed to have enough time to go on dates," Gene said.

The two of them stopped in the queue in front of the mess hall. Ecklund, Morris, and Fuller were ahead of them.

"I'll tell you one thing, Harry. When I do get married, it will be with someone I truly fall in love with, and it will be forever. I don't want to get married just because a girl thinks it's time or anything. If your girl at home doesn't want to get married right now, don't keep bringing it up. But I suppose she wants you to get down on one knee and ask her," Gene said. He craned his head to see past the long line and into the mess hall.

"That's good advice, Gene. Thanks. I'll do as you say. Now I just need to live through the war and save up for a ring," Harry said. They both laughed.

After lunch, they split apart again and met up in a wooded area just outside the base. Ecklund showed Gene a shaded area with a fallen tree where they could sit. There were cigarette butts and a few empty soda cans strewn about. It was apparent that they were not the only ones who knew of this hideaway.

For over an hour, they chatted and joked around. The group talked about home and their families. Gene kept silent for most of the time. His work for Mr. Molfetta would have required explanations that they would not appreciate, he thought. Running numbers and helping to smuggle booze at such a young age would either impress them or cause them to dislike him. Gene listened in on the conversation.

"Someone's coming." Ecklund stood up. He looked in both directions. To their right, a sergeant walked onto the grass from the dirt pathway. He was tall with broad shoulders and stern, brown eyes. His voice was deep and intimidating. The sergeant pointed at them. They all stood at attention.

"What are you soldiers doing here? Don't you have anywhere to be or something to do? Come with me, all of you, now!"

They put their hats on and walked behind the sergeant all the way back to the camp. The sergeant let them to a building with a small lobby, and they were told to wait outside. There was an office door with a translucent window, and they could hear the sergeant talking to someone inside. Lettering on the window read: *Lieutenant Rossi.* One at a time, the sergeant called them into an office. Ecklund went in first. He was inside for less than a minute. The door opened, and Ecklund came outside with a grave expression. He cast his eyes down as he walked and furrowed his brow.

"Good luck in there, fellas," he said. He placed his cap on his head and left the building. Fuller went in next and then came out with the same expression as Ecklund. Morris took his lumps after him and then Harry. Harry came out after about two minutes with a grim look.

"I got kitchen detail. I'll see when I see you, buddy." Harry patted Gene's shoulder and then exited. Gene gulped and then squared his shoulders. The sergeant opened the door and motioned for Gene to enter. Gene stepped inside and stood at attention. The sergeant stood next to the lieutenant with his hands behind his back. He looked at Gene with a menacing grin. It was clear to Gene that what he thought earlier was correct. While his newfound pals had enough guile to hide from the officers, they weren't smart enough to evade them for too long. Gene had the sense that this sergeant prided himself on hunting those shirking duty.

"You were caught off base without leave by Sergeant Hynes. What was it that you and the others were doing in the woods, private?" Gene clenched his jaw.

"Sir, we were smoking cigarettes, talking, and laughing, sir," Gene said. Lt. Rossi stared at him with his mouth open. Then a smile appeared on his face.

"Is that so, private? I asked the others what you were doing, and I got different answers from all of them. Is this the story you're going to stick to?"

"Sir, yes, sir." Gene swallowed hard. Lt. Rossi sat back and looked Gene up and down.

"Sergeant Hynes. Will you excuse us, please?" Sgt. Hynes looked at Lt. Rossi with raised eyebrows.

"Yes, sir," he said. He glared at Gene and left the room, closing the door behind him.

"At ease," Lt. Rossi said. Gene placed his hands behind his back at parade rest.

"Where are you from, private?" Lt. Rossi asked.

"Brooklyn, sir."

"I know you're from Brooklyn, private. I recognize your accent. Where in Brooklyn?" Lt. Rossi leaned back and folded his hands over his abdomen. He had dark hair and eyes, and his skin was dark like all the Italians he had met. Gene noticed that his upper torso was muscular, as well as his neck. The lieutenant's arms were thick, though he did not appear to be as tall as Sergeant Hynes.

"Bay Ridge," Gene answered. "East 73rd Street."

Lt. Rossi's eyes opened wide.

"Is that so? I'm from Bath Beach." Lt. Rossi stood up and walked around to the front of his desk. He sat on the edge and folded his arms.

"Your last name is Koenigsmann? Any relation to Alphonse Koenigsmann, the man everyone called Big Al Kane?" Lt. Rossi looked Gene in the eye. Gene felt his stomach roil with anxiety. He could only imagine who it was that his father or one of Mr. Molfetta's associates had beat up who was related to the lieutenant.

"He was my father, sir!" Gene said. He looked out the window behind Lt. Rossi's desk and the multitude of people and vehicles moving about. Gene wished he was among them, on his way to whichever fate awaited him. The sidebar he was having with the lieutenant was uncomfortable, especially since his father had been brought into the conversation.

"Al Kane *was* your father, huh? What happened to him?" Lt. Rossi stood, walked behind Gene, and then around to his right side.

"My father died in thirty-seven. I was twelve years old, sir."

"I'm sorry to hear that."

The lieutenant pulled a chair away from the side of the office and placed it in front of the desk. He motioned for Gene to sit.

"Take a seat, private," he said. Gene eyed Lt. Rossi for a second and then sat down. The lieutenant sat back in his chair.

"What's your first name, private?"

"Eugene. But everyone calls me Gene, sir." Gene breathed shallow breaths.

"I'm only a few years older than you, Gene. Back in thirty-one, my father lost his job at the factory where he had worked for over fifteen years. He found work here and there as a bartender and doing odd jobs, but it wasn't enough to raise a family. I was nine years old, and I had to work after school doing what I could to help pay the rent." Lt. Rossi leaned on his elbows and rubbed his hands together.

"Matters became worse when my sister got sick. Medicine was expensive and so were the doctor's bills. Someone my dad met at the local pub where he tended bar told him to visit Al Kane. Ordinarily, my father wouldn't take a handout, but he was desperate. He sucked in his pride and went to your house on East 73rd Street and met with your father, Alphonse Koenigsmann." The Lieutenant paused. He watched Gene for a reaction. Gene sat still. His stomach quieted down. Scenes such as the one Lt. Rossi was describing had played out on his front step for as long as Gene could recall.

"Your dad gave my father an envelope with fifty dollars and slip of paper with an address inside. My father took the envelope, shook your dad's hand, and then visited the address. He was given a job, a good job as a pressman, and we were finally able to pay the rent, the doctor, and buy medicine for my sister. My father paid your father back the fifty dollars he loaned him, and my mom baked lasagna and meatballs for your family. To your dad's credit, he never asked for a favor in return. That was Big Al Kane."

Gene felt his eyes well up. He wiped his eyes with his hands.

"When was the last time you saw your mother?" Lt. Rossi asked.

"Back in August, sir," Gene said.

"Why aren't you being shipped out with your unit?"

"My glasses broke yesterday, sir. They said it will be about a week before I can get new ones, sir."

"Well, the best I can do is a five-day pass, Gene. I think you should get going." Lt. Rossi took a form out of a drawer and filled in the blanks. The form was in triplicate. He removed the copy from the bottom and stood. Gene rose to his feet at attention. Lt. Rossi walked around to Gene and handed him his leave paper.

"This is in no way enough to repay your father for how he helped my family. But hopefully, it helps you in some way."

Gene took the paper from him, folded it, and then placed it in his top pocket. He removed his cap from his waistband and put it on his head.

"Thank you. It does help, sir," Gene said. Then Gene saluted him.

Lt. Rossi returned the gesture.

"You're dismissed, Private Koenigsmann. My regards to your mother."

"Thank you, sir." Gene pivoted on his heels and walked out of the office.

Back at the barracks, Harry sat alone. None of the others were around. He was dressed in dungarees and a tee shirt and looked like a condemned man. He saw Gene come in, and he placed his hands on his hips.

"So what's the verdict?" Harry asked.

"You don't want to know." Gene sat on his bunk and removed his hat.

"That bad, huh?" Harry stood in front of him.

"I didn't say it was bad. I just said you don't want to know." Gene laid back and placed his arm behind his head.

"Actually, I do want to know. I'm going to be scrubbing dirty pots and pans until I ship out. Whatever punishment they gave couldn't be any worse. Come on, tell me." Harry nudged the bed with his toe.

Gene reached into his pocket and handed the folded paper to Harry.

"I got a five-day pass," he said.

Harry stared at the form as if it were a magical amulet. His eyes widened, and his lips parted. He took it from Gene's hand, unfolded the paper, and read it while moving his head back and forth.

"Cheese and crackers, how the hell did you luck out like this?" Harry dropped the pass on Gene's stomach. Gene quickly folded it and placed it back in his pocket.

"It's a long story," Gene said.

"I have time. I want to hear it." Harry sat on the bunk behind him and leaned on his knees.

"Lt. Rossi asked me what I was doing in the woods, and I said I was smoking cigarettes, laughing, and telling stories. I think he respected the fact that I told the truth." Gene rolled on his side, facing Harry. He leaned on his elbow.

"Son of a bitch," Harry said. He sucked his teeth and rolled his eyes. "Wait a minute. That can't be all. You said it was a long story. What really happened? When you walked in you looked like you were going to bawl your eyes out."

"Harry, it's not something I really want to talk about." Gene lowered his voice, careful not to sound agitated. He liked Harry, but he did not appreciate his prying, no matter how unfair it seemed that he was rewarded while the others were reprimanded.

"What did you do? Promise to wash his Jeep or something?" Harry slapped the pillow next to him.

"He knew my father. My dad once helped his dad. You're asking me to talk about things that you're nowhere near able to appreciate or understand. But my neighborhood is nothing like wherever the hell it was you grew up in cow country."

"Are you talking about mobster stuff? You city folks see that all the time."

"Shut your mouth!" Gene yelled.

Gene stood and lifted his duffel bag. Harry pulled his feet up and let Gene pass by. Gene stopped by the doorway.

"Look, I'm sorry you're peeling potatoes or washing dishes or whatever, but don't ever make assumptions about my father ever again. My dad was kind to strangers, but he could fend off dangerous men with a flick of his finger. He was a good man — a respected man — and Lt. Rossi is someone who remembers what he meant to the neighborhood. Too bad if that doesn't suit you." Gene breathed hard, his chest visibly rising and falling.

Harry got up and walked over to Gene. He fumbled with his fingers.

"Hey, Gene. I'm sorry, pal. I was upset, you know? I guess I got jealous. I didn't mean to say anything bad about your father."

Gene sighed and dropped his shoulders.

"It's all right. Don't be sorry. I just miss him, that's all," Gene said. He stretched the corners of his mouth and tapped Harry's arm.

"Listen, I have to catch a train out of this place. I'm not sure if we'll see each other again, but it was sure nice to meet you," Gene said.

"Give me your address. We can write to each other," Harry said. Gene smiled and put his cap on with his free hand.

"Three seven five East 73rd street, Brooklyn New York. We're the only Koenigsmanns in the neighborhood.

"How am I supposed to remember that?" Harry said.

"See ya, pal. Maybe you'll still be here when I get back." Gene stepped outside and squinted in the sunlight. He had gotten used to his near-sightedness since his glasses broke. His vision wasn't so bad that he was blind but needed them to read signs.

Gene asked several different soldiers where the train station was, careful to avoid sergeants and officers. Because he had arrived at the depot that morning, he was unfamiliar with the sprawling military base. Finding his way back to the railway platform was proving to be a daunting task. He hitched a ride with a sympathetic corporal driving a truck. At the station, Gene thanked the young corporal and set about finding the next train to New York. After he bought a round-trip ticket, he found a bench outside under the awning. The station bustled with soldiers and civilians alike. This was Newport News, Virginia. Gene could see the Liberty ships moored in the distance. Each day thousands of young Americans shipped out to Europe, Africa, and Asia from those docks. He lit a cigarette and inhaled deeply. He let the smoke escape from his nostrils. When he saw the large, gray, navy vessels, he felt a tinge of anxiety. In one brief week, he would walk up the gangplank onto a boat and be carried off to war. He almost wished he did not have this brief reprieve to visit home. He wondered if there was any way he would be able to return to the army, having seen his mother and his old room again. Before long, the train arrived, and he boarded, taking a seat by a window. The train departed, and soon he found himself dozing off while admiring the Virginia countryside at dusk.

In nearly two days, he was home. Gene emerged from the subway near his house and discovered a bounce in his step. Soon he would be back. It was morning, and his mother was sure to be at work. Gene knew the door would be unlocked. No one would dare break into the Koenigsmann's house for fear of what Mr. Molfetta would do to them if they were caught. If the door was secured, his mom kept a spare key hidden underneath the doormat. Gene arrived home. He paused and looked up at the welcoming façade of the family brownstone. He ascended the steps and turned the doorknob. As he expected, the door was unlocked. Gene stepped inside and set his duffel bag down by the stairs. In the kitchen, he poured himself a tall glass of cold water from a pitcher his mom kept in the refrigerator. After a few sips, he carried the drink with him the living room. His body ached after the cramped and bumpy train ride. The sofa by the window offered him familiar comfort. Gene sank into the cushions and sighed. Though he did not want to take a nap, in moments he was asleep.

"Gene, wake up. Wake up."

Gene sat up and noticed his mother standing before him. She held a shopping bag full of groceries, and she wore her office work clothes. She beamed at him and set the sack down on the coffee table. "Come here, Gene," she said.

Gene stood and went to her. She opened her arms and hugged him. Gene could hear muffled sniffling coming from where her head was buried against his chest.

"Why didn't you call and tell me you were coming home? I would have cooked your favorite pot roast." She stepped back while holding his lapels and smiled.

"This was unexpected. My glasses broke before I shipped out, and a lieutenant gave me leave." Gene felt his throat tighten. As happy as he was to see his mother, he wished his dad would enter the room from the kitchen to greet him as well.

"You look so handsome in your uniform. I am so proud of you," she said, choking on her words. Tears formed in her eyes once more.

"It's okay, Mom. It's okay." Gene felt a knot form in his stomach. He rubbed her arm for a moment and then took his hand away. Suddenly, his mother stood straight and smiled at him.

"Well, I am so glad you decided to come home." She lifted the grocery bag and carried it into the kitchen. Gene followed her. She placed the bag on the table and emptied the contents.

"You look like a grown man in that uniform. I must snap a photo of you before you go back." She placed some vegetables in the refrigerator and then paused with her elbow leaning on the counter.

"When do you return?" she asked. Her voice cracked, and she swallowed hard.

"I should leave tomorrow if I am to get back in time. It took forever to get here. The train seemed to stop at every station." Gene pulled out a chair and sat.

"That's hardly any time at all." His mother folded her arms and pushed out her lips.

Gene sighed and hung his head. Then he sat upright and smiled.

"We'll make the most of it. I won't have to leave until nine tomorrow morning," he said.

"I'm just happy to see you before you…" She took a tissue from her pocket and covered her mouth. Gene got up and stood next to her. He rubbed her shoulder to console her.

As a thirty-nine-year-old widow, she had many potential suitors, and she was choosy at best. After marrying Alphonse to pay off her father's gambling debts, the next time around she wanted to marry for love. A petite woman with light brown hair and a fair complexion, she wore beautiful dresses and had a sense of style and fashion unlike many of the neighborhood mothers. Gene hated that his mother was all alone, even though Mr. Molfetta and his crew looked after her. Uncle Edward and his wife, Adele, visited her often. His Aunt Joan, her sister, lived a few blocks away. Still, Gene wanted her to meet a nice man; though whoever dated his mother would have to endure his scrutiny.

"Before you get too comfortable, come with me," his mom said. She went into her bedroom and returned with her camera.

"Upstairs," she said. She pointed up with her finger.

They walked two flights up to the roof of their brownstone.

"Stand over there," she said, pointing to the front of the building overlooking the street. Gene complied. He felt a bit awkward, but he understood how significant this moment was to her. His mom realized that this could be the last time she would ever see her son again. This photo was to memorialize what could potentially be their final moments together. Suddenly, he felt queasy.

"Smile." She raised the camera and peered through the viewfinder.

Gene squared his shoulders and did his best to stretch his lips into something resembling a smile. He imagined how he might have appeared in his uniform. He had no unit insignia, rank, or patches. The looming war and the battlefields full of Allied casualties still seemed like rumors to him. Yet this moment symbolized his fate. There would be no more avoiding the fact that he was going off to war.

Gene turned his head and eyed the street below. A short distance away sat Mr. Molfetta in the back room of his tiny shop. Gene knew that if he visited Mr. Molfetta, the man could make a call to a politician who could then make a call to someone in the War Department who could have Gene assigned to a non-combatant role stateside. However, as much as Mr. Molfetta would be obliged to do so, Gene would find no glory in that. His father went into combat when he was a young man, and Gene believed it was his duty to honor his dad's service fighting for his country. His stomach settled. He looked at his mother. She held her camera with both hands and beamed. She snapped the photo and then lowered the camera. Gene started to walk away. "One more," she said. Gene went back to the same spot and posed. His mom lifted the camera again, aimed, and then snapped another picture. "That should do it," she said. "Come on, I'll make dinner." Then she walked downstairs. "I'll be down in a minute," Gene called after her. She did not answer him. He watched as she stepped through the door to the stairs.

Gene stayed on the roof for a while. He smoked a cigarette while he spied on the pedestrians below. There were some folks he recognized, others he did not. But none of them were about to travel overseas and storm enemy lines while dodging machine gun fire and artillery. His queasiness returned. He watched a man in a suit holding an attaché case emerge from the subway down the block. Gene suddenly wished he had the nerve to visit Mr. Molfetta and ask him for the giant favor of keeping him alive. But he squelched the temptation. He dropped his cigarette, crushed it under his heel and then went downstairs. His mother had already begun preparing meatloaf, his second favorite meal.

That night Gene slept on the couch in the living room. If he slept in his own bed, he thought he would never leave. The sofa offered him the comfort of home but not enough to prevent him from returning to his base.

In the morning, his mother walked him to the subway. She had planned to take a later train to work, and she had already dressed for the day. Gene placed his duffel bag on the sidewalk and faced her.

"Stay safe and listen to your sergeants," she said. "I already lost your father. I can't stand to lose my boy too." A tear streamed down her cheek, and she wiped it away with her hanky. She smiled as only a mother can while she wept, and then she hugged him. Gene placed his arms around her back. He kissed her cheek and then pulled away from her.

"I'll be okay, Mom. I know what to do. I'll stay safe," he said. Gene lifted his duffel bag.

"Goodbye, Gene. I love you. Make sure you write to me." She touched his cheek. He held her hand, then he smiled.

"I'll write to you every day, Mom. Goodbye," he said. He turned and walked away. He considered visiting Mr. Molfetta, but he did not want to risk returning to the base late. A growing sense of anxiety began to swell in his abdomen. As soon as he returned, his glasses would be ready for him. There would be no more delays. Soon he would ship off to war.

After traveling all day and night, the train pulled into Newport News.

He went to see Lt. Rossi to thank him. Gene permitted by the lieutenant's secretary to enter his office. Their conversation was not an informal chat, but Lt. Rossi inquired about his visit home. They talked for a while, and then Gene was dismissed. Before Gene left, the lieutenant told him to receive his orders from the secretary. Outside the office, Lt. Rossi's secretary handed Gene his orders. Gene read the print and gulped. *Africa*. He cocked his head and chuckled. He never once contemplated being sent to Africa.

Gene folded the paper, stuffed it in his top pocket, and walked out of the building. Next, he went to pick up his glasses. There was no line or wait. There was a young woman, a clerk, who asked for his name. He told her and waited. The clerk disappeared into a back room and returned with a small, black case in her hands. Inside it were his new, government-issue, gold, wire-framed glasses with round lenses. She handed them to him with a smile. Gene tried them on. It was satisfying to be able to see again after walking around nearsighted for almost five days. When he was satisfied with the fit, he set out to find his bunk from memory. After a few minutes, he located the barracks. He hoped that someone he recognized would be in there.

Harry saw Gene come in. He had been laying on his bunk, reading a newspaper. Four other GIs were sitting on beds and talking on the other side of the room. They looked up at Gene as he entered. Gene greeted them with a nod.

"Welcome back, Gene. How was your visit?" Harry got up and greeted him.

"Too short," he said. "You don't know how hard it was to come back." Gene tossed his duffel bag on a bunk next to Harry.

"I can only imagine." Harry sat up and placed his newspaper next to him.

"So, did you peel potatoes the entire time I was gone?" Gene snickered and sat down. He removed his cap and placed it on the bed.

"Nah, I lucked out. Lt. Rossi took pity on me and cut me loose after one day. He gave me a two-day pass, but that wasn't long enough to get home. So I explored the town and saw a few movies. In fact, I haven't done much of anything since you left. I've been keeping a low profile and trying not to get noticed." Harry leaned over and tapped Gene's knee. "Hey, did you get your orders? Where are you going?"

"Africa. I leave tomorrow." Gene produced the papers from his shirt pocket and showed them to Harry.

"Well, I'll be damned. That's where I'm going too. In fact, we all are." Harry smiled and pointed at the rest of the guys. Gene looked down and shook his head.

"I guess this is it. We're actually going off to fight," Gene said in a somber tone.

Harry looked at his feet. "You bet. And I can't say that I'm too excited about it. But if the army went through all the trouble to teach me how to shoot a rifle, I might as well put it to good use. I can't spend the whole war washing pots and pans in the mess hall. Ain't that right, Gene?"

"I suppose that's true. But I have no right to complain," Gene said.

"How's that?" Harry cocked his head and looked at him.

"I enlisted." Gene sat up straight and cleared his throat.

"No shit. You enlisted too? Damn, Gene." Harry shook his head, leaned back, and put his feet up.

"I only signed up because my dad was in the army and my mom could use the extra money I'll be sending home." Gene rubbed his palms together. The fact was that his mother didn't need money since she had a job, and Gene had also worked for Mr. Molfetta up until he went to basic training.

"I would have thought a New Yorker like you would have been drafted. The mail takes longer to reach us out in the country." Harry sucked his teeth and chuckled.

"That's the dumbest thing I ever heard," Gene said. He laughed and shook his head. "I'm gonna go into town and see if I can get something to eat. You want to come along?" Gene asked Harry.

"It's a little early, don't you think? Besides, we can get chow at the mess hall." Harry sat up and put his feet on the floor.

"I want to have some real food before we ship out. Come on, let's go." Gene tapped Harry's shoulder and stood up. Harry got up as well and picked up his cap. Together they walked outside.

"Your dad was in the army? Was he in the first war?" Harry asked.

Michael Kannengieser

"Yeah, he was in a motorcycle unit, one of the first out of Camp Upton on Long Island," Gene said.

"Motorcycles? I wish they would let us ride motorcycles. I bet he must have seen a lot of action." Harry trudged along next to Gene.

"I don't know how much combat he saw, but according to my mom, he brought home every silver knife, fork, spoon, oil painting, Luger, timepiece, and other valuable he could get his hands on. He shipped so much stuff home that he was able to open his radio store after the war by selling most of it."

"So, he was a looter?" Harry stared at Gene as he walked.

"Looter or entrepreneur or someone who planned for his future. Either way, that's what he did. It doesn't matter anymore, because he died when I was twelve years old." Gene peeked at Harry from the corner of his eye. They approached the gate and were waved through by the guards.

"You lost your father when you were only twelve? I'm sorry about that, Gene. I didn't mean to judge." Harry put his hand on Gene's shoulder.

"Don't apologize, Harry. Not many people hear that story and think too highly of my dad. But he loved me, and my mom and I miss him. There isn't a day that goes by when I don't think of him or how he would have handled something. I like to think that I'm still learning from him." Gene paused at the corner bus stop and removed his cigarettes from his pants pocket. He offered one to Harry. He accepted and put it in his mouth. Gene used his lighter to ignite both of their cigarettes. They waited for the bus in silence. Then Harry spoke.

"You think it would be a good idea if we, you know, gathered some things we find for ourselves and ship it home like businessmen?" Harry flicked the ash off the end of his cigarette and looked at Gene.

"Harry, I'll be happy if we make it home alive. Of course, I'm open to opportunities." Gene blew smoke out from his nostrils. Then he turned to Harry.

"What do you know about business, anyway? Your family owns a ranch."

"A ranch is a business. We sell cattle, city boy." Harry smiled and flicked his butt into the gutter.

"I guess that qualifies as a business. I imagine you learned something from feeding cows." Gene chuckled. The bus arrived, and they both climbed aboard. Gene chose a window seat. Harry explained how ranches operated, livestock is sent to market, and how much profit was involved. Gene's mind drifted as he reminisced about his father. Alphonse had secreted cigar boxes full of cash around their home in various hiding spots. After his funeral, he and his mother searched the entire house until they were convinced there were none left. Gene remembered his mother telling him the story of Alphonse shipping home his pilfered goods and selling it for capital to open his radio store with Mr. Molfetta's help. He recalled his dad seated in the rear of the flower shop, collecting debts owed to him from the numbers racket and from loan sharking. Memories of excursions on the family cabin cruiser in Sheepshead Bay watching his dad heave the giant anchor overboard came back to him. Gene was aware back then that his father smuggled whiskey into the neighborhood on that boat. Lawbreaking was the business Gene learned while growing up. As he listened to Harry tell tales about his father, the hard-working, successful rancher, he admired his own dad, the gangster, even more.

Chapter 2

June 1969

For Ray's eleventh birthday our parents gave him a Civil War battle set. The box came with miniature, blue and gray, plastic soldiers, a single artillery piece, and some brown, plastic barriers. Ray and I used a tub of Lincoln Logs to construct forts and other barricades to orchestrate epic battle scenes. Because Ray lost the dart for the spring-loaded cannon soon after opening the kit, he got the idea to use pieces of dry spaghetti as projectiles.

We would spread out across the living room carpet on Saturday afternoons and play. During one of our brutal, staged combat scenes the Union Soldiers were facing heavy *pasta* fire from the cannon, which the rebel soldiers stole with the aid of a pickup truck and an armada of Matchbox cars. Dad tiptoed around the array of figurines and structures we had built as a battleground.

"They didn't have trucks and cars in the Civil War," he said with a grin.

"I know Dad," said Ray. "We're pretending this is World War II, just like the war you were in." He looked up with wide eyes and a broad smile.

"I fought in the Civil War," Dad said.

"Yeah right," Ray said. "You'd be over a *hundred* years old."

"Did you ride a horse in the army, Daddy?" I asked. I looked up from the diorama of inanimate conflict before me with my eyebrows raised. My glasses slid down my nose, and I pushed them back up. Dad chuckled and walked away. Then I noticed his scar; a semi-circular, reddish depression just under his right ear. At that moment, the wound had a whole new connotation for me. That meant he had been shot. Back then, I believed that men who got hit with a bullet *died*—just like the plastic figurines spread out in imagined agony before me.

Somehow after making the connection between the lesion on his neck and his army service, he became even a mythical figure to me. Yet he never actually answered my question. I needed to hear it myself.

Ray went back to racing the cars around, knocking over gray plastic troops in their permanent, fixed-bayonet poses. I didn't understand the sarcasm in my brother's remark, and it didn't occur to me that Dad was teasing us. For all I knew, in my six-year-old mind, he could have been a century old. At the time, he was in his early forties. Yet, as a boy in the first grade, I was unable to put age into perspective. Anyone over the age of eighteen was an adult—and to me *old*. My father might as well have been a hundred-year-old Civil War veteran.

Once a month, we took a weekend trip to visit Grandma, who lived on the North Fork of Long Island. My earliest recollection of driving from Copiague to her home in Southold included the sensation of getting tossed around in the rear-facing seat of the Dad's station wagon. We did not have a lot of money. Each vehicle he bought was used, needed some work, and kept him busy on the Saturdays changing oil and repairing the engine.

Grandma moved out to Southold, Long Island after marrying a tall, happy man named Pat O'Brien. Grandma went from being named Lillian Koenigsmann to Lillian O'Brien. Alphonse had died long ago, and Grandma was far removed from her former role as the wife of a gangster. A native of an obscure town outside Dublin, Pat came to the United States in 1923 and ended up in Far Rockaway, Queens. Lillian and Pat met on the subway. She was on her way to work, and he was a conductor. The year was 1955, and Pat had retired early and collected a pension. Lillian was through with city life and wanted to settle on Long Island, just as Gene did after he married Ann and moved to Copiague in Suffolk County.

Pat wanted to travel further east, out near the farms, which reminded him of where he was raised. Suffolk's east end was a lush terrain of cultivated fields which yielded potatoes, cabbage, cauliflower, corn, and more. Also, the famed Long Island duck farms provided fresh fowl for restaurants up and down the east coast.

They settled into a nineteenth-century colonial home with a front porch that took up the entire width of the house. Half of it was screened in, and it served as a playground for us during our visits.

Since I was the youngest kid in the family, I got to sit in the rear of the station wagon. Like most cars of that type, Dad's car had a rear-facing bench seat, which meant that I had to view the vehicles behind us and make uncomfortable eye contact with strangers on the highway.

In those days, before the completion of the Long Island Expressway, it took about two hours to drive to Grandma's. The length of the trip added to the allure of the more rural setting where she and *Poppa*, as we called Pat, made their home. Down the block from their house was part of the diesel line of the Long Island Railroad. The engines would whistle as they passed the crossing and the gates went down, lights flashing. A potato farm was further down the narrow, asphalt lane which abutted their property line, about fifty feet or so from the front porch. There were no sidewalks, like I was accustomed to in town. But we did not have woods with a trail like the one which began in the backyard belonging to Mr. and Mrs. Wells next door.

The ride was a hot and uncomfortable one. Cindy sat next to me, and I could not stretch out and relax. The aroma of cauliflower from the nearby farms filled the car, because Mom and Dad had their windows open. This was because our car did not have air conditioning. My father did not own a car with an air conditioner until the late nineteen-seventies.

Mom turned on the radio. There was a newscast about soldiers getting killed in a place I heard repeatedly mentioned on TV called *Vietnam*. In those days, I believed that there was a never-ending conflict going on somewhere in the world, and one day I would have to fight in that battle. On the six o'clock news, they showed footage of young men in olive green fatigues carrying cool-looking rifles—black with a handle on top and a pointy-sight at the end—just like the toy one my friend George had.

That got me thinking about playing *war* with my friends in the woods next to Killie's Lake near the edge of town and what it would be like to fight in an actual war. I sat up, turned around, and looked at Dad. The scar on the side of his neck was visible from my vantage point.

The mark was a depressed, circular, dark pink blemish where part of the bullet had exited after he had been shot. Dad had been shot twice, strafed by automatic gunfire as he crouched and fired his weapon. As I understood the account at that time one round had entered his mouth, shattering his teeth and damaging bone. The slug had split in two, with one half exiting the right side of his neck and the other half lodging close to his spine. The other shot hit his right arm at the elbow and did severe damage to the tissue and bone. Doctors did not remove the fragment next to his spine for fear of complications that would cause him to become paralyzed.

My grandmother told me more and more about Dad's battle experiences each time we visited. I would sit, transfixed, at her feet and listen with my utmost attention. While I was fascinated by the details, I was also bothered by the fact that Dad had told his mom his stories but not his children. Grandma would change the topic whenever Dad entered the room. This would leave the story with a cliffhanger, and I would have to wait for Dad to either go outside and sit on the porch with Mom or take a walk with Pat. I could tell Grandma was proud of her son. She marveled at his bravery, and she wanted his children to hear about his daring exploits. Dad spent most of his life shielding us from what he had seen and experienced. As I grew up, I often speculated if Dad felt betrayed by his mother for recounting his conversations with her to me, which undoubtedly were told to her in confidence.

I sat on my knees and looked forward at my family. Mom looked like she was dozing. Dad caught a glimpse of me in the rearview mirror.

"Daddy, did you get shot when you were in the army?" I asked.

Dad did not answer right away. I heard Ray groan.

"Yes, but I'm fine now," Dad finally said.

"Michael, turn around and sit. You'll get hurt," said Mom.

"Did you get shot by a rebel?"

"Who?" Dad asked.

"Did a confederate soldier get you?" I asked.

The smirk on my father's face should have offered me a clue as to my naivety, but I could not decipher it. My youth, gullibility, and lack of historical context had me confused. Dad was amused by my query but reluctant to answer.

"Daddy fought against the Germans," Ray said. He grunted and looked back at me through narrowed eyes.

"Do we have to talk about war? This is annoying," Cindy said. She made a *tsk* sound and folded her arms.

"Yep, that's it, Mike. A rebel got me," Dad said. My mom turned and was about to tell me to sit again. Dad touched her arm and shook his head.

"You see that field out the window? That's where I was deployed in the Union Army. We fought the Confederates right there."

My head snapped in the direction he pointed. All I could think was *wow*. The murmuring among my parents, Ray, and Cindy were stifled by the revelation that my father was a

45

soldier, and this is where he *fought*. I was in awe even though it was not true.

"Daddy wasn't in the Civil War, Mike." Ray turned around and laughed hard at my gullibility. "He'd be so old we'd have to light all the candles on his birthday cake with a flamethrower." Both Ray and Cindy giggled. My mother turned her head and frowned at my father. Naturally, Dad had teased me, and I felt foolish. My eyes welled up with tears. My throat ached, and my skin was flush with embarrassment. It hurt to be made fun of by Ray and Cindy, but my father's joking stung the most. In my elementary school mind, I could only see war as a game that I played with my buddies in the nearby woods. Our cap guns, plastic rifles, and make-believe *rat-a-tat-tats* were our homages to our fathers and uncles who came home from Europe, Asia, Korea, and now a new part of the world called Vietnam. I didn't comprehend this consciously then; it was innate. It was the process of envisioning my father as a warrior from my young perspective.

"Look, he's crying," Ray said.

"Michael, your father was joking. Stop crying." Mom's tone was harsh, though her annoyance was directed at Dad. He gripped the wheel and watched the road, not reacting to her indirect reprimand.

I folded my arms and sat back down. As I gazed out of the rear window at the farm stands and fields of sprouting vegetables, my annoyance faded.

"Michael," Dad said. "Michael, look at me." His deep voice resonated in the car. I didn't answer.

"When we get home, I have something for you."

"What is it?" I asked, remaining in my backward position. I had been experiencing post-crying hiccups, and I let on that I was still upset.

"It's a genuine, U.S. Army issued canteen. You can have it."

Immediately, I smiled wide, and I had the same excitement as when I thought I was getting a BB gun for my birthday. I'd seen this relic before. Dad kept an old M1 cartridge bandolier, a belt, a helmet, and the canteen hanging in his closet. Ray and I never dared to hold these valued possessions of his in our hands, but often enough, we would enter his closet when he wasn't around and ogle them.

"How come *he* gets the canteen?" Ray held his arms in the air and let them drop. "Relax, Ray, I have something for you too," Dad said.

It didn't matter what he was giving my older brother. I was getting something fascinating. It was in a *war.*

Chapter 3

March 1944

"Don't look up, boys. You'll get kicked in the face," a sailor standing by the rail warned the troops. This was Gene's first attempt at scaling down the side of a ship. At every other opportunity, they were all afforded a gangplank. This time, they had to disembark while climbing down a rope net. Gene swung his leg over the side. Others queued up behind him, waiting their turn. The sailor turned his attention to him.

"Move it. You're holding up the line!"

Gene hurled himself over. All he could do was fixate on what was below. Gene saw the bobbing helmets of dozens of GIs gripping the web and trying not to fall. They were raw, untested, replacement troops for the nearly depleted Texas 36th Division. Yet even combat veterans would do a double-take when they realized, as Gene and his pals did, that they had to jump off the vessel and run across the side of a shipwreck to reach the shore.

Though he had no relatives from Italy, Gene had always wanted to visit the country. The allure of Italy came from being around Mr. Molfetta and his wife. Mr. Molfetta was born in Naples and never missed an opportunity to talk about his childhood there. Gene wondered how Mr. Molfetta would react upon seeing the crumbled buildings, cratered cobblestone streets, and piles of rubble. Naples appeared grand, regardless of the devastation caused by bombers and artillery. He recognized the vestiges of Italian architecture, crumbled and charred, unfamiliar compared to what he was used to back in Brooklyn. Gene was anxious to return home and tell Mr. Molfetta what he saw of his hometown, even though much of it was in ruins.

Gene slipped when he landed, nearly falling backward after he got off the rope net. The surface was slick. He spread his arms out for balance. Others around him held each other for support. A sergeant grabbed his shoulder.

"Move along, soldier. Keep the line going!"

With his hand atop his helmet, Gene caught up to his buddies. When they reached the end of the hull, they jumped into the shallow surf. The Mediterranean's clear water welcomed Gene's boots. Together, they ran onto the beach.

A few yards ashore, they paused. Gene marveled at the sky ahead. There was no avoiding the spectacle of Mount Vesuvius erupting in the distance. Ash fell around them like snow. It was mid-morning, yet tough to pinpoint the sun on the horizon.

"All right men, hustle up, fall in." Sgt. Thames waved his hand over his head in a circular motion, waiting for the platoon to assemble before him. Other sergeants were tracking down their men as well. Gene liked Sgt. Thames. He was an affable, twenty-five-year-old man. At home, he was a police officer. Like most cops, Sgt. Thames was cynical, sarcastic, and he always expected the worst. Yet he was protective of his men in the same way cops were protective of the public. Sgt. Thames was over six feet tall and athletic, with a lean build. Gene suspected Sgt. Thames could wrestle and brawl with the best of them. Though Alphonse taught Gene to be wary of the police, he grew fond of Sgt. Thames as soon as he met him. Somehow Gene could not envision Sgt. Thames accepting bribes and gifts from men like Mr. Molfetta or even his father.

The Germans had long since been pushed back. Gene and the others were to be transported to an area outside the city to be assigned their new units. Gene hoped he would not be separated from his friends, especially Sgt. Thames. He had been with them since landing in Africa back in September.

Of mild concern and greater curiosity was the looming volcano, which was causing the war to grind to a near halt.

"Hey sergeant," his buddy Pete called out. "Those Germans must be genuine masterminds if they figured out how to attack us with a volcano."

Several soldiers in the platoon chuckled. Sgt. Thames raised his hand. The young men stopped laughing.

"Enough with the wisecracks. I know you boys are anxious to get into this fight, but this eruption you see is no joke. We lost over fifty bombers at an airfield to the smoke and ash already."

The mood of the group shifted. The sergeant's face took on a solemn expression like someone about to deliver grim news. His eyes narrowed, and he sucked in his cheeks. The men in the platoon stopped chatting and looked straight ahead.

"You see that, boys? That's God talking to us, telling everyone to stop murdering each other." He pointed at the raging Mount Vesuvius and frowned. "These cinders hitting the ground, looking like snow. Those are the tears of angels."

He looked down and swept a little pile together with his boot.

"We're getting ready to join a division that's been getting chewed up in the past few months. They landed at Salerno and have been clawing their way across Italy, fighting hard and taking significant losses. The last thing they want to hear is a bunch of replacements telling dumb jokes."

The men did not respect Sgt. Thames only because he was older and he outranked them. They knew he had seen action. He may have wanted to look like a rough, cinematic action hero, but he could not lose the paternal tone in his voice or his sympathetic leadership style.

"As gigantic as that volcano is and as much ash, smoke, and soot as it spews down all over everything, you can still see it from hundreds of miles away. You know it's there," he said, pointing at the blackened skyline behind him. He faced the platoon and put his hands on his hips, making eye contact with the young troops in the front rank.

"Let me tell you something. You'll never see a kraut sniper gunning for you. And those eighty-eight rounds fall from the same sky that ash is raining down from. They blow up tanks, trees, and whole squads of men." He paused and eyeballed the group. The platoon kept their gaze on Mount Vesuvius.

Gene figured that it'd probably be better to charge toward a volcano than a German panzer. The newsreels showed kraut tanks blasting everything in their course—including American Shermans. Still, his training and the high morale amongst his peers kept him eager to fight, despite any anxiety he experienced watching the German Wehrmacht and the Waffen-SS on film.

"Listen to me, and I'll do my best to keep you alive. That's my promise. I can't hold back molten lava, but I know a few tricks to outsmart the enemy."

Finally, the sergeant dismissed them. A few of the soldiers wandered down the debris-strewn road to get a better view of the volcano from between bombed-out buildings. Gene walked off with his friends. Though they didn't speak, it was apparent what they were all thinking. This was the last stop before facing the Germans. Soon they would board trucks and be taken to a camp in Campania.

The previous July, in 1943, Gene walked into a recruitment center in Bay Ridge, Brooklyn to enlist in the Army. It was a week before his eighteenth birthday. The sergeant wrote his name on a form and told him to come back in a week when he was old enough to join. While it was Gene's idea to enter the military, his mother also prodded him to in her own, gentle way.

Since he was twelve years old, his mom had told him that he had to earn money. After Alphonse had died from complications due to diabetes, Gene went to school and worked as much as he was able. Mr. Molfetta had plenty of deliveries for Gene to make and other odd jobs that paid well. But his mother never let Gene rest. However, Gene did not have to become the chief breadwinner in the house since his mom also worked. Also, there were plenty of folks in his neighborhood who owed his father favors. His dad commanded respect even in death. In addition to all this, his mother had also received a large sum of cash envelopes from his father's *business* associates at his funeral. Mr. Molfetta had ensured that all of Alphonse's debts were paid to Gene and his mother.

Gene's *man of the house* role was mostly figurative. His mother never wished to place such a heavy burden on him. She wanted to teach him to be independent and fend for himself should something happen to her.

"Gene? Are you going to sign up before all the other boys on the block? You'll make me so proud," she'd tell him. Gene suspected that his mother saw the army as a chance for her son to mature into a man.

Gene also viewed military service as a rite of passage. His father, if he were still alive, would have found a way for Gene to stay home, maybe work in the family business running numbers, loan sharking, and other illegal activities associated with organized crime.

Like most other teenage boys, Gene detested Nazis and the Japanese. The war had a profound impact on his neighborhood. There were shortages, gas rationing, and occasional air raid drills. What was an inconvenience for most Americans became an opportunity for Mr. Molfetta. He sold war ration stamps on the black market. These were used to buy food and gas. Gene never knew how he obtained them. However the stamps were either counterfeit or stolen. Gene heard Mr. Molfetta joke with his nephew, Salvatore, once. They were both in the back office of the florist shop. Gene was outside the screen door, waiting for Mr. Molfetta to give him a package to deliver. He had just parked his bicycle, and he gripped the door handle to enter the store. Mr. Molfetta and Salvatore stood next to a folding table. On it was placed a large, cardboard box. Mr. Molfetta picked up a ration book from inside and flipped through the pages, admiring the stamps. He said, "This racket is putting bread on our tables and in our pockets." Mr. Molfetta, never one to laugh out loud, smiled wide and patted Salvatore on the shoulder.

On the day Gene enlisted in the army at the induction center, the sergeants and soldiers there displayed a toughness that Gene admired. Before he knew it, he had reached his eighteenth birthday and was shipped down south to Camp Wheeler in Georgia for basic training.

Being a Brooklyn boy, many of the other recruits in his platoon mocked his lack of skills in the outdoors.

You can't shoot a rifle? My dad took me hunting since I was three years old.

It was that type of ribbing which was mostly fun. Still, others were displaying true ignorance.

Koenigsmann, are you a Jew? He heard this more than once, and it was generally from someone who did not like those of the Jewish faith.

Gene was a city boy who biked through tough neighborhoods delivering various goods and contraband for the local crime boss. He played baseball and football and being from New York City, he was used to dealing with people of diverse backgrounds. Alphonse raised him to be tough. There was not much that Gene feared. The guys who teased him typically never set foot outside their hometowns and were from needy families. Part of Gene felt sorry for them.

Gene made friends quickly. One of his new buddies, Josh, a kid from Louisiana, handed him a plug of chewing tobacco on a long march through the rural countryside. By that time, they were three weeks into basic training, and it was a sweltering August afternoon.

"It's to keep you from getting thirsty," he said. "We all chew it where I come from."

Yet, Josh never told him not to swallow the juices. Before long, he was vomiting along the side of the dirt road with a sergeant screaming in his ear to move it along.

"City boy," jeered one of the recruits. As the rest of the platoon marched past him he stayed squat on the ground. The sergeant didn't worry him, neither did the rest of the guys in the unit he was training with.

Gene grew up in the city, but his dad took him deep sea fishing on a regular basis. Alphonse's thirty-six-foot cabin cruiser that he had moored in a Brooklyn marina was given to him as payment for gambling debts. Often his parents took him on summer weekends to a bungalow, which they rented in Babylon, on Long Island. From there, they went fishing on party boats which sailed from Captree.

Part of Gene's childhood was spent on the Atlantic Ocean. He long dreamed of being the captain of a great ship. After the war, he planned on buying his own boat, just like the one his father had owned.

The voyage overseas was eleven days. Seasickness was rampant. Aside from the sailors who manned the ship, Gene was one of the few who already had his sea legs.

"Mmm, pork chops. Anyone care for a bite?" Gene walked among the bunks coming back from the mess hall. Most of the GIs were vomiting into their helmets, and they freely handed him their meal tickets. At one point, so many soldiers were puking over one side it caused the ship to list at an angle.

The abundant amount of food he consumed did little to ease the rising tension he felt as they cruised closer to Africa. One part of him was excited to join a unit and to take part in defeating the Germans. Another part of him winced as he remembered the war newsreels that played in movie theaters. Explosions, machine gunners, and dead bodies flickered in black and white in his mind.

The fighting in Africa had ended before they arrived. Immediately the fresh troops were boarded onto trains and sent across the continent to Tunisia. Once there, they learned that Italy was where they would be deployed next.

It seemed an odd place to be inserted into the war. After spending the preceding weeks in Africa with nothing to do but train, run, write home, smoke cigarettes, and sit around; they were back to doing the same. But this time they were doing it outside a town in Italy.

"Texas?" Why I am getting thrown in with a bunch of Texans?" his friend said. They jumped off the truck at their latest camp in Maddaloni, Italy.

"I'm from Brooklyn. Imagine what my buddies from home will think," Gene said. He climbed down and stood on the dirt road with his backpack on and his rifle slung over his shoulder. Gene pushed his glasses up and looked around at the countryside. From where he stood, there were no indications of any battles taking place. This offered him some relief from his enduring anxiety.

The fact was that Gene and his unit were replacements for the severely depleted 36th Infantry Division, which had suffered massive losses in the most recent battle at the Rapido River. The division, originally from Texas, wore a light-blue arm patch with a gold letter T at the center.

Gene was assigned to the 141st Regiment, Company L with the rest of the men he had been grouped with since shipping over. From a distance, he could see hills, and fields, and an old, Roman aqueduct. It was vastly different scenery than what he was used to at home. That included the backwoods of Georgia and the relatively metropolitan Newport News, Virginia.

During basic training, his voyage at sea, and across the African continent by rail everything had seemed like a camping trip to Gene. There was always, however, the looming threat of combat. The M1 Garand he was issued was meant for one purpose and that was for killing the enemy. Gene was afraid that if he aimed his rifle at a German soldier, he might lose his nerve to pull the trigger—even if that soldier was about to kill him. Gene imagined his father fighting in the Great War. Indeed his father did not hesitate to shoot krauts back then. If his father fought in combat, then so could he.

Once in camp, the troops began training for the upcoming push by the Allies toward Rome. Sergeant Thames acted more like the coach of a football team than a sergeant. He gave rousing speeches, and he offered advice that came from his experiences on the front lines. Sgt. Thames had fought at the Battle of Kasserine Pass. A grenade exploded nearby, peppering him with shrapnel. At home, his father pulled some strings with politicians he knew and had his son sent back home. When Sgt. Thames recovered, he visited his father, thanked him, and then asked his commanding officer that he be sent back into combat. While many shook their heads at his decision, the men he served with gave him their utmost respect.

Sgt. Thames armed himself with a Thompson sub-machine gun. Also, he carried two Colt 45 caliber pistols, one on each hip. Gene figured that his display of weaponry was more of a morale booster than a necessity.

"Forget what they told you in basic training," he said as he marched up and down behind the platoon on the firing line. "When you're in combat, shoot, and keep shooting. Don't wait for Jerry to stick his head from out behind a tree, cut the damn tree in half!"

It was on the third day with his new division that Sgt. Thames issued Gene a Browning Automatic Rifle. The BAR weighed almost twenty pounds when loaded.

Sgt. Thames sized him up. "You're one big, goddamned Brooklyn boy, Koenigsmann." He patted Gene on the shoulder and strode away.

A few feet away, he turned and grinned. "You sure you can see through those coke-bottle glasses, private? It's a good thing I gave you that BAR. Spray and pray, soldier. Spray and pray." Sgt. Thames snickered and continued walking.

Chapter 4

September 23, 1973

Sunday evenings meant going to bed early for us kids, especially on a school night. After dinner, Cindy and Ray would take their showers first. When they were finished, it was my turn to use the bathroom. I was ten years old and still took baths. Mom and Dad would sit in the living room and have an evening cup of coffee. We'd come downstairs in our pajamas and relax with our parents for a family night that consisted of popcorn and TV. First, we'd watch *The Wonderful World of Disney*, followed by *Mutual of Omaha's Wild Kingdom*. Ray was fifteen years old by then, and Cindy almost eighteen. Our strict adherence to our family bonding routine rarely changed and that included viewing choices. On that night, however, Dad had taken control of the television.

"Gene, why do you want to watch this movie?" Mom looked around the room at Dad. He kneeled in front of the TV and changed the channels until he found the station he wanted. In his other hand, he held a copy of TV Guide.

"There's something I want to see." Dad stood and walked back to his chair next to mom. She shook her head and made a *tsk* sound. When the program started, it was clear that it was about World War II.

"This is what you want to watch? You don't like war movies. You said so yourself," said Mom.

"This is a documentary. Not a movie." Dad clenched his teeth. His annoyance showed.

"I just don't want the kids to see anything bloody." Mom looked back down at her needlework and sighed. Ray groaned, and Cindy rolled her eyes.

"And neither do I if I have anything to do with it, not in real life anyway," Dad said with a tinge of sharpness. He sat back and grabbed both arms of his chair like he was waiting for lift off.

Dad turned on PBS to watch *The World at War.* The mini-series covered all aspects of WWII from the battles to the Holocaust. I witnessed the exchange between my parents while sitting on the carpet. This was my usual spot in the living room, because Ray and Cindy claimed the couch for themselves. Mom and Dad had their own comfy chairs. Just like in the station wagon where I was relegated to the rear seat, I had to sit on the floor. Because of Dad's insistence on watching his show, I was going to miss an episode of *Mutual of Omaha's Wild Kingdom,* which aired before *The Wonderful World of Disney.* I folded my arms and sat crossed-legged. Although I was annoyed because my father had hijacked the TV, I was also intrigued. Dad watched the screen as if he were searching for clues. I eyed him, gauging his reactions to the grainy, black and white video. He had removed his dentures, as he typically did after dinner. His lips puckered, and he looked like a toothless, old man. While I was used to seeing him without his teeth, I once again made the connection between the scenes on TV and his wounds. Because Dad rarely mentioned his time in the army, his sudden interest in a WWII documentary was unusual and captivating.

My fascination with my father's army life took root that very night. If ever before I was curious about what he did during the war, I became nearly obsessed with his story after that Sunday evening. Somewhere in the middle of the program, my father leaned forward and rested his forearms on his knees. He studied the film like he was trying to identify specific details.

On screen, Adolph Hitler stood on a balcony in pre-war Italy, 1938. Below, a throng of fervent supporters hailed him with their upraised arms. Suddenly, Dad's eyes opened wide, and he pointed to the TV.

"Kids, do you see that building over there?"

There were a lot of buildings depicted in the footage my father referred to.

"Which one?" I focused on where he was pointing.

"It was a grammar school before the war."

My mother stopped what she was doing and looked up. We all paid attention. Ray leaned forward, his face scrunched up and eyes squinted. Cindy peered at the television with her eyebrows raised. I crawled closer to the TV and sat down again.

"Over there was a church. There was a market, and there were shops all along the avenue there." Dad leaned closer and pointed at all the landmarks he recognized.

"How do you know all of this, Dad?" I asked.

My father fell back into the cushioned chair. He exhaled and breathed through parted lips. For a moment, he spied the TV. Then he looked at me.

"The elementary school became a hospital during the war. That is where I spent two months after I was wounded."

My eyes widened. I turned my body to face Dad, and I wanted to ask so much more. Ray read my mind. He reached over and tapped my shoulder. Before I could protest, I saw the expression on Ray's face. His eyes narrowed, and his lips pursed. Slowly he shook his head. My shoulders sagged, and I heeded my brother's caution.

Dad stood up. He looked down at my mother. "Put on what you want. I'm going to bed," he said. And then he left the room.

"I told him not to watch that," my mother said under her breath. She caught me looking at her and went back to her needlepoint.

"Why don't you put your show back on, Michael."

I no longer wanted to watch *Wild Kingdom* or *Disney.* The documentary had my complete attention. The scene shifted from Hitler to American troops marching in formation into Rome. For a few brief seconds, I watched intently for any signs of a young enlisted man from Brooklyn carrying a rifle. How could I tell Dad from thousands of other GIs shown in dozens of battles? I knew nothing of where he fought or even what unit he was in except what I had just learned about him having been in a makeshift hospital in Rome. What I still did not know then was that Dad arrived in Italy in March of 1944. Of course, he survived. Yet how close he came to dying, I would not discover until decades later.

Chapter 5

April 1918 - November 1931

Very little is known about Alphonse's life before he fathered Eugene. The few details I have about my grandfather I gleaned from my grandmother and Dad. The same way that Grandma told me stories about Dad while he was in the army, she regaled me with tales of Alphonse and his life as a mob associate in Bay Ridge, Brooklyn. Dad shared tidbits here and there when he was feeling nostalgic. I swallowed every detail that they tossed at me.

I would sit at Grandma's feet in the living room at her home in Southold or at our house when she visited. She would wait for Dad to leave the room and proceed with her storytelling. Grandma enjoyed my reactions to her stories. Often, I saw a gleam in her eye when she spoke about her son. She recalled taking his photo on the roof of their Bay Ridge brownstone. Her face took on a somber expression when she explained the extent of Dad's injuries. Grandma recognized that I was proud of my father, and that I wanted to absorb as much as I could about him, so she obliged. I surmised that she also told me about Alphonse to differentiate them as men. Perhaps, I thought, she desired to depict my father as a positive role model. Also, I believe that she considered their life stories as a family heritage. No matter what her motivation was for sharing those memories with me, I was grateful.

The contrast between my criminal grandfather and my religious, hardworking dad was unambiguous. Again, it occurred to me that my grandmother must also have betrayed the trust of her long-deceased husband by revealing his secrets and life choices—as scarce as they were. Grandma was kept in the dark about many of Alphonse's dealings. What she was privy to was damning, indeed. She made no secret of her contempt for him. Yet she had remained a loyal wife, because he fathered Eugene, whom she adored more than anything.

Alphonse died long before I was born. His tale begins in my mind when he was thirty years old. Alphonse and two members of his crew were arrested for burglary. The three of them worked for the notorious Mr. Molfetta. One of the men in his crew had worked for a dressmaker in the garment district in Manhattan. He had made a copy of the key to the back door. In those days alarms were uncommon. Late one evening in April 1918, the three of them broke into the shop. They loaded racks full of dresses onto the bed of a truck. Two police officers on foot patrol stumbled across them during their routine building check. Alphonse's partners fled on foot. They abandoned Alphonse, who was caught red-handed in the truck along with the swag.

Alphonse did not resist arrest. Back at the precinct, he did not rat out his buddies either. The next morning, he was arraigned in the courtroom of the Honorable Henry Rodham. Judge Rodham was all too familiar with Alphonse. It was not the first time Alphonse had been arrested. One of the perks of working for Mr. Molfetta was the protection he afforded his crew. Alphonse stood tall. He turned and saw Mr. Molfetta sitting in the front row of the gallery. Seated next to him was Alphonse's first wife, Madeline, and their two children; William, age five; and Doris, age three. Alphonse winked at his kids and smiled at Madeline.

Alphonse's attorney, a man whose name is lost to antiquity, had worked out a plea bargain with the district attorney. Judge Rodham called the court to order. According to the deal, Alphonse was given a choice between serving jail time or joining the military. America had declared war on Germany and was sending troops to fight in France. Without hesitation, Alphonse chose service in the army.

Ordinarily, the option of military service instead of incarceration was offered to juvenile delinquents or much younger men deemed capable of being rehabilitated. In Alphonse's case, Mr. Molfetta's influence was substantial. Judge Rodham was a married and a respected pillar of the community. He had also amassed a considerable gambling debt and had a proclivity to visit brothels. In Brooklyn in those days, these operations were controlled exclusively by none other than Mr. Salvatore Molfetta. The district attorney, on the other hand, was a man who was easily bribed with envelopes of cash and tickets to Dodgers games.

Alphonse completed basic training and was assigned to Camp Upton on Long Island. Camp Upton was the home of an army motorcycle unit. Since Alphonse was much older than the typical recruit, he was chosen for the assignment by his superiors for his maturity. Upon completion of his training, he was shipped to France. He was assigned to a regiment and acted as a messenger. Grandma could not remember, or perhaps never knew, which unit he belonged to. Riding a motorcycle gave Alphonse the freedom to scour the French countryside in search of goods to send home.

There were things Alphonse did on the battlefield which he would never tell others in his platoon, and it did not involve killing. Because of his advanced age, he was more street-smart than the idealistic, and often frightened young men he served alongside. Alphonse regularly volunteered for details which took him away from the others. As part of the motorcycle squad, his job was to run messages back to headquarters. Sometimes he would drive a truck and carry the wounded to the hospital behind the lines and return with supplies. Alphonse was not above pilfering from the crates and sacks he was delegated to transport. At night, he would head out of the trenches to scout enemy positions. Most of his time was spent searching through the pockets of dead German soldiers. Yet he made it a point to return with accurate reports of the enemy's whereabouts. While Alphonse was a thief, he did not want Americans to get killed because of his extracurricular activities. Besides, he wanted the officers to trust him. If he were wrong most of the time, they would not deploy him as a scout anymore, and he would have fewer opportunities to rob the dead. The officers loved him for his resourcefulness and his ability to survive. As far as Alphonse was concerned, there were many areas to plunder. Abandoned homes, bombed-out shops, and dead bodies—including those of Americans—all yielded gold watches, rings, coins, and other pickings. Alphonse stuffed his goods into a duffel bag. Then he would load the duffel bag into his motorcycle's sidecar.

In a bombed-out house he visited during one of his jaunts, he sliced a painting out of its frame using his bayonet and rolled up the canvas. He was careful not to damage it, and he secreted the pilfered art inside his shirt. Using this technique, he filched many more paintings that he came across.

Alphonse also had a knack for finding hiding places for valuables that owners abandoned in their haste to flee artillery barrages and enemy soldiers. By the end of his service, he needed eight duffle bags to haul the treasure he amassed during his tour of duty. He was savvy enough to collect Lugers, which were issued to German officers and prized by American doughboys. If the soldiers in his outfit asked questions or snooped around, he would offer them cigarettes or provisions, which he had pinched from the supply trucks. Anybody who demanded more would be given a right hook to their jaw—Brooklyn style. Alphonse was not one to be taken advantage of.

His lieutenant and the other ranking officers were too busy fighting the war to take notice of his activities. Plus, they valued his skills too much to question him. If anyone in command took note of his pillaging, they turned a blind eye because he was the only one they did not have to order to crawl into no man's land.

Alphonse was surprised that he could bring his bounty of stolen riches home unchecked. Yet he would not have risked losing his cache of wealth if he did not think that there was a chance he could smuggle all of it home. Alphonse shipped everything back to Brooklyn. Of course, Mr. Molfetta ensured that none of the items were filched by any longshoremen. Mr. Molfetta oversaw the docks. No one dared to steal from him.

Alphonse returned to his family November 1918, soon after Armistice Day. He opened a radio store using the profits from his war exploits. Soon after, in January 1919, his beloved Madeline was struck by a car two blocks from their home and killed. Grandma could not swear to it, but she had heard rumors throughout the years that the driver of that car died in a similar mishap some months after her death. While Alphonse could not be connected to the accident of the driver, there was no doubt that he reveled in it. Many suspected him of killing the driver. Yet the most likely culprit was none other than Mr. Molfetta. Whether or not Alphonse requested the favor of him was sheer speculation.

With Madeline gone, Alphonse raised William and Doris by himself. He sent them to school in the morning. While they were gone, he sold radios out of the front of the store and plied his nefarious trades from the back door. During Prohibition, he smuggled whiskey from Canada. Buyers from local speakeasies bought liquor from him in the back alley behind his shop. Alphonse also took bets on the horses, ran a numbers racket, and engaged in loan sharking. As always, he gave Mr. Molfetta his share.

Alphonse's reputation preceded him. Because of his quiet demeanor, people chose to do business with him as opposed to more notorious men from the underworld. Folks from all classes of society went to his shop to place a bet, borrow money, or buy whiskey or bathtub gin. Alphonse remained a single parent until 1924.

The Heart of Velletri

Grandma rarely mentioned William and Doris to me. She preferred to tell me about Dad. She described how he sat on Alphonse's lap in the back of the shop while Alphonse conducted business and how fast he grew—much like I did. William married his high school sweetheart, a woman named Mary. They lived in New Jersey and had a son, William Jr. Doris died in 1962, one year before I was born. She had slipped in the bathtub of her home and was knocked unconscious. The hot water of the shower scalded Doris so severely that, when she was discovered, she had second and third-degree burns over most of her body. She lingered in the hospital for two days before she died. Grandma shed tears when she told me what had happened to her. My Uncle William was also someone whom I did not meet until much later in life. In the photos I had seen of Uncle William, he was the spitting image of Alphonse. Perhaps, I thought, that was the reason why Grandma did not stay in touch with him.

Chapter 6

May 9th, 1944

In Campania, Gene and his buddies; Harry Beasley and Paul Skinner, or *Skinny* as he was known; made themselves scarce. They found a spot to hide behind a supply tent. None of them wanted to be spotted loafing and then get assigned a detail like digging latrines or unloading trucks. Gene and Harry learned their lesson back in Newport News, Virginia. Their camp consisted mostly of tents and a few wooden structures. This became the staging area for the eventual breakthrough toward Rome. Sgt. Thames sneaked up and caught them smoking cigarettes behind the tent. The wafting scent of tobacco must have attracted him to their location. "You boys need something to do? I have the perfect job for men who know how to be sneaky." Sgt. Thames led him to his tent and ordered them to wait outside. After a few moments, he emerged holding a map. He unfolded it and held it up for them to see.

"We have reports that the Germans might be scouting this road. You boys go ahead and see if you can spot them. Don't go too far now. A mile or two that way should be enough," said Sgt. Thames. He pointed to a location to the north and then looked at them.

"Corporal Skinner, you're in charge of this detail. Stay sharp, watch out for booby traps, and come back before dark."

Skinny's eyes opened wide. "Uh, Sergeant?" said Skinny. Gene smirked. Skinny saw Gene's expression and sighed. Skinny looked like a kid with his hand raised in class asking for a pass to the nurse's office.

"What is it, Skinner?"

"Nothing, Sergeant," Skinny said. He sighed and gave Gene a sideways glance.

"Good. Now get going," said Sgt. Thames. He folded the paper, handed it to Gene, and walked away. Skinny was a corporal, and Gene and Harry were privates. Yet Harry and Skinny looked at Gene; who by possessing the roadmap, became their leader. Gene tucked it into his shirt and left part sticking out. Not only should Sgt. Thames have dispatched an entire squad out for this detail, he should have led it. However, what Gene, Harry, and Skinny did not know was that intelligence reports indicated that after recent fighting in Caserta, the Germans pulled back to just outside Rome. This detail was Sgt. Thames's way of keeping Gene and his buddies busy.

"That's just great. We're being sent out as bait," Harry said.

"Hey Gene, I'll lead the way. I'm really good at tracking." Skinny placed his hands on his hips and grinned.

"We're not tracking anything," Gene whispered. He watched Sgt. Thames walk out of hearing range.

"Come on. We'll get some ammo and rations, fill our canteens, and find someplace with a scenic overview. Pretend we're tourists," Gene said.

The trio plodded along a cobblestone street in the war-torn town of Caserta. It had been two hours since Sgt. Thames gave them orders, and Gene wanted to be far enough away in case he came looking for them in a Jeep. Gene wanted to find an abandoned building comfortable enough for the three of them to hide in.

"There aren't any Germans around here for miles. Harry picked up a rock and threw it far ahead of the three of them.

"What are you doing? Stop that." Gene snapped his head around and gave Harry a cold stare.

"I'm checking for landmines." Harry shrugged his shoulders.

"If you want to check for mines, walk ahead of us." Gene shook his head and turned back around. Harry walked past Skinny and Gene.

"What are you doing?" said Skinny.

Harry looked back. "I'm doing like he said, checking for mines."

"No, you idiot. That's how God makes angels." Skinny and Gene laughed out loud, and Harry raised his eyebrows.

"They don't bury mines under cobblestone, Harry." Gene walked over to him and slapped him on the shoulder.

"Well, aren't you the comedian. I'm the only one here who wants to do real work. You two goof off all day getting us in trouble with the Sergeant." Harry waved his arms as he spoke for emphasis.

"The only work we have to do is stay alive. If you think for one second Thames believed there were snipers out here, don't you think he'd send more than three of us out here?" Gene sucked his teeth and took his BAR from his shoulder. He cradled his weapon in his arms due to its heft.

"Gene is right, Harry. We're just taking a Sunday stroll." Skinny nudged Gene's arm with his elbow and looked at Gene for approval.

"Then this is bullshit. I ought to be taking a nap," Harry said.

"There aren't any Germans around here for miles, at least no live ones," Skinny continued.

Gene looked over his shoulder at Skinny. They had been together since they had left Libya months before. Skinny was from Wisconsin, and he was delighted to be pals with someone from the tough streets of Brooklyn. Gene liked him, but he learned fast that Skinny talked—a lot.

"Let's knock off this bickering. I am bored. I'm going to find a place to relax for a while. In another hour, we'll head back. Thames will be happy that we survived."

Gene walked point along the debris-strewn street. Harry and Skinny trudged behind him. They were just within the town of Caserta, surveying the destruction resulting from Allied bombardments from both artillery and bombers. The air was thick with the putrid odor of dead German soldiers. These weren't the first bodies Gene had seen. However, these Wehrmacht corpses rotted and crawled with maggots. He did his best not to look at them. He listened to Skinny talk as he tried to keep his mind off the carnage and stench and concentrated on finding a resting place that did not stink. A reflection caught his eye, and he looked to his right. The body of a young enemy soldier was seated upright. A wooden beam sticking up from a mound of rubble supported him. At first, Gene thought he was alive. He aimed his BAR at the body and recognized immediately what had caused the reflection. Skinny and Harry caught up with him with their rifles pointed at the dead soldier. Gene shouldered his weapon and walked closer. He examined the lifeless young man. His uniform shirt was tied around his upper thigh and that left him with just an undershirt on. A gold crucifix on a thin, gold chain hung from his neck. Blood soaked through the makeshift bandage. Gene leaned forward and closed the young man's eyes. He paused and looked back at his buddies.

"Gene, the boy's dead. Looks like for just a few hours, though. Must have made it through the fight but couldn't hang on," said Skinny.

"I know, the chain on his neck caught my eye."

"Probably a sniper," said Harry.

"You don't strike me as the grave robbing type," said Skinny.

"I'm not." Gene straightened up and looked at him. "I'm not taking anything. I feel bad for him, that's all."

Skinny took off his helmet and walked over to the body. "I don't see why you'd feel sorry for him and not all the other blown up krauts drawing flies around here."

Gene stared at the crucifix. The small carving of Jesus dying for the sins of mankind seemed futile amid the butchery and ruin they found themselves in.

"This kid probably just gave up. He's wearing this. He must have believed in God…I don't know." Gene pursed his lips and shook his head.

"That leg wound looks nasty. No amount of praying would have helped him," said Skinny.

"We need to keep moving. I mean, it's nice that both of you feel bad for dead guys, but this one would have blown your damn head off if our boys didn't get to him first," said Harry.

Skinny tapped Gene's arm with the back of his hand and nodded. Then he put his helmet back on. Gene took his BAR from his shoulder, and they turned around and continued walking in the direction they were headed in. Gene took his position up front with Skinny right behind him. They walked a few hundred feet, and Harry caught Gene by surprise.

"Hey Gene, this is for you," he said.

Gene stopped and looked at the gold chain and crucifix dangling from his fingers.

"You took that from him?" Gene raised his eyebrows.

"I thought you wanted it but didn't take it because we were around."

"I might take a Luger or a bayonet, but I'm not stealing someone's crucifix." Gene looked over at Skinny who smiled and shook his head.

"Just go on and take it. It didn't do that last boy any good," said Harry.

He dangled it in front of Gene's face. Gene inhaled and then snatched it from his hands. "Fine," he said, "but only because you *gave* it to me."

He put the gold chain in his shirt pocket and walked ahead without acknowledging him.

"That's really messed up, you know?" Skinny said. "They tell us to come over here and blow shit up and shoot the enemy, but we still feel guilty about taking things from the men we kill."

"Hey not for nothing, but aren't we supposed to be looking for snipers? We should keep quiet," Harry said.

"Snipers are far away. That's why they're called snipers," said Skinny. "They can't hear us down here."

"Skinny's right," Gene offered. Yet he did not slow down or even turn around to see the others. In all, the three of them were sent out as scouts to see if they make enemy contact.

"The Germans are holding up just outside of Rome, in the Velletri Gap. I heard Thames talking about it with the other sergeants. There are none of them left around here," said Gene.

As he spoke, he saw two men approaching dressed in civilian attire. They appeared well-fed, wearing clean clothes, and despite the devastation of the town they were in, they seemed to be out for an afternoon stroll.

Gene held up his arm, and they stopped. It was clear that these men were locals, most likely residents of the town searching for food and supplies. The men approached, slow at first, with their hands out at their sides. Gene stood firm with his BAR held out in front, and the other two held their rifles about waist-high.

"*Non abbiamo alcuna arma, ci sono amici,*" said one of the men. He was about thirty years old, and the pair looked like brothers. The other man seemed a bit younger.

"*Chi sei? Dove abiti?*" Gene asked. The men looked at each other and then shrugged their shoulders.

"Hey Koenigsmann, you speak Italian?" Harry asked.

Gene looked back at Harry and raised his eyebrows. "What was your first clue?" he said, and then he shook his head. Turning his attention back to the civilians, he sized them up.

"*Sei italiano?*" the older man asked.

"*No, sono americana. Da Brooklyn,*" Gene said.

"What are they saying?" asked Harry.

"I asked who they are and where they live, and they asked if I am Italian," Gene said.

"What'd you tell them?" Harry asked in a whisper.

Gene cocked his head and turned around to face him. "I told them I was the Pope and that I took a stroll out of the Vatican to get some fresh air."

Skinny laughed. "Good one, Gene."

"Are you guys for real? I didn't say that. Now let me ask them if they know where the Germans are, alright?"

Harry and Skinny looked at him and then at the ground.

"*La nostra famiglia abita in fondo alla strada, stiamo cercando per la benzina e medicine.*" The first man pointed behind him, and Gene turned his attention back to them. He cradled his BAR in his arms. Harry and Skinny did the same.

"*Quali sono i vostri nomi?*" Gene asked.

"*Io sono Samuele, e questo è mio fratello Vincenzo,*" the first man said. He had told Gene that their names were Samuel and Vincent.

Gene looked back at his buddies who had nothing to contribute to the conversation. Though their orders from Sgt. Thames were to scout ahead of the column for any signs of the enemy, so far Samuel and Vincent were the only people they came across. There was an awkward pause between them as Gene couldn't decide whether to question these men further or to say goodbye and let them go on their way.

"*Sei ragazzi fame?*" Samuel asked.

Gene raised an eyebrow. "*Avete cibo?*"

"*Sì, la nostra azienda è finita quella collina,*" He pointed south and both he and Vincent smiled.

Skinny and Harry stepped in closer, still not knowing what was being said. But it was evident to them from Gene's expression that the conversation had become a bit more interesting. Gene and his friends had K-rations, but they were hardly appetizing. Any opportunity to eat a hot meal— especially authentic Italian food—was an opportunity any Brooklyn born young man was unlikely to pass up.

"What'd he say?" Skinny asked.

"They want to know if we're hungry."

"I could eat." Harry's face lit up. "I always wanted to try spaghetti."

"They're not going to have spaghetti here," Gene said. "They're farmers. Most likely, they'll kill a chicken for us."

"You trust these guys?" Skinny asked as he pushed his helmet back above his eyebrows.

"Why not? They aren't armed, and the locals here hate the Germans."

Gene looked at the two men. "*Sei amico di uomini con i tedeschi?*" He asked if they were friends with the Germans.

"*Tedeschi? Odiamo tedeschi. Hanno preso le nostre mucche!*" Vincent pumped his fist and then spit on the ground next to him.

"See? I told you. They hate the Germans," Gene said. Then he turned back to the civilians. "*Vi saremo grati se ci gavce po 'di cibo.*"

"*Eccellente, vi porteremo a casa per incontrare pappa e mamma. Saranno così felici di vedere i soldati americani!*" said Samuel. Then they turned toward the direction of their home and waved for Gene and the others to follow.

"Where are we going?" asked Harry. "You sure we're allowed to do this?"

"We're going with them, boys. It's chicken soup for dinner." Gene chuckled and motioned for them to follow. He held his BAR at his hip and tried to point the muzzle anywhere but at the backs of his new friends. He was excited at the prospect of eating a meal with folks who weren't wearing olive drab uniforms and ready to shoot at the sound of a snapped twig. If Vincent and Samuel's mother cooked as well as Mrs. Molfetta from back home, then Harry and Skinny were in a for a pleasant surprise.

Gene remembered sitting in Mrs. Molfetta's kitchen one Sunday afternoon after mass. He was about eight years old. Gene sat at the kitchen table and watched Mrs. Molfetta stir pasta sauce while his father conducted business with Mr. Molfetta in their living room.

While Gene's visit with Mrs. Molfetta was routine, this instance stood out in his mind. Just as always, he watched her prepare a big pot of sauce. She arose before dawn; attended an early mass; and then returned home to crush tomatoes, cook the pork and meatballs for the sauce, and then stir in garlic, oregano, salt, and a dash of sugar to lessen the acidity. For the rest of the day, she had to make pasta and stir the pot. She also taught Gene Italian.

This Sunday she had a different tone.

"Gino," she said in her thick accent. "Why's a boy like you here with your papa? Why you do not play the stickball with the other boys?"

She sat at the other end of the table rolling cavatelli on a wood board placed on top of the table and sprinkled with a layer of flour. She would boil them after they dried. Mrs. Molfetta always had several pounds of pasta already made, and this was to replace what she would cook for supper.

"My dad brings me with him while he does business," he said.

"*Gino, parlano italiano.*"

"*Sì, certo, la signora Molfetta,*" he said. "*Mio padre mi porta con lui mentre fa affair.*"

She paused and looked past him, through the door into the living room. She could see her husband from the side, comfortable in his leather, winged chair, sipping a glass of red wine as he spoke with Alphonse. She wasn't supposed to listen to their conversations. Later in life, Gene learned that his father brought him there to distract Mrs. Molfetta so she would not be able to eavesdrop. But she wasn't as ignorant as they supposed her to be.

"*E 'questo il tipo di attività si vuole fare da grande un uomo, Gino?*" She raised an eyebrow and kept her eye on the living room.

Is this the type of business you want to do when you grow to be a man, Gino? Gene remembered those words as clearly as he could recite his own name. As young as he was then, he was worldly enough to understand that his father's business was unlike that of a druggist or a butcher. Yet for Mrs. Molfetta to hint at dissatisfaction with her husband's line of work was weighty.

"*No, voglio essere il capitano di una nave,*" he said.

"Oh, you are a good boy!" she said. She got up and walked over the pot of sauce, or *gravy*, as she called it. Using a wooden spoon, she scooped a meatball from inside and deftly placed it on a small dish. Then she put the steaming treat in front of him and placed a folded, cloth napkin next to it and a fork on top.

"There you go. The captain of a ship must eat to become big and strong. You use muscles to steer and raise sails."

"*Grazie signora Molfetta,*" he said. Then he used the fork to slice his treat into pieces before eating. Mrs. Molfetta sat down and hummed as she continued rolling her homemade cavatelli.

Gene didn't know why he recalled that incident, but as they walked to the Vincent and Samuel's farmhouse, his mouth watered for a home-cooked meal.

Harry's voice woke him out of a daydream.

"Aircraft, nine o'clock!"

Skinny grabbed Gene by the arm and led him to a small flank of bushes to their right.

"They're ours," Harry said. He jumped behind the shrubs and joined Gene and Skinny. The Italian brothers continued to run down the road, zig-zagging to avoid debris and cracks in the street.

"Do you guys have a flag or a white hanky or something?" said Gene. He pushed his glasses up and then tilted his helmet back to see the aircraft better.

"They won't pay attention to any flags. As far as they know, it is a trick," Harry said.

"They're heading right for us. Run…" Harry got to his feet and ran towards the crumbling buildings behind them. Skinny followed soon after him, jogging while crouched forward. The sound of the plane's machine gun caused Gene to shudder. Bullets shredded a dual-line path from a point just to the left of the bushes where Gene hid. More rounds kicked up chunks of stone around Skinny as he ran. Gene watched Skinny fall face forward on the cobblestone road. Harry took cover behind a pile of rubble. The Mustangs flew overhead and continued over the abandoned town and out of sight.

Harry reached Skinny first. "Gene, Gene…He's hit bad, really bad!" Harry removed his helmet and then tore open Skinny's shirt. His abdomen was drenched in crimson, blood-soaked from a wound that went through his body.

Working together, Gene and Harry pulled his shirt off and wrapped gauze bandages from their first aid kits around his waist.

"Skinny, talk to me. You're going to be okay," Harry said. He looked up at Gene with his mouth open and breathing heavily. Gene removed his canteen, opened the cap, and put it to Skinny's lips.

"Take a drink, buddy. Have some water," he said. From behind, they heard footsteps. Gene dropped his canteen and pointed his BAR in the direction of the noise. Samuel and Vincent jogged up and stood over them.

Skinny breathed fast, trying to speak. He choked on his words. His eyes widened, and he darted his head back and forth, looking at Harry and Gene for help. Gene lifted Skinny's shoulders and cradled him in his arms while he knelt next to him. Skinny relaxed, felt his stomach, examined his reddened fingers, and then closed his eyes. Gene felt the air leave his lungs. Skinny's shoulders slumped, and his eyes faded, leaving a cold, unfocused gaze.

"He's gone," said Harry.

"*In nomine patris et filii et spiritus sancti.*" Vincent crossed himself and bowed his head. Samuel did the same and clasped his hands at his waist.

Harry knelt down next to Skinny's lifeless body. He watched as Gene took the gold cross he acquired only minutes earlier and placed it in Skinny's shirt pocket.

"What's you go and do that for? I just gave it to you." Harry wiped his eyes and breathed hard. His lower lip quivered, and his hands shook.

"You didn't give me anything. This belonged to that kraut."

"Then why are you giving it to Skinny?"

"I'm not." Gene looked at Harry and down the street to where they found the German young man's body. "This is for his mother."

"That's good, Koenigsmann."

The brothers looked down at Skinny and crossed themselves. Without saying a word, they turned and walked away.

Harry stood first. "Hey, where are they going? They could help us carry Skinny back."

"Let them go. If I were them, I'd want to get back home too."

Harry started to pant. He scanned the sky for the American aircraft that killed their buddy. "What the hell was Thames thinking, sending only three of us out here? Why'd he give us this bullshit detail anyway? Skinny's mom is going to feel even worse knowing her boy was shot by our own planes. He never even saw real combat."

"Harry, Harry…" Gene stood at Skinny's feet. Harry looked at Gene bent down and grabbed Skinny's ankles. Harry's eyes were red and his mouth open. Tears streamed down his face.

"We need to get going. Let's take Skinny back. Thames can have a look at what he's done."

Harry wiped his eyes and took Skinny from under the arms. They trudged for a few hundred feet, pausing near the young German soldier's body. They rested every quarter of a mile or so until they reached camp. Sgt. Thames wouldn't respond to requests to speak with Harry and Gene, and he retired to his tent for the evening. By morning, Skinny was shipped on a truck to the rear along with the outgoing mail. A tear-stained letter crammed in one of the mail sacks contained the hand-written apology from Sgt. Thames to Corporal Paul Skinner's mother and a small, gold crucifix on a chain.

Chapter 7

1924 - 1932

The Koenigsmann family of East 73rd Street in Bay Ridge, Brooklyn had an embarrassment of riches throughout The Great Depression. Gene's father, Alphonse, was a bear of a man with a full face, deep-set eyes, and dark hair which he kept combed back. Alphonse drove a large Ford sedan at a time when many families could not afford a bus ticket. He also owned a 36-foot cabin-cruiser, which he kept docked at a marina in Sheepshead Bay.

Young Gene remembered an episode which took place when he was about six years old. It was the first of many scenes of its kind that would occur on his front stoop. A man who lived down the block knocked on their door with his head down and his hat in hand. He pleaded for a little bit of cash or a handout. Unlike many bookies, Alphonse took pity.

"Mister Kane," the man said. Alphonse would sometimes use the last name *Kane* instead of Koenigsmann, because his surname was frequently mispronounced by anyone attempting to say it. "My family has no food. We have nothing. I am out of work." The man's lips quivered as he awaited a reply from Alphonse.

Gene stood at his father's side. The hard-luck neighbor combed his hair with his hand, then swallowed. Alphonse looked up and down the street and then disappeared into the house. There was an awkward moment as the neighbor, who was the father of one of Gene's playmates, smiled at him and looked back down at his shoes. Moments later, Alphonse returned with a scrap of paper with an address scrawled on it. "Go to this store. Tell the manager, Henry, that Al Kane sent you. Your family will eat tonight."

Alphonse grinned and patted Gene's head. The man nodded, not daring to shake Alphonse's hand. Then he scurried off to get groceries for his wife and kids. This turned out to be a routine over the years. Alphonse's generosity tempered his notorious reputation. Though men feared Alphonse, he was respected. Much of the time Alphonse sent those who asked for help to the shop owned by someone who was in debt to him. While this bit of charity was never enough to erase what was owed, it was a reminder that the money was due.

Alphonse was an imposing figure of a man, just under six feet tall, perhaps two-hundred and twenty pounds. He walked with a slight hunch forward and kept his right hand in his vest pocket. Always dressed in a suit, he was also fond of donning wide-brimmed Fedoras. Holding a cigar in his mouth, most of the time unlit, was a habit which Lillian wanted him to quit, not for health reasons, but to keep the house from stinking of tobacco.

Of all the people who could have told Gene the story of how his father and mother met, it was Mr. Molfetta. Admittedly, Gene was not proud of the way his father came to marry his mother, but as he grew up, he came to terms with the story.

Alphonse did not court Lillian the way couples traditionally did. Their marriage was arranged. Lillian's father, Martin Torrence, was a pianist who earned his living playing with various orchestras and at nightclubs. His sole vice, though, was betting on horses. Martin chose to place his bets with Alphonse, and he would collect his winnings with a broad smile and a tip of his hat. Alphonse was smart enough to lay-off his bets with Mr. Molfetta. While Alphonse did not suffer fools lightly, he accepted Martin's cockiness as part of doing business.

Along with Alphonse's success as a bookie and a loan shark, there came the misfortune of others. Martin Torrence's luck ran out with a large wager on a long-shot horse that few had heard of. Martin gambled two-thousand dollars on the horse after overhearing a conversation at a nightclub between two men whom he mistook for local mobsters. Thinking that the fix was in, he bet with Alphonse more than he had on the horse. It was standard practice for Alphonse to see a gambler's money before he recorded the bet. However, Martin Torrence was a regular and Alphonse believed that he possessed that sum of money. Martin was a successful musician, and he always wore a tailored suit and expensive shoes. Alphonse also thought that if he did not have the cash, then he could come up with something of value instead. After all, that was how Alphonse had obtained his boat.

"You want two-thousand dollars on Grandmother's Quilt? I'll gladly take your money, Mr. Torrence; but I have to ask, are you crazy?" Alphonse characteristically had a stone-faced glare, rarely smiled, and viewed the world with the narrow-eyed scrutiny of a hard-boiled detective.

"Yes, that's the horse. And put every nickel on her in the fifth. She's a winner." Martin smiled, showing his teeth, and rocked on his heels. Alphonse recorded the bet in his book and shook his head.

"Ordinarily I don't wish anyone luck, but in this case, you'll need plenty of it," said Alphonse.

"Thank you, Mr. Kane," said Martin. He tipped his hat and left through the rear door of the flower shop. He stumbled when he heard Alphonse chuckle through the window screen.

The next day, after Martin's horse had finished last, he returned to the florist wearing a grim expression. More importantly, he only had five-hundred dollars. He had been so confident in what he thought was a valid tip that he acted recklessly as a result.

Alphonse sat behind his desk and kept his eyes focused on the ledger opened before him. Alphonse never greeted anyone or initiated a conversation unless it was necessary. Martin stood before him with the brim of his hat gripped in his fingers.

"I am guessing by your silence that you do not have the money you owe me. Am I correct?" Alphonse said. He closed his ledger and leaned back. He placed an unlit cigar in his mouth and folded his hands on his belly.

"Well, I had it... I mean I have some of it," Martin said.

"You only have some of it? You mean to say that you placed a bet with me, and you did not have all of the money?" Alphonse leaned forward and rested his arms on the desktop. He looked Martin in the eye. Martin fumbled with his hat and looked at his feet.

"I have five hundred dollars. I can give it to you now." He gulped and wiped his forehead with a handkerchief.

"You owe me two-grand."

"Yes, I do. I can give you this now, and I will get you the rest."

Alphonse stood up, walked around the desk, and faced him. Martin took a step back.

"Do you think I am a foolish man, Martin? Do you think I am someone not to be taken seriously?"

"No, no, not at all, Mr. Kane." Martin dabbed his brow again.

"Then why do you treat me like I am a fool?" Alphonse folded his arms.

"I'm not. I never would. You're no fool," Martin stammered and stepped backward again. There was a chair behind him, and he plopped down on it. Alphonse moved closer and loomed over Martin.

"You have been coming to my place of business a long time, Martin. You have also won a lot of money. I think that you thought you were going to win big on a sure thing, so you bet more than what you had. Since you only had five-hundred bucks, and you bet two grand, that means that you think I am a fool."

"Of course not." Martin held his hat over his chest.

Alphonse sighed, walked over to the window, and peered into the alley. He took the cigar out of his mouth and placed it in his shirt pocket. Then he put his hands on his hips. He faced Martin.

"Any other man in your position would find themselves in a lot of trouble. I'm talking about the kind of trouble that leads to a long stay in the hospital or perhaps worse. But I like you, Martin. However, Mr. Molfetta, he does not know you at all." Alphonse put his hands in his pockets and walked over to him. Martin breathed quickly, and the color drained from his face.

"Please, Mr. Kane... Mr. Kane... I will get you the money. I promise. I will get it to you as soon as possible." Martin's voice cracked.

"Stop it. Stop lying to me. If you had the money, you would not be in this situation. And if you could get it, you would have already. Unless you still believe that I am a fool, don't speak another word." Alphonse pointed at him. Martin pursed his lips and blinked several times. Alphonse sat on his desk and crossed his arms.

"Your daughter Lillian, how old is she?" Alphonse tilted his head.

"Why do you ask?" Martin swallowed hard.

"I would like to meet her."

Martin's head dropped. He placed his hat on the desk and covered his face with his palms. Then he took his hands away, put them on the arms of the chair, and sat straight.

"She's old enough," he said.

"Good. When do I meet her?" Alphonse glared at him.

"She will be at my performance tonight. I am playing with the orchestra." Martin's shoulders sagged, and he shook his head ever so slightly.

"Tickets to this event are expensive, are they not?" Alphonse raised an eyebrow.

"I will leave one for you at the box office. Lillian was going to bring a friend. Now she will be with you. Oh God," Martin said. He sobbed and wiped his eyes with his hankie.

"Don't cry, Martin. Be a man. After all, she will be with me, and I am a perfect gentleman. Think of it this way, I can give Mr. Molfetta the ticket, and you will have an excellent reason to cry for your last time." Alphonse put his cigar back in his mouth and lit it with a lighter. Martin remained still for a moment and then stood up fast.

"I must go. Rehearsal is in a few minutes, and I cannot be late." He put his hat on and stuffed his hankie in the top pocket of his jacket. He held out his hand for Alphonse to shake. Alphonse regarded it as if he were being handed a rotten fish. Martin withdrew his hand and nodded to Alphonse.

"I will see you tonight, Mr. Kane." Then he walked out the rear door.

Alphonse retrieved his ticket at the box office as Martin had promised. Lillian expected Alphonse to be there, and she was genial. Martin told his daughter about the debt he owed Alphonse and about his desire to meet her. Though she did not protest, she was not happy. Alphonse and Lillian were married two months later. She had just turned twenty, and Alphonse was thirty-six years old. Martin and a group of fellow musicians played music at their wedding reception. The debt was paid as far as Alphonse was concerned. Lillian resigned herself to a life with a much older man, and in turn, she saved her father's life.

Eugene was the only child of their union. Gene was the apple of Lillian's eye. She loved him more than anything. Lillian did not try to be a mother to William and Doris. She cooked for them and washed their clothes, but she was more of a big sister than a stepmother. Her relationship with Alphonse was distant at best. Though he never mistreated her, he treated their relationship like any other business arrangement. He needed a wife, and she provided him with a son. In return, Lillian married a man who could provide for her in the worsening economy of the nineteen-thirties. Their marriage dissolved her father's debt. Martin never placed another wager on a horse again.

As much as Alphonse loved his family, he was a reserved and emotionally detached man. That is why he was so feared in his line of work. The men he dealt with could not read him. The roundness of his face made him appear younger than he was and some likened him to Al Capone. However, Alphonse was quick to dismiss that comparison.

Alphonse's steely countenance did not prevent him from being close to his son. If they weren't spending time at Mr. Molfetta's with young Gene learning a new language, chatting it up, and eating pasta with Mrs. Molfetta; Gene was on the boat with Alphonse. The *Sea Angel*, as she was christened by his half-sister, Doris, was the stuff of fantasy for Gene. For as long as he could remember, he had wanted to be a ship's captain when he grew up.

At the library, Gene read about ships and water vessels of all types. He could name every class of U.S. Naval warships. He would spend time in his room on his bed with the pages of a book open, staring at photos of ocean liners and warships.

The Sea Angel became his ship while he daydreamed all those summer afternoons. With a fishing line in the water, he'd stare at the horizon and become excited when he saw another vessel in the distance. His father was content to watch him scamper about the deck and wave at the distant ships. Years later, an eighteen-year-old Gene would charge down the ramp of a U.S. Navy landing craft and onto the beach at Anzio.

Chapter 8

May 22, 1944

"That's Anzio Annie. The krauts have been pounding sand here with that gun for months," said Sgt. Thames. Gene, Harry, and the sergeant crouched in a crater on the beachhead. Thames led the way with self-confidence, much like a movie viewer who notices the zipper on the monster's costume in a horror film and realizes that the danger isn't real. The muddy battleground at Anzio did not appear to present much of a challenge for Sgt. Thames. He was experienced in combat, and he guided his men in and around the craters and dunes on the beachhead with little effort. His younger charges, Gene and Harry, had taken a disliking to him after Skinny's death, and Sgt. Thames sensed this. Since the sergeant's order to scout for Germans left Cpl. Skinner dead, Sgt. Thames had become over-protective—and softer. A lot of his attention was focused on Gene and Harry. Still Sgt. Thames' bravado and age provided them with comfort as they made their first foray into battle. If anything, Thames had a reputation as a fighter, and while the rest of the platoon struggled to keep up, Thames made it his mission to keep Gene and Harry alive.

The Heart of Velletri

The Germans had held Anzio under siege for months since the initial Allied landing in January 1944. Anzio Annie was a rail-mounted artillery piece which could fire a 560-pound artillery round for forty miles. Shells would land, causing deafening explosions and massive damage. G.I.s could hear the *whooshing* sound of incoming rounds when they tumbled end-over-end through the air. Immediately, they'd duck for cover—just as Thames, Harry, and Gene were doing.

"Here comes another." Sgt. Thames pushed Gene first and then Harry. Neither one needed to be told to lay down flat. The blast erupted about fifty meters to their right. Mud, sand, and seawater rained upon them. Immediately after, screams from the wounded filled their ears. Gene exhaled. He was alive. Sgt. Thames jumped to his feet and ran to the fallen soldiers.

"Medic, medic!" he cried. He grabbed the front of his helmet and sprinted, crouched over with his Thompson in his other hand.

"Harry?" Gene looked to see if his buddy was hit.

"Yeah, I'm okay," Harry said.

"You hear those boys over there? I'm surprised anyone can live after that explosion," said Gene.

They pushed themselves up and peeked over the edge of the crater. Sgt.Thames saw them and jogged back, waving his hand at them.

"We have to get off this beach," he yelled.

Gene looked at Harry and shrugged. "What do you think?" Gene asked.

"I guess he's giving us an order," said Harry. He climbed to his feet and stepped out of the crater. Gene stood to follow Harry. The whoosh of another artillery round filled the air. The noise grew louder and neared their position.

"Get away from there!" Sgt. Thames yelled and ducked for cover.

Gene and Harry had no time to duck, much less lay flat in their hole. The round hit about five yards in front of them.

"Holy shit." Harry dropped his rifle and removed his helmet. He looked back. Gene had put down his helmet also.

"I don't believe it. It's a dud." Gene took Harry by the shoulder. "Get your stuff, and let's get the hell out of here."

Harry picked up his rifle and helmet and then put his helmet back on his head. He followed Gene toward the dunes. Sgt. Thames cut them off.

"You two are the luckiest sons of bitches I ever saw. I told you to stay down. What if that thing exploded?" he said.

"We'd have been buried alive," said Gene.

Sgt. Thames cocked his head, never considering that, if it had gone off, a blast from a shell that large would have killed them no matter what position they took.

"From now on, you two stay with me. Got it? Wherever we are, no matter what we're doing, you stick to me like glue, understand?" He looked each of them in the eye and breathed hard. Gene still did not like him for what had happened to Skinny, and he certainly did not like being favored, either.

"What about the rest of the platoon?" Gene asked. He pointed with this thumb over his shoulder at the men who were huddled up on the beach behind them. Sgt.Thames raised his shoulders and neared Gene.

"I'm not losing another man ever again, not for the rest of this God damn war. You hear me? Now let's move out before the Luftwaffe takes their turn." Sgt.Thames did an about face and stomped forward toward the dunes where other commanders and their platoons began to assemble. The area was abuzz with intense activity. The wounded were being carried away to waiting troop carriers. Soldiers arrived and disembarked landing crafts while fumbling with large packs, weapons, and other gear. Occasionally, shells from smaller enemy artillery exploded along the expansive shore, and the threat of the Luftwaffe kept everyone moving. In all the frantic activity, Gene watched Sgt. Thames from behind. His purposeful gait portrayed a man who was in denial about having to sacrifice the lives of his men while he led them on their mission. The aversion Gene had for him dissipated at that moment. It was then he realized that this man was not infallible and never claimed to be. He wanted to run to his sergeant and pat him on the back in the same way a baseball manager tells a struggling pitcher not to worry and to stay in command of the game. However, he knew he had no standing to do that.

Another artillery round whooshed toward them. Harry and Gene ran to catch up with Sgt. Thames. The blast landed about one-hundred yards out in the sea.

Sgt. Thames looked over his shoulder and saw his Gene and Harry following him. Gene saw Sgt. Thames glance at them. Gene did not mention it to Harry, but Sgt. Thames smiled when he saw them.

Chapter 9

September 1978

Gregory was the tallest of the high school boys at the bus stop. On the first day of school, he showed up with a denim jacket, a black Sabbath tee-shirt underneath, and blue jeans with a tear in the knee. He was the new guy in the neighborhood. I sized him up and figured that he probably smoked pot and did poorly in school. My friends, Ricky and Mark, spied on him as if he were a sideshow freak. None of us were dressed formally for classes. We each wore jeans and collared button-down shirts. Yet Gregory took dressing down seriously.

I noticed right away that Gregory's mannerisms were odd. He wrote backward in his notebooks. We had not even been issued textbooks or given homework, and he had bizarre entries scrawled into the pages of his brand-new, spiral notebooks. He made it a point to show us.

"Hey, read this." Gregory shoved his handiwork under my nose. Although Gregory was over six-feet tall, he was not intimidating like the muscle-head jocks in gym class. Gregory's hair was sandy-brown and looked like he had a *perm*. His bean-pole physique made him look like a frizzy-haired Abraham Lincoln reincarnated as a lower-middle-class kid from the south shore of Long Island.

"It's' all backward," I said. Ricky and Mark were unimpressed. In the high school social order, we were hardly bookworms, yet considered smart. None of us had girlfriends, but we weren't freaky like Gregory either. Indeed, we had scaled enough rungs on the high school societal ladder to be able to blow off this new guy who looked like a misfit.

"It's funny. That's why I do that," he said. I stepped back and looked up at him. I had to give him credit for trying. It wasn't that he wanted to impress us with writing backward, it was his exuberance that caught my attention.

"What's your name, man?" Mark was the one who held the highest *cool* rating in our clique. It was natural that he would open up the investigation into who he was and where he came from.

"I'm Gregory, Gregory Schuster." None of us stepped forward to shake his hand.

"I'm Mark."

"Rick."

"Mike."

"Mark, Rick, and Mike?" He pointed to each of us as he repeated our names. "That should be easy to remember. You sound like the members of a sixties pop band. I could see you on the Ed Sullivan show wearing black suits with skinny ties and Beatles haircuts." Gregory laughed. None of us reacted.

"Where are you from, Greg?" Mark asked.

"It's *Gregory*. And I am from Hicksville." We nodded. Long Islanders always ignore the irony in the name of that town since we're all supposed to be hip New Yorkers.

"Well, Gregory from Hicksville, the bus is here," said Mark as he walked over to the bus stop. I broke away and caught up with Mark.

"What's with that weirdo?" he asked. I shook my head. Gregory was behind us. I overheard him asking Rick if he ever went hunting or if he owned any guns. He spoke loudly, and with his height and his tightly-curled hairdo, he was difficult to ignore.

A few weeks later I was alone on the bus for the ride home. Mark and Rick were staying after school for football practice. Though I enjoyed playing baseball, handball, and football with my friends, I did not belong to any organized sports teams in school. It was a Friday afternoon. Since I did not have a girlfriend, I was doomed to spend the evening watching TV with my folks. Gregory appeared from behind. It was inexplicable how I could miss him when I boarded the bus.

"Hey man, where are your pals?" I looked up. Gregory sat next to me.

"They're at practice."

"Baseball?"

"In November?" I shook my head.

"Oh, that's right. I don't really follow baseball." Gregory wedged his notebooks between the two of us. My habit was to leave my books in my locker for my glorious two days away from Copiague Senior High School unless I had homework, which I did not.

Gregory rambled on about how much better it was in Hicksville, and how his parents decided to move when they did not like their neighborhood anymore. I guessed that the neighbors could not stand Gregory, and they had moved away rather than face a mob of townsfolk armed with pitchforks and torches looking to burn them out of their home.

"Hey, you want to come to my house tonight? My dad is bringing home a new rifle."

"Uh, a new rifle? Really?"

"Yeah, he goes hunting all the time, and he's getting a Weatherby 300 magnum."

Not that I was desperate for a friend, but anyone who asks someone to come to their house to check out a new gun has got to be in even more need of companionship than I was. Mark and Rick were cool guys, but they were jocks. I was a *tweener* who was not smart enough for nerds and not athletic enough for the sports crowd. Before I could think about it, my mouth said *yeah*.

After dinner, I told my parents I was going to Gregory's house. Mom was busy with her needlepoint. Dad was watching TV. They weren't curious about him, and I was relieved that I did not need to explain who Gregory was, because he was such an oddball. By then, my mother had heard that his family had moved in two blocks away from us. The other moms in town did not offer any negative reviews about them apparently.

Since my mother didn't raise an eyebrow, I felt more comfortable with my decision to hang out with him. Besides, the lure of seeing his father's rifle was too much of an attraction to pass up. Many of my friends' fathers owned guns, but I had only seen them encased in cabinets or hung high on a wall on a rifle rack. My Dad strictly forbade firearms in our home. He would not permit me to own so much as a BB gun. Because of my father's extreme dislike of all guns, I became more fascinated with them. That was even more of a reason why I so curious to see one up close at Gregory's house that night. Maybe Gregory's father would allow me to hold it.

"Be home by ten," my father said.

"Eleven," I countered as I grabbed my hooded sweatshirt and ran out the door.

Gregory's father was a threatening man, taller than his son and with broad shoulders. He had a crew cut and a stern expression. He reminded me of an older, bad-tempered state trooper who had locked up a lot of bad guys.

Gregory and I met him in the basement. Both rooms appeared to be dedicated to the care and storage of firearms. I must admit that I was impressed. Mr. Schuster loaded his own ammunition. There were boxes of empty shell casings for different calibers on a wooden bench and other paraphernalia. I noticed a gun safe in the corner, which must have held at least twenty rifles. Mr. Schuster saw me admiring the gun safe.

"It's bolted to the floor," Mr. Schuster said as he walked past me. I watched as he stopped next to the four-foot high, black gun vault and placed a hand on top of it. "You need dynamite to get into this." He smacked the top and smiled as if he were showing off a gleaming, new Mercedes-Benz.

"Or the combination," Gregory quipped. Mr. Schuster glared at him.

"What, Dad? I was kidding."

His father folded his arms and looked at me.

"You ever fire a gun?"

"No."

"Does your father own any guns?"

My heart beat a bit quickly. He had a law enforcement demeanor about him. And Gregory told me that he was a corrections officer. That meant he spent most of his time around bad guys.

"No. He doesn't like them."

"Why not? What's he going to do if someone breaks into the house?"

"Someone tried that once. He ran outside with a baseball bat."

Mr. Schuster laughed and stuck his thumbs through his belt loops. "A baseball bat? That's funny. And if the perp were armed with a gun, he'd be dead."

His mocking tone irritated me. Even though my parents taught me to respect my elders, I pushed back.

"It worked, the guy ran."

"He's was lucky."

"I don't think luck had much to do with it. Not many people mess with my father."

"He's a tough guy, huh?"

"Yes, he is."

"What does he do for a living?" Mr. Schuster walked over to his workbench. Overhead was a cabinet that was secured with a hasp and a padlock. Everything was tidy and ordered, and the brass casings were lined upright in plastic cases.

"He's a mechanic. He fixes oil burners, refrigerators, and air conditioners."

"Oh, that's good…I guess." Mr. Schuster looked at Gregory and grinned. He was full of himself. I don't know if it was because of all of his firearms or if it was because he considered himself to be some sort of super-hero because he was a corrections officer. I decided to keep my mouth shut because it was only eight o'clock, and I did not want to go home. Although I was just a sophomore, it a social taboo to be seen walking around the neighborhood, or even on a bicycle, on a Friday night when there were all kinds of social events I could be attending with cooler kids.

"Mike's dad was in the army," Gregory offered.

"Really?" He raised his eyebrows and looked down at me. By that age, I was approaching six feet tall myself, but I was no giant like Greg and his father.

"I never served in the armed forces."

I just nodded.

"What did your father do in the army?" He leaned both of his hands on the workbench and pursed his lips together.

"He fought against Germans," I said.

"Germans? World War II? How old is your father?" Mr. Schuster sneered at me and sucked his teeth. Mr. Schuster's disrespect toward my father angered me. I was ready to leave and go home. However, I was too intimidated to abruptly walk away from an adult and ruin any sort of friendship I might have with Gregory.

Gregory smiled, proud of his dad. Yet I doubt he realized that his father felt challenged by my father's service. I suspected that Mr. Schuster would not have been jealous of his wounds, though.

"We have a small family. I'm the last child out of three. He's fifty-three years old."

"What did he shoot, an M1 Garand?" Mr. Schuster walked over to his big safe and leaned forward. He twisted the knob on the door as he waited for my answer.

"Well yeah, that's what he was issued at first. But they gave him a Browning Automatic Rifle." The only reason I knew any of this was because of my uncles—my mother's brothers. Dad was so unwilling to share anything about the war, especially combat, that he had to practically be dragged into any conversation about history which involved the years between nineteen-thirty-nine and nineteen-forty-five. Whenever Uncle Richard and Uncle Bob came to visit, they'd sit at the dinner table and start rambling on about the Japanese and the Nazis and offer their opinions about how each battle was fought. This irked Dad because they were too young to have experienced combat, and they both missed *The Big Show* as he termed it.

Uncle Bob had been in the Army and had served in the post-war occupation of Germany. Uncle Richard had been in the Merchant Marines. It didn't hurt that each of them urged my father to talk about the war. Dad typically intervened when there was an error of fact.

The real value in any of these exchanges was that I was a child who sat at the same table and kept a keen ear open for anything my dad said, which would give me a clue to who he was before I was born and what had happened to him when he was a soldier. Those details about the weapons he used were byproducts of those family dinners and the awkward history lessons which accompanied them.

Mr. Schuster unlocked the door of the safe. It opened towards me, so I could not see inside. My heart rate quickened, because I was so curious to see a gun and there were so many of them. I was also a bit nervous, because my dad would most likely get angry if he knew another father was so casual with rifles around his son.

"Well, that's good. The M1 Garand was a piece of shit."

"Really? My dad said it was a great rifle." I became defensive since Mr. Schuster was acting like a know-it-all. I had no idea what my dad's opinion of that rifle was—or any weapon for that matter—since he never talked to me about it.

"It only holds eight rounds. And they were held together by a metal en-block. When a soldier fired the last round, the en-block was ejected along with the last shell casing. It made a distinctive, metallic sound that let the enemy know that the

G.I. was out of ammo. A lot of guys were killed that way." He raised himself to his full height, folded his arms, and stared down at me. I lowered my head and looked away from him.

"I never knew that," I said. "Maybe that's how my father got shot?" It was moments like that one when I understood how little I knew about what happened to my father in the war.

"I'd bet my house on it," said Mr. Schuster. "He should have stuck with the BAR."

Though Gregory's dad made me feel uncomfortable, he provided me with insight, and I was appreciative. He may have been rough around the edges, but in the end, he was more affable than I had initially deemed him to be. He showed us his new rifle and then took out some others he had collected over the years. Some of the firearms had belonged to his father. He was proud to own them and considered them to be family heirlooms.

That night I had trouble falling asleep. After marveling at all the guns I had seen that evening, I kept imagining what it must have been like for my father in battle and getting shot— *twice.*

Gregory arrived at my house early the next day. He parked his ten-speed on its kickstand in our driveway and introduced himself to my father. Dad was under the carport, painting an outdoor, Adirondack chair. When I came outside, it took me by surprise to see them talking to each other.

"Hi Gregory. Hi Dad," I said.

"Good morning, Mike," Dad said. He looked up at me and then at Gregory's bike. I could read his mind. He would like me to stick around and help him with chores, but he didn't want to ask.

"I was telling your father that my father showed you his gun collection last night."

I gulped. Apparently I misread Dad's emotions. Clearly, he was annoyed but didn't want to say anything in front of Gregory. Not only did Dad hate guns, but he also didn't want his kids anywhere near them.

"Oh yeah. Well he just held them up for us to look at. We didn't hold them or anything," I said.

Dad stopped painting and looked up at me. The chair was on its back, newspapers were spread underneath to catch drips, and he was kneeling next to it. Dad placed his hand on an unpainted part of the chair. He appeared as though he wanted to say something, but he held back.

"Mr. Koenigsmann, Mike tells me you were in World War II. Did you ever use the M1 Garand?" Gregory asked. I could see the confusion in Dad's eyes. What should have been the two of us saying a quick hello and then taking off was turning into an awkward conversation. Both my father and I did not want this to happen. For one thing, I didn't want to get roped into working around the house all day. And I could tell that Dad was not pleased to learn about Mr. Schuster exhibiting his gun collection to me.

"Yes. It was standard issue," he said. I could tell he was cordial for my sake.

"Hey Gregory, let's get moving. I want to see if Mark and Rick are down at the ball field," I said.

"My dad says it's a piece of junk," said Gregory. Dad kept painting. I tugged at Gregory's arm.

"Did you use the Thompson, the sub-machine gun too?" At that point, I could tell that my father was annoyed. Gregory had no clue that Dad was peeved. I noticed the stern appearance Dad's face took on and the bold brush strokes he was using on the chair. Only his rigid sense of civility kept him from telling my new buddy to shove off.

"Yes," he said through clenched teeth.

"Gregory, let's go." I walked away to get my bike from the backyard where I left it the night before. I stopped after taking a few steps when I saw that Gregory had continued his questioning.

"How about the BAR?"

"I used that," said Dad.

"My father says that was a piece of junk too." Gregory folded his arm and touched his chin. He wanted to appear knowledgeable and engage my dad in a topic which both he and Mr. Schuster were avid about. What he didn't understand was that to a veteran, he came off as smug and uninformed.

"Was your father in the military?" My father pressed his lips together and narrowed his eyes.

That was it. Dad had endured enough of Gregory's banter. My shoulders dropped, and my mouth opened.

"Uh, no. But he knows all about guns." Gregory took his hand away from his face and let his arms fall to his sides.

"What does he do, read about them? Does he shoot at the paper targets?"

"We go hunting all the time. Last year my dad shot a deer. It was an eight-point buck." Greg smiled, full of pride and unable to comprehend where the conversation was going.

"A deer, huh?" Dad stood up. He wasn't as tall as Mr. Schuster, but he was broader, more muscular, and had a distinctive, deep voice which frightened many of my friends, including Rick and Mark. Gregory remained unaffected by my father's countenance.

"Deer don't shoot back. They don't hide in bombed-out buildings and pick off dozens of your friends, fire artillery rounds into your positions, or strafe your platoon in the streets of a town in ruins. And they certainly don't cry for their mothers as they lay dying, tangled in barbed wire while no one can help them because they are being held down by machine gun fire."

Gregory gulped and looked at me. I shrugged my shoulders.

"So, what does your father know about guns? He never saw a shot fired in anger in his life."

Gregory didn't respond. Dad glared at him. Finally, he looked at the chair, then at me.

"You boys run off and have fun, okay?" He pointed toward the street with his paintbrush. I didn't have to be told twice. In a moment, I jogged away to get my bike. Dad nodded at me as I rode past him and down the driveway. Gregory had already mounted his ten-speed and rode away and onto the sidewalk.

"Be home in time for dinner," Dad called after me. Without looking back, I raised my hand over my head and waved.

"I'd listen to him if I were you," Gregory said. We rode in tandem up Warwick Avenue to the schoolyard in hopes of finding my friends.

"I do, all the time."

We didn't speak again until we made it to the schoolyard and saw Rick and Mark playing handball on the courts. We pulled up, dismounted our bikes, and left them leaning on their kickstands.

"Hey Gregory," I said. He paused and looked back at me.

"I'm sorry about my dad," I said. Mark cut me short.

"You guys want to team up?" Mark asked.

Neither of us answered.

"Don't be." Gregory bit his lower lip and then took a deep breath.

"I saw the scar on the side of your father's neck. How'd he ever survive that?" Gregory turned to me and cocked his head to one side.

"It's Mike and I against you and Rick," said Mark.

Yeah, how did he live after all? I thought about it and reran the scene in my head. I should have stayed home to help him paint and do chores. The image of my father, alone on a Saturday working around the house, when he should be relaxing made me feel guilty.

"Are you playing or what?" Rick threw me the ball.

"We're up first," I said as I caught it and took a spot next to Mark. Dinner time came quickly, and I didn't have to be reminded to go home. Dad's booming voice had echoed in my head before he had the chance to call out my name while standing at the end of the driveway.

101

Chapter 10

October 1932

Alphonse buttoned his jacket and straightened his Fedora. His reflection in the wall mirror in the master bedroom included young Gene at his side. The family had just returned from Sunday mass. Gene's mother had walked to the market to buy groceries for dinner. Alphonse would not walk the usual route to Mr. Molfetta's house to give him his envelope full of cash. An unusually warm day for October, it was likely that Mr. Molfetta would meet Alphonse along the way. Gene enjoyed it when his father and Mr. Molfetta conducted their business outside. Typically, they would sit on a bench in the park and talk while Gene played with the other boys there. Mr. Molfetta's nephew, Salvatore, a tall, burly young man in his early twenties, would stand with his hand tucked inside his jacket nearby and keep a watchful eye on those walking past them.

That day, Alphonse stepped on the sidewalk and held Gene's hand. Together, they made their way up E. 73rd street to the corner where they would wait for Mr. Molfetta. Salvatore appeared first. Gene, from the vantage point of a seven-year-old, recognized Salvatore's black, wide-brimmed hat. His expressionless, deep-set, piercing brown eyes always frightened Gene. The two had never conversed except once, when an older boy at the playground shoved Gene to the ground. Salvatore had chased the kid away. Looking down at Gene, he held out his hand and had said, "Come on, get up." That incident had happened almost a year earlier, and Salvatore had never said a word to Gene before or since.

Alphonse took his son's hand and pulled him close. Gene felt an unusually strenuous tug and looked up at his father. Alphonse squinted, focusing his attention on something far away. His lips were thin and whitened as he pursed them together. Gene looked up the block and recognized Mr. Molfetta's charcoal-gray hat. His black overcoat framed his face. Mr. Molfetta walked with his usual, confident stride. Salvatore waited for Mr. Molfetta to catch up with him. He was much taller than Mr. Molfetta, younger and more muscular—the perfect bodyguard. A black car pulled alongside them.

Alphonse lifted Gene and carried him up the front stoop of one of their neighbor's homes. The front door was unlocked. He yanked the door open and put his son in the small vestibule.

"Stay on the floor. Don't look out the window!"

Gene disobeyed his father and watched him walk quickly down the steps and head in the direction of Salvatore and Mr. Molfetta. Alphonse reached inside his jacket and produced a Colt .45 caliber pistol. With his left hand, he racked a round into the chamber and leveled his weapon at the car. Gene pressed his face against the windowpane. The car stopped, and a passenger emerged from the back seat. He was a young man, well dressed just like Salvatore. He aimed a pistol at Alphonse and fired. The shot missed. The blast made Gene's body jerk. He felt it up his spine, and his already roiled stomach tightened. Alphonse fired three shots at the man. All three bullets hit the gunman. Gene opened the door and ran onto the sidewalk.

"Daddy, Daddy!" he yelled.

Alphonse spun his head around. "Gene, get back in the house," he said. Alphonse did not holler at him. His deep voice reverberated in Eugene's ears. He watched his father march confidently toward the car and the crumpled man he had just shot. He lay on the street a few yards away from Salvatore and Mr. Molfetta. Gene saw Mr. Molfetta crouching behind a garbage can. Salvatore chased the car as it raced down the block. Salvatore fired several shots at the fleeing vehicle. As the car passed Alphonse, the driver aimed a gun at him. Alphonse spun around, his arm outstretched, and fired the last of the rounds in his handgun at the gunman behind the wheel. Gene stood on the sidewalk with his mouth open, witnessing the events unfold with a mix of excitement and terror. Salvatore rushed over to Gene and scooped him up into his arms, carrying Gene up the steps of his home. Salvatore opened the door, put him inside, and then shut the door.

"Stay down!" he yelled. Then he rejoined Alphonse.

Gene watched as his father reloaded his pistol. The driver crashed into a parked car in front of the house next door. The car door opened, and the driver collapsed onto the pavement. He raised his hands and begged Alphonse not to shoot him.

"You could have killed my son!" Alphonse hollered. He aimed his pistol at the man's face. Salvatore approached Alphonse, placed his hand on his pistol and shook his head. Alphonse nodded, put his gun in his pocket, and walked away. The man on the ground dropped his arms. Salvatore looked up and down the street. Mr. Molfetta came into Gene's view. He ranted at Alphonse loudly, speaking in Italian. Gene's attention turned back to Salvatore.

Salvatore pointed his pistol at the downed driver's head. The man closed his eyes. One shot rang out. He squeezed the trigger again and hit the man in his chest. Alphonse turned and walked up the stairs, blocking Gene's view. Gene heard Salvatore's voice.

"Go to your family, Signore Kane. I'll talk to the cops," he said in his heavy, Italian accent. The front door opened.

Alphonse looked down at Gene like he did not expect to find him there.

"Go inside. Your mother will be home soon."

Gene obeyed him. The activity outside reached a crescendo with police sirens, and a crowd of onlookers gathered around to see two dead men on their block. Gene parted the curtains and peeked outside. Salvatore stood next to a police sergeant on the sidewalk. Several police officers were next to each body, one in front of Gene's house and the other further up the block where Mr. Molfetta and Salvatore had come from. The sergeant was animated, pointing at Gene's home. Mr. Molfetta was nowhere to be seen. Salvatore's face was stone-cold—expressionless. Occasionally Gene heard his father's name or Mr. Molfetta's being mentioned by the sergeant. Finally, the sergeant dropped his hands and nodded. Salvatore patted the sergeant's shoulder, and they shook hands. Then Salvatore looked up and locked eyes with Gene. Gene's body stiffened. Salvatore touched the brim of his hat and nodded, then turned his attention back to the sergeant.

"What are you doing? Get away from the window." Alphonse stood behind him and pointed toward the upstairs. Gene climbed the steps quickly. A few minutes later, he heard the front door open. He knew it was his mother returning home. Nothing was said between her and his father. Gene went to his room and laid down on his bed. The events of the morning replayed in his mind, especially his father shooting with cold determination at the men who were about to kill Mr. Molfetta. Outside, the street was still abuzz with neighbors talking and the sound of the dead man's car being towed.

"Gene, come down for lunch. Wash your hands first." It was his mother. Doris should have been home with the rest of the family, but she was out with friends. His mother sounded calm and unaffected considering that her husband and son could have been shot to death. Gene would have felt better if she ran to him, threw her arms around his shoulders, and wept at the thought of losing him. But, in his young mind, he was equally impressed by the heroics of both his father and the typically cold and closed-mouthed Salvatore. Gene hesitated at the top of the stairs. Beyond the safety of his house were terrible people whom his father did business with. Yet his dad was more dangerous than all of them. Gene could not help it, but he smiled. He bit his lower lip to hide it, because he did not want his parents to see him so proud of his father's actions. Yet he was.

Chapter 11

July 1968, September 1980

The first time I saw the book was on my fifth birthday, July 20th, 1968. I spent my entire summer wondering what it would be like to be in kindergarten. It was not unusual to see Mom or Dad reading. Their home had shelves filled with fiction and history books. The latter belonged to Dad. Mom read Victorian romance novels and the occasional spy thriller that Dad had finished. My father had a veritable library of non-fiction. Underneath the stairway in the living room was a cubby hole. A pair of doors opened to reveal a space about three feet wide and almost four feet deep. The area was big enough for him to crawl inside. Yet it was not a large enough space to move around comfortably. There were shelves on either side of the cubby. My father filled all of them and stacked some books on the floor in the rear. When he wanted a book from inside, he had to get on his knees and crawl halfway in with his legs outside. He would find what he wanted, leave the doors open, and go off to read. I would sometimes wander over and snoop around, looking at his hardcovers and paperbacks. So, when that book caught my attention, I knew it was special.

The Heart of Velletri

The cover was black, jet black like an old west preacher's Bible. On the cover was a pale blue arrowhead with a gold letter *T* emblazoned on it. It was morning, and I came down for breakfast. The book was laying on the kitchen table. Next to it was a pad and a pencil. My father snatched the tome, the pad, and the pencil up before I could read the cover. He did not say anything, yet he carried it away under his arm as though it was a secret document. Dad went into his bedroom and placed the items in the bottom drawer of his dresser.

In high school, the book emerged again. By that time, I had completely forgotten about it. However, my curiosity about my father's service was persistent. My mom mentioned that Dad had lost his Purple Heart and that made me press him even more. Some of my friends had fathers who kept memorabilia from their tours of duty. My buddy, Rocco's father, had a bayonet and an ammo belt for an M1 Garand. A pal of mine from school, Joe Kendall, showed me his father's unit patch and a photo of him loading an artillery round into a cannon. I had no such keepsakes. Dad's stubbornness emboldened me. I felt like a detective working for years endeavoring to solve a mystery.

I was a high school senior, and it was one of those rare occasions when I did my homework at home. Theresa was at home studying for an exam, and I was annoyed that I was not able to be with her. It was late September, and the weather was warm, making me even more frustrated that I had to stay in and write a research paper. Typically, I finished my assignments during study hall. The term paper assigned to my history class was too long for me to scribble in forty-five minutes. I had no choice but to complete the project during my own time. I came home from school and plopped my books on the dining room table. Mom was out shopping, and Dad was still at work. Ray, who was in college at the time, was upstairs also doing homework. Cindy had already graduated college and was renting an apartment with a friend.

The subject matter was World War I. The textbook given to us had a smattering of information about the conflict, and my teacher, Mr. Diehl, instructed us to use more than one source of material. This was long before the days of the world wide web. If you needed information, you either went to the library or referred to an encyclopedia. Since I was too lazy to go to the public library, I decided to see what my father had available. I went into the living room and pulled the couch away from the wall under the stairs. Then I opened the doors to the cubby where Dad stored much of his non-fiction, such as books on the Civil War, old ships, and of course, World War II. I was sure he owned a few titles covering the Great War. I got on my hands and knees and sorted through the stacks. Then my hand touched the cover. I paused. Immediately I flashed back and recalled my fifth birthday when I had first laid eyes on the cover. With the same reverence a museum curator would use when handling a rare or significant artifact, I took the book from the top of a pile and then sat down with my back against the wall.

On the cover, I recognized the same light blue, flint arrowhead with a gold letter *T* emblazoned on it. Then I read the inscription. In gold-lettered script from left to right, moving upwards at roughly a thirty-degree angle, read the words *The Fighting 36th*. I opened the cover. Inside were accounts of the *Texas* 36th Division in action during World War II. My heart raced. This was more information in my shaky hands than I had ever gleaned from my father in almost eighteen years. My sweaty fingers flipped through the pages. I marveled at the photos of the Italian countryside and the various maps throughout. I forgot all about my term paper and sat there reading. I lost track of time and when my parents were due home.

"Put that away now!"

My body jolted. I closed the book and looked up. Ray stood over me with his hands on his hips.

"Are you crazy? If Dad sees you with that, he'll flip out. Put it back." Ray snatched the book and knelt next to me.

"Ray, what the hell was that all about? It's a book, not the Declaration of Independence," I said.

"What stack did you find it on? Show me," he hissed. I leaned over and pointed inside the cubby.

"That one, in the back. It was right on top." I crawled out of the cubby. Then I stood and folded my arms. My face felt flush, and I was shaken from being startled. Also, I could not understand why Ray was acting like a jerk.

Ray arranged the books in order and then closed the doors. He stood up and looked at me.

"Help me push the couch back. Dad's going to be home any minute."

I rolled my eyes and shrugged my shoulders. I resented being scolded for doing something that I did not think was a big deal. However, deep down I knew that my initial instincts about the importance of the book were correct considering Ray's reaction to me reading it. We moved the couch to its spot. Ray motioned to me.

"Come upstairs," he said.

"Fine," I said. I followed him.

In our room, I sat on the edge of my bed. Ray sat on his also and rubbed his palms together. He took a deep breath, preparing himself as if he were going to deliver a speech, and then faced me.

"Dad hides that book because it is special to him." Ray lifted his eyebrows and watched for my reaction.

"No shit," I said.

"Don't be a smartass." Ray leaned back on his hands, stretched his legs out, and crossed his feet.

"Mom found me in the same spot doing the same thing you were about two years ago, and she nearly ripped out two of my fingers when she pulled it from my hands."

"What's so important about it? I know Dad doesn't like to talk about the war, but Jesus, from what I read it's nothing but a collection of articles written about his unit during battles. I'm happy to finally learn what division he belonged to." I grinned and shook my head.

"Did you open the second half? Did you read the rest of what's in there?" Ray pulled his legs up and leaned forward, resting his elbows on his knees.

"No." I cleared my throat.

"I didn't think so." Ray sucked his teeth and scratched behind his ear.

"Tell me the big deal then," I said.

"In the back are the names and addresses of all the men who fought in the 36th Division during World War II," Ray said. He paused for effect. I shrugged my shoulders.

"So… Dad's name and address are in there too?"

"Yes idiot. So are the names and addresses of all of his buddies."

"I don't understand," I said. I climbed further onto my bed and rested my back against the wall.

"Mom told me that for years he wrote to everyone he fought with, all of his friends. He learned that they never made it home. They all died in later in France after D-Day. Dad also wrote letters to the families of guys he fought with who were killed and told them how close they were and that their sons were brave in battle. He would correspond with the mothers and fathers and sometimes with the wives of people he hoped would still be alive. But he became heartbroken when he learned that they never made it back. Mom said it tears him apart that he is the only survivor among them." Ray got up and walked to the window. He checked the driveway for Dad's car. My shoulders sagged, and I released a long sigh.

"No wonder he never talks about the army," I said.

"Yeah, no wonder. Stop pestering him about it. You're beginning to annoy me too."

"Don't tell me what to do," I said.

Ray walked over and tapped my shoulder.

"Hey, I'm not kidding. This shit seriously upsets him. We're lucky he doesn't drink or gamble or run around with other women. All he does is work, come home, sleep, and go to work again. He doesn't have any hobbies, and he doesn't splurge on anything for himself, because he does not think he deserves it."

"Who are you? Sigmund Freud?" I sat up straight and looked him in the eye.

"Very funny. Mom told me all of this. Anyway, just keep your hands off the thing and don't ask any more questions, okay?"

"I'll ask my father whatever I want. All my other friends talk to their dads about it, and for some weird reason, I'm not allowed to? Leave me alone. That's what I have to say to you." I huffed and got up. I brushed past Ray and walked out of the room and downstairs.

That night, when everyone was asleep, I took that book from the cubby while clenching a penlight in my teeth. I brought it to bed with me and hid under my blanket like a tent for the entire night until I had finished reading the whole text. I had found my father's name and old address on East 73rd Street in Bay Ridge, Brooklyn. Also, I noticed the small check marks in pencil next to the names of his deceased buddies. The fact that my father felt guilty for surviving angered me. My adolescent mind did not understand the concept of survivor's guilt. I wanted to tell him that because he survived, he had a wife and children who loved him. Yet I was in no position to present that case to him.

Before dawn, while my parents and Ray slept, I sneaked the book back into the cubby. In about an hour I would be up again and on my way to school. For an entire night, I delved into the intricate details of a conflict and its effect on my father that left me feeling emotions ranging from grief to anger. I was angry that Dad experienced immense anguish and guilt from the war when, in my mind, I believed he should be reveling in glory for his role in an American victory. There had to be something I could do to put his mind at ease. That made me even more determined to get Dad the honor that he deserved. However, at that time I did not know in what form that recognition would be.

Chapter 12

May 29th, 1944

"Move it along, Koenigsmann, this hike is longer than your last name. You've got to keep up the pace." Sgt. Thames looked back at Gene and smiled. The entire division had left Anzio about two days earlier. The march had taken them through the battle-torn streets of Cisterna. Now, at seven o'clock in the morning, they trudged along the dusty road towards the town of Velletri. Sgt. Thames and his squad of eight men were given point.

Sgt. Thames stopped and held up his hand. The men ducked and took cover on the side of the road. Sgt. Thames kept Gene close by his side. He carried the Browning Automatic Rifle, and Sgt. Thames used him to probe potential trouble spots. The weapon required a lot of ammo. It needed twenty round magazines, which Gene used plenty of when under fire. His buddy, Harry Beasley, was assigned to carry cans of ammo for Gene, along with his own M1 Garand and ammo pouches. Gene and Harry kneeled next to a large tree on the roadside. Sgt. Thames crouched in front of them, peering through a pair of binoculars past some bushes on their left.

"That farmhouse way back in the woods. You two go check it out," Sgt. Thames whispered. He craned his head and looked back at them. Gene squinted and stared at the house about fifty yards away from their location. It was a two-story building that appeared abandoned. The windows were broken and the front door, from what Gene could see, was dangling from a single hinge. Harry set down the two cans of ammo for the BAR and unshouldered his weapon. The pair did as they were ordered. Still hunched over, they entered the tree line. Gene became acutely aware of his heartbeat. For some reason, the sounds of birds chirping caught his attention, as did the scent of morning dew. The muzzle of Harry's rifle tapped the back of Gene's helmet. Gene turned around.

"What the hell is wrong with you?" Gene snapped at him in a hoarse whisper.

"Sorry, I'm just jittery. I have to pee," Harry said. He pushed his helmet back and grimaced.

"I don't care if you wet yourself, just don't blow my head off." Gene glared at him for a moment. Then he covered his mouth and suppressed a laugh. Just then, a pebble ricocheted off Harry's arm. They both turned their heads toward the road.

"Move it, you idiots!" Sgt. Thames hissed at them.

Gene held his BAR at his hip and moved towards the farmhouse. He observed the windows and the front door. He could hear Harry breathing hard behind him. When they got within twenty-five yards of the house, they stopped.

"I can't take it anymore. I have to go, man," Harry said. He hung his rifle over his shoulder and kneeled behind a bush. After he relieved himself, he readied his M1 and tapped Gene on the shoulder.

"Let's go," he said.

Gene started to move but then stopped.

"What's that sound?" He looked up through the overhead branches.

"Incoming!" Harry yelled. They both hit the ground and covered their heads with their hands. The shells landed on the side of the road where they had left their platoon. After the explosions, they heard screams of pain. More shells flew overhead. Harry stood and turned toward the lane. Gene got to his knees and grabbed him by the belt. He yanked Harry back down.

"Stay here. You'll get blown up with the rest of them."

A shell landed about ten yards away and detonated. Gene and Harry were pelted with branches and twigs. They sat up and examined themselves.

"I'm okay. What about you?" Gene asked.

Harry ran his hands up and down his torso. "I'm good," he said.

They waited for the barrage to stop. The shelling lasted for about two minutes. When it was over, Gene and Harry made their way back to the road. The screaming and yelling had ceased. They saw Sgt. Thames on the grassy shoulder of the road with a soldier cradled in his arms. Gene didn't know the kid's first name since he was new the platoon, but he knew he carried the radio. The young soldier was apparently dead. His eyes fixed on the cloudless sky. His shattered radio lay next to him. Several men were strewn like tattered dolls along the roadside. The squad; except for Sgt. Thames, Harry, and Gene; were all dead.

"Sergeant, we have to go," Gene said.

Sgt. Thames placed the young soldier on the ground with care. He wiped his hands on his shirt and turned his head back and forth to check for the enemy. He stood and took a deep breath. Sgt. Thames removed his helmet and wiped his hands through his hair. After he put his helmet back on, he paced back and forth and examined the men strewn all about. Finally, he straightened himself and walked over to Gene and Harry.

"Gather any weapons, ammo, grenades, K-Rations, canteens, anything we might need, and let's get out of here," he said. Sgt. Thames picked up his Thompson and pointed the muzzle upright with the butt on his hip. Gene and Harry took whatever they could from their fallen comrades. But they had been already fully laden before the artillery wiped out the squad. Sgt. Thames removed dog tags from the dead and carried what supplies he could. They gathered near a crop of bushes a few feet into the woods.

"We don't have a radio. Calling for help isn't going to work. We need to remain here for the rest of the company to catch up to us. That could be by nightfall." Sgt. Thames pulled a pair of binoculars from his pouch and spied on the farmhouse.

"Why don't we go back?" Harry asked.

"That's not an option. The Germans know we're scouting their lines. They could be ahead of us, behind us, or we could be surrounded. We need a place to hold up." Sgt. Thames stretched the corner of his mouth and shook his head.

"How close did you get to the building?" Sgt. Thames pointed into the woods.

"We got within about twenty yards before the shelling began," Gene said. The three of them bent forward and stared at the structure.

"What do you think, Koenigsmann? Any krauts in there?" Sgt. Thames looked at him.

"If there were, they'd be attacking us by now," Gene said. He wiped his brow with a handkerchief and stuffed it into his pants pocket.

"Good point, Koenigsmann. I'll have you promoted to sergeant before this war is over."

"I learned everything from you, sergeant," Gene said.

"What about the barn? Anyone hiding in there?" Sgt. Thames asked.

Gene adjusted his glasses and looked deep into the woods past the farmhouse.

"There's no barn there, sergeant," he said.

"Good. Let's move out." Sgt. Thames smacked Gene's arm.

Sgt. Thames chuckled and waved them forward. Sgt. Thames and Gene walked towards their objective, weapons pointed ahead. Harry carried the ammo cans he had left at the roadside earlier. Gene was in the middle, Sgt. Thames to his right, and Harry to his left. They kept about six to eight feet between each of them.

"Jesus, we sound like a herd of pack animals. We're gonna have to dump some of this gear," Sgt. Thames said.

At that moment, a bullet struck a tree branch to Harry's right. It came from behind. Gene spun around and aimed at the road. German Wehrmacht soldiers took cover at the spot where they had just left their dead squad mates. More gunfire erupted from the enemy position. Tree bark and leaves showered them. Gene sprayed their line with an entire magazine. Just as fast as he dropped the empty magazine, he slapped a new one in and racked a round in the chamber.

"To the house!" Sgt. Thames yelled.

The three ran as fast as they could. Bullets whizzed through the air past them.

"How many, Gene?" Sgt. Thames yelled.

"Twenty, maybe thirty," Gene called back.

Harry reached the front door first. He did not bother to clear the room before he entered. Sgt. Thames and Gene ran in behind him. The took cover under the window facing the area where they had just left. A hail of gunfire ripped through the front of the structure. Bullets hit the wall opposite them. Gene stuck the barrel of his BAR out the window and fired in the direction of the enemy without looking.

"Don't waste your ammo. If you can't see them, don't shoot," Sgt. Thames pulled on Gene's trigger hand. Gene removed his weapon from the window and cradled it.

"They stopped shooting. They must be moving in on us." Sgt. Thames dropped to his knees and removed his helmet. He raised the helmet just above the window frame. After a few seconds, he peeked outside.

"Damn it. There's a platoon heading this way," he said. "Harry, cover that window. Gene, you cover this one. I'll be over there." Sgt. Thames pointed to a window on the opposite side of the doorway. Like the others, the glass was blown out. Sgt. Thames held his Thompson close, took deep breaths, and then ran past the door. A shot rang out. The bullet missed him and hit the wall.

"On my signal, fire at will," he said.

Sgt. Thames craned his head around the door and then pulled it back.

"Fire!"

Gene got to his knees and aimed outside. His first target came within fifteen feet of him. Gene released a quick burst, and the soldier fell face first. Harry fired into the trees until his depleted clip popped out. Just as fast, he slapped in another clip and continued to shoot. Sgt. Thames fired full auto. He aimed his volley at the advancing enemy. Thames' expression had a ferocity that Gene had never seen before. With all the violence that he had witnessed as a boy, the beatings and pistol shots had always seemed cold-blooded and business-like.

Gene continued shooting at the Germans until they pulled back. Harry finished a clip and reloaded.

"Cease fire," Sgt. Thames yelled.

"We can't stay in here, sergeant. They'll call in artillery just like they did on the road," Gene said. Sweat dripped down his forehead, and he wiped it with his forearm.

"Sergeant, we really should go back. We'll die out here," Harry said.

"Relax, boys. I'll get us out of this." Sgt. Thames poked his head around the doorway. In an instant, he fell to the floor. Blood poured out of his forehead. The shooting continued. Gene looked down at Sgt. Thames. He covered his mouth and breathed hard. His heart pounded, and adrenaline surged through his body. He felt like he could vomit. Gene wanted to rush to Sgt. Thames and do something—anything—but he knew he was dead. An overwhelming sense of helplessness overcame him. He closed his eyes and grasped his weapon with both hands. Then, he summoned the courage to continue fighting.

Gene and Harry picked up their weapons and gear and ran toward the back of the house. The extra weight of their kits and the additional ammo they carried hindered them as they made their escape. Harry stopped when he reached the kitchen. Bullets ripped through the broken windows and poked holes in the walls. Gene fired at two approaching Germans, and they both collapsed. Harry tossed the ammo cans to the floor and raised his weapon and shot through the opened back door. Gene watched an enemy soldier clutch his abdomen and fall forward.

"Holy shit, we're gonna die," Harry said as he reloaded.

"We'll take a whole bunch of them with us," Gene said.

They continued shooting at the enemy through the window and the doorway. Bullets pierced the walls, creating puffs of plaster and puncturing the walls around them. Harry heard footsteps coming from the front of the house where Sgt. Thames lay dead.

"They're getting in the front door!" Harry yelled.

Gene spun to his left and shot at two soldiers. The one who led the charge fired his rifle before he collapsed. The round hit the ceiling above Gene's head. The German soldier behind him raised his rifle and aimed at them. Gene fired a single shot at the man and dropped him.

"Come on." Gene tugged Harry's arm.

"Leave the ammo. We'll come back for it. They probably think there's more than two of us in here," Gene said.

Harry did as Gene suggested. They stepped over the bodies of the German soldiers in the hallway and reentered the front room. Gene took Sgt. Thame's lifeless body by the arm and pulled him out of the open entrance. The enemy had ceased firing once more. Harry poked his head in the window and then pulled his head down.

"They're retreating," he said. Harry's voice was hoarse. Gene breathed fast, and he tried to calm himself down. He thought of his father and how he would have handled himself in this situation. Then a reassuring calm came over him. Alphonse would have attacked. Gene smiled at the romantic image he conjured of his father wielding a BAR and chasing Germans into the thickets. His demeanor would have been cool and collected as it had been all the times he did Mr. Molfetta's bidding back in Brooklyn. Gene thought of his father when he was in the Army, climbing out of the trenches and charging across no man's land.

"They'll be back. And they'll bring reinforcements. That's why we're going to do our best to fake them out and get the hell out of here." Gene returned to the front room. He removed one of Sgt. Thames dog tags and put it in his shirt pocket. He found the other dog tags that belonged to his dead squad mates killed in the barrage. Then he took Sgt. Thames' Thompson, ammo pouch, and the extra bandoliers of ammo Sgt. Thames had collected earlier. All the while, Gene marveled at Sgt. Thames resourcefulness and foresight. Gene and Harry would have been throwing rocks at the Germans by then if they had not scavenged what they could carry after the artillery assault. Finally, Gene removed Sgt. Thames's pair of forty-five caliber pistols and his remaining magazines. He handed one to Harry. They each hung the extra bandoliers across their chests. Harry and Gene pocketed their handguns and the magazines. Gene then took a long look at Sgt. Thames. He closed his eyes and folded his hands across his abdomen. Gene removed his helmet and recited a silent prayer.

"They're back," Harry whispered.

Gene put his helmet back on and peeked out the window. A pair of Germans were setting up a belt-fed, MG-42 machine gun. Others hid behind trees and bushes. Gene could not count how many there were, but he knew they could not hold out for long.

"I'm going to use two mags. As I'm shooting, grab the last two cans and run out the back door into the woods as far as you can and don't stop. Not even to pee, got it?"

"Funny, Koenigsmann. You can't help yourself, can you?" Harry shook his head.

"Just do it. I have a feeling we're going to get shelled in a minute."

"Whenever you're ready," Harry said. He slung his rifle over his shoulder and readied himself as if he was about to sprint at a track meet. Gene took three quick breaths and then thrust his BAR out the window. He aimed at the machine gun and emptied his magazine. Harry leaped over the two dead Germans, picked up the ammo cans, and ran out of the back door. There were gunshots from behind, and bullets hit the trees before him. He made it to the woods and kept running. The German machine gun buzzed like a chainsaw. A moment later, Gene ran from the house. He sprinted across the backyard grass to his right, using the house as cover. He ducked into the woods and hurried with his head down.

"Gene, over here!" Harry yelled and waved at him.

"Keep running that way." Gene pointed in the direction they had come from before the squad was almost eliminated. Harry stood and waited for Gene to catch up. The jogged alongside each other, nearly out of breath and sweating profusely. Though they could not see the Germans, they could hear their rifle fire and the deadly machine gun. Bullets zipped past them and snapped twigs and branches.

For over an hour, they ran as far as they could until they almost collapsed. They would rest while they sipped from their canteens, careful to ration their water. Then they would wait for the Germans to almost catch up to them, exchange gunfire, and then run away. Gene had used up all the ammo for the BAR in the cans and on his belt. Since the BAR weighed almost twenty-one pounds fully loaded, it became a burden. Gene reluctantly left it behind. Before he did so, he leaned it against a tree and kicked it as hard as he could until he snapped off the stock. Then he switched to Sgt. Thames' Thompson. Since he had only four magazines for the weapon, he wished he had picked up another M1 as well. Gene made sure they could see the road or could make their way back to it if they strayed too far.

Harry took cover behind a large tree. Gene found one about four feet from Harry and sat down behind it, keeping an eye out for Germans.

"Got any more water?" Gene asked. They both breathed hard. Harry removed his helmet and placed it on the ground next to him. Gene did the same, and he wiped his glasses with his handkerchief, then put them back on.

"Here. There's about half left." Harry leaned over and handed Gene the canteen. Gene unscrewed the cap and took a sip. He savored the water in his parched mouth before he swallowed. Then he put the cap back on and handed it to Harry.

"Why the hell are they chasing us? We're only two guys," Gene said. He rested the side of his head against the tree.

"How should I know? You're the man who would be *sergeant*. Didn't Thames teach you any of this shit?"

Gene laughed, but it was not a cheerful giggle. He put the Thompson down.

"Damn it," Gene said.

Harry rolled his head to the side and looked at him. "What?"

"I have to pee," Gene said.

"I wish I had something sarcastic to say, but I'm gonna have to take a rain check." Harry grinned and looked away. Gene knelt with his back to Harry. When Gene was done, he leaned against the tree and placed his weapon on his lap.

"Psst Gene, look. I think they're here again," Harry said. Gene's shoulders sagged, and he turned his head to investigate. A quick count showed ten or fifteen Germans tracking them. They were about thirty yards away in the sparse woods. Both Harry and Gene could see them clearly.

"Are you kidding me? Do both of us amount to an offensive? Why won't they leave us alone? I'm not doing this shit all day." Gene stood up and put his helmet on. He slid the bolt back on his Thompson and made sure there was a round in the chamber.

"What are you doing? Get down. They'll see us!" Harry waved his hands at Gene. Gene cradled his Thompson and removed a grenade from his pocket. He pulled the pin and squeezed the handle, holding it closed to delay the blast. Harry fumbled with his helmet and put it on.

"Gene, what the hell?"

"Screw these clowns. Where I come from, my buddies and I would beat the crap out of all of them," he said.

"This ain't Brooklyn, Gene. These guys have guns." Harry grappled with his M1 and got to his knees. He looked up at Gene.

"They're just as many guns in Brooklyn as there are in the entire kraut army, Harry," Gene said. He looked down at Harry and winked.

"You're crazy."

"That's right. And that's why we're going to attack. On my signal, we toss the grenades and then charge while giving them everything we got."

"Gene, wait a minute." Harry started to pant.

"Do you want these krauts to bayonet you while you crouch behind this tree, or would you rather die shooting these bastards?"

Harry groaned. "If we survive this, I'm gonna kick you in the ass so hard you'll land back in Brooklyn," Harry said. He stood up and held his M1 under his arm. Harry took a grenade from his belt, pulled the pin, and kept it closed.

"If we live through this, I'll come out to Oklahoma and work with you on your father's ranch," Gene said.

"That I absolutely must live to see," Harry said.

"Ready?" Gene looked at Harry and back at the advancing enemy. Harry nodded. A bead of sweat dangled at the end of his nose.

"Hey, morons!" Gene yelled at the Germans. They halted in their tracks. Several of them looked around, not knowing where the shouting came from.

"Eat this!" Gene threw his grenade at the center of the group. Harry left his cover and hurled his at their line also. Then the Germans took cover behind the trees. One explosion, and then a second, rang out. A man screamed.

"Charge!" Gene emerged from his position, firing his weapon. He hollered as he ran straight at them. Harry followed, yelling and shouting while shooting his rifle. Gene dropped an empty magazine while still running, slapped another one in, and racked the bolt. Harry reloaded as well. They passed a fallen soldier who had been killed by the grenades. The Germans returned a volley at them and then fled. Harry and Gene dropped to their knees and continued firing at the escaping soldiers.

"Yee ha!" Harry yelled. He fired until his expended clip ejected from the breach. Then he reloaded and closed the bolt.

"You're a goddamn genius. I can't believe that worked." Harry slapped him on the back.

"I'm only a genius if we get back alive. Let's get to the road. We can move faster, and we should run into other Americans soon." They got up and walked to the lane in a crouched position, ready to take cover if the Germans counter-attacked.

Once back to the narrow lane, Gene scanned back and forth to get his bearings. Also, he wanted to ensure that the Germans did not have the same idea that they had.

"I can't believe Sgt. Thames is gone, Gene. I liked him a lot." Harry walked with his head down.

"Neither can I. And those other guys, we were just getting to know them," Gene said. "They had all seen a lot of fighting. Sgt. Thames told me that nearly the entire regiment got chewed up at the Rapido River. Imagine living through that fight only to get blown up on the side of some dusty road?"

"I'm still trying to believe that we outwitted those krauts back there and that we're still breathing," Harry said. "You got some big set of balls, Gene."

"Stop it. It's what Thames would have done."

"Exactly, and that's why Thames liked you so much. Damn shame he isn't around to put you in for a medal."

"I don't want any medals. As soon as I get home, I want to forget all about this. The dead bodies, the stench, the goddamn krauts. All of it." Gene kicked a rock, and it veered off the road and hit a tree.

"You aren't gonna forget about me, will you Gene? After all, you're gonna come work on my family's ranch with me." Harry smiled.

"I didn't forget. I'm looking forward to riding horses and roping cattle." Gene lit a cigarette with his lighter and offered it to Harry. Harry shook his head. Gene took a drag and blew the smoke out of the side of his mouth.

"I'll teach you how to ride," Harry said.

"No need to. I already know how to ride a horse. My dad took me to my Uncle Charlie's a lot when I was a kid. We weren't related to him. Uncle Charlie was a man Dad knew from work. He wanted me to call him uncle, so I did. Anyhow, he had a small farm and a stable with some horses. He even had cows, chickens, and goats. He mostly grew cauliflower though." Gene took another drag and checked over his shoulder. Then he looked at Harry.

"You're telling me that there are farms in Brooklyn?" Harry scoffed.

"Out on the island, Harry. Long Island is mostly farmland out east. I might even move there one day."

"I thought you were coming to Oklahoma with me?"

"What's that? Up ahead... Go for cover!" Gene took Harry by the arm, and they ran back to the trees.

Down the road, a cloud of dust obscured what appeared to be vehicles approaching them.

"Can't be Germans. They're all that way," Harry said as he pointed in the direction from where they came.

"You can't be too sure. Thames said that we could expect our unit to catch up to us by tonight. It's not even eleven hundred hours." Gene peeked from behind the bush and squinted at the convoy.

"Did you take Thames' binoculars?" Harry asked.

"Nope. I was kind of in a hurry when I was grabbing shit." Gene looked at him from the corner of his eye.

"I was just asking." Harry stuck his head out of the bushes, and Gene pulled him back by the shoulder.

"You want to get shot?" Gene crushed his cigarette in the dirt and took a knee. He used the Thompson for support.

"You hear that?" Harry whispered. He scanned the woods behind them. Gene turned and looked along the tree line.

"There're maybe three, four guys. I'm not sure." Gene removed his glasses and wiped his eyes with his sleeve, then put them back on.

"They're Americans," Harry whispered.

"Hold on. We have to make sure that they…"

"Hey, hey guys. We're over here!" Harry yelled. He stood and waved.

"Harry, get down!" Gene hissed at him.

A shot rang out. Harry fell forward and groaned.

"Shit, Harry!" Gene pulled Harry close to him.

"One hundred and forty-first! Company L. Our squad is all dead. I'm coming out!" Gene yelled.

"You're in the hundred and forty-first? Who's in command of your squad?" One of the GIs asked. The young soldier was taller, older than the others, with a cleft chin and earnest eyes. He looked to be about twenty-five years old, and he had corporal stripes. The soldiers stopped about ten yards from them. Gene could make out their faces. They were young replacements, just like he and Harry were.

"Sgt. Thames. But he's dead. It's just my buddy who you just shot and me. You better pray he lives," Gene said.

"Jesus, they're Americans," said the corporal. "Call for a medic," he said to one of the others who carried a radio. The soldier did as he was ordered.

There were four soldiers in total as Gene counted. They rolled Harry on to his back and checked his wound. Harry had been hit just below the right knee. He winced in pain.

"Don't worry, private. We'll get you patched up. Looks like you'll be going home," the tall soldier said.

"Who does he have to thank for that?" Gene asked.

"Look, it was an accident. We thought you were Germans, okay?" the tall soldier said.

Gene held Harry's hand while the others stopped the bleeding and applied a bandage. A jeep arrived. Two men hopped out. One was a medic, the other a sergeant. Harry was placed on a stretcher. Two men carried him to the jeep, and he was put in the back. The sergeant asked Gene what happened, and Gene gave him a brief account of their skirmish. Gene described the artillery barrage, how it took out the bulk of the squad, how Sgt. Thames led them into the farmhouse, and that he was shot. Then he told him about running from the Germans all morning, and how they got away. He reached into his shirt pocket and handed the dog tags to the sergeant. The sergeant held them in the palm of his hand and examined them.

"Sgt. Thames is *dead?*" The sergeant closed his fingers, clasping the tags.

"Yes, they're all up the road about two miles," Gene said. His lower lip quivered, and he fought back tears. It took him a moment to compose himself, because he did not want to break down and cry in front of everyone. Losing nearly all his squad was bad enough but seeing Sgt. Thames killed in front of him caused him grief. "Sgt. Thames is in a small farmhouse off the side of the road, about fifty yards in."

The sergeant shook his head and removed his helmet. He pocketed the dog tags and then scratched his chin. Finally, he put his helmet back on.

"Good job, soldier. And, thank you for bringing me these." The sergeant tapped his pocket. "You're now with my platoon. Corporal Pollard here will introduce you to the others." The sergeant pointed to the corporal.

"What is your name, soldier?" The sergeant looked at Gene.

"Private Eugene Koenigsmann, sergeant." Gene pursed his lips in anticipation of the sergeant's response.

"Koenigsmann? Are you a damn Nazi?" The sergeant chuckled.

"No sergeant. I shoot Nazis," Gene answered. The sergeant slapped him on the shoulder.

"You'll fit in just fine in my platoon, private." The sergeant walked around the Jeep and sat in the passenger seat. The medic sat with Harry. Gene started to walk over to him. The driver started a three-point turn to head back to the line.

"Harry, you're gonna be okay," Gene called out to him.

"Don't worry, Gene. I'll be back. Damn it," Harry answered. The Jeep rode away and left a cloud of dust. Gene waved his hand in front of his face. Cpl. Pollard stood next to him.

"Your buddy was just grazed, private. He'll get patched up and rejoin us soon," said Cpl. Pollard.

"I wish he were sent home," Gene said. He wiped his forehead with a hanky and turned to the corporal.

"What's the sergeant's name?" Gene asked.

"That's Sgt. Warren. He's going to win this war all by himself." Cpl. Pollard snickered.

"By the way, this is Dave Hansen, Roger Price, and Hamlin. His first name is Morton. No one calls him that." Cpl. Pollard pointed to each man as he said their names.

Gene sized up his new squad mates. On the surface, they appeared no different than the other young GI's he had left camp with who were now all dead. Dave and Roger looked like they played football and stacked bales of hay with equal proficiency, and Hamlin looked like he wanted to be an accountant when he grew up. It wasn't his glasses that made him look wimpy, Gene wore glasses also. It was his slouched demeanor and his plump cheeks. Gene raised his hand and acknowledged the guys.

"You prefer Eugene or Gene?" Cpl. Pollard asked.

"Gene. And don't even attempt to say Koenigsmann," Gene said.

"You bet," said Col. Pollard. He slapped Gene's back, and they started back up the road in advance of the convoy. Gene paused. Cpl. Pollard eyed him.

"What's the matter, Koenigsmann?"

"My friends. They're up there, Sgt. Thames, all of them. They're blown up and shot." Gene panted, and he could feel tears welling up in his eyes.

"We'll cover them with honor, Gene. Don't worry. And they'll be taken back when the trucks get here. Sgt. Warren will make sure of it. You didn't know this, but he and Sgt. Thames were close. They grew up together in Michigan."

"Michigan?" Gene looked at the ground and then back at Cpl. Pollard.

"It just goes to show, as much as I knew the sergeant, I didn't know all that much about him from back home. I would have bet he was a New Yorker," Gene said.

"You're lucky Sgt. Warren didn't hear you say that," Cpl. Pollard said. "Come on. Let's go. We're walking to Rome. Ain't this a nice vacation, boys?" Cpl. Pollard waved his arm over his head and took point. Gene fell into line behind Roger and Dave, ahead of Hamlin. All of them followed Cpl. Pollard. Gene bit his lower lip and fought back the tears as he prepared to return to the farmhouse and see his favorite sergeant for the last time.

Chapter 13

September 2, 2001

Dad was such a devoted husband that he ignored his own health to care for his wife. While Mom was undergoing chemotherapy for colon cancer, Dad did not want to leave her side. As a responsible adult who owned a working telephone to call for an ambulance, he only asked for help when the pain and discomfort he had experienced became unbearable. After waiting for Mom to take a nap, Dad ambled across the street to Mr. Langdon's house. Jake Langdon was a retired auto mechanic who earned extra money by repairing neighbor's cars in his garage. Dad walked up the driveway and saw Jake and his son-in-law, Brendan, toiling under the hood of a pickup truck.

Our family and the Langdon's had always been friendly. They were always welcome in our house for coffee or a barbecue, as were we at their home. The Langdon family were the type of folks who would go out of their way to help someone in need.

"Oh, hi Gene." Jake popped his head from under the hood. He grabbed a nearby rag and wiped grease from his fingers. Dad shook his hand. Immediately Jake noticed that something was wrong with him.

"Gene, are you feeling okay?"

By then, Brendan came over and looked at Dad too. His friendly smile gave way to narrowed eyes and an open mouth.

"I think I need to go to the hospital," Dad said.

"You need to sit down, Mr. Koenigsmann." Brendan took Dad by the hand.

"I'm fine. I just have some chest pain." Dad waved Brendan off but managed a grin so as not to offend him.

"I'll call an ambulance," Mr. Langdon said.

"No, no, just drive me there. I don't want to cause a big scene. Ann will get scared, and she's too sick to handle all of that."

Mr. Langdon shrugged and let out a sigh. "If that's what you want, sure. We'll drive you. I think you should have the paramedics here," he said. Mr. Langdon walked to the garage and grabbed the keys to his truck from a hook on the wall.

"No, Jake. We'll take my car."

"Gene, let me drive you." Jake held up his keys and dangled them.

"Yes, okay. Drive me. But use my car. I have a full tank."

Jake threw up his hands and walked down the driveway and across the street to Dad's light-blue Toyota Corolla. Dad followed him. He paused when he got there and leaned on the hood of the car. Dad's breathing was rapid, and he was sweating in the early September sun.

"Wait, hold on a second," he gasped. Jake came to his side and placed his hand on his shoulder. Brendan ran across the street and stood by, ready to act if necessary.

"What is it Gene. Do you want me to call nine-one-one?"

Gene wiped the sweat from his upper lip with a handkerchief he produced from the pocket of his slacks and stood straight, his face contorted from the aching in his chest.

"I need to tell Ann where I'm going." Then he trudged back into the house. Jake and Brendan waited, confused and anxious, for him to return. Their discomfort was amplified as they both comprehended that our mother, weak from cancer treatment, and Dad, most likely experiencing a heart attack, were alone together. The reason Mom and Dad lived alone was that they flatly refused any help from their children. They still saw themselves as caregivers to their children, not as dependent seniors. Dad's insistence on not causing a scene was dangerous, to say the least. If a myocardial infarction couldn't kill my father, delaying help—especially when his wife was ill—could do the trick.

Cindy called me and broke the news. Mom had phoned her just before she left the house. She summoned the strength to get dressed and ride in Mr. Langdon's car with him while Brendan drove my father in his Corolla.

Mandy met me at the emergency room entrance. She looked me in the eyes and said, "He's having a heart attack. He's awake, and the doctors are with him now." Inside the emergency room, I could see him. My mother stayed in the waiting room, as she was too weak and upset to stand. Mr. Langdon and his son-in-law went home but asked to be updated, and Ray was on the way. I stood next to my father. He opened his eyes and noticed me. The doctors had administered medications, and nurses had prepped him for the cardiac catheterization lab.

"Hi Dad. How are you feeling?" I asked.

He was alert and wearing a hospital gown.

"I'll be okay," he said. He tried to smile, but I could tell that he was uncomfortable. He had a pale complexion, and his eyes were watery. A nurse came over and checked the heart monitor he was hooked up to.

"You're going to be moved in just a moment, Mr. Koenigsmann. The doctors are ready for you there."

I stepped back and allowed the nurse to unlock the wheels of the gurney. Another nurse arrived to help wheel him away.

"I love you Dad," I said with a gulp. My eyes were teared up, but I tried to hide it from him. For no reason, I smiled, perhaps to remain defiant.

"I love you too," he said. His breathing was heavy, and he reached for my hand. I had to walk to his side for him to take it. "You have a beautiful wife. She's like one of my own."

"I'll tell her you said that," I said. Dad released his grip on my hand.

Then the nurses wheeled him out of his curtained stall and pushed him down the central aisle and out of my sight. For a moment, I stood and eyed the invisible wake they left behind. It dawned on me that unless the doctors could stop his heart attack that would be the last time I spoke to him. Also, I wished there was time to bring my mother back in to see him.

Later that evening, we learned how severe the damage was to his heart, and how lucky he was to be alive. Dad was suffering for three days. He kept his symptoms to himself, because he wished to continue caring for Mom. While the doctors and nurses considered his actions foolish, Ray, Cindy, and I understood that this was definitely in his character.

In the hall outside his room, a young cardiologist took my mother aside. She was confounded by Dad's inflexibility when it came to him caring for her. Her tears were laced with guilt. Somehow, she had her husband convinced that her needs were more important than his. Because of Dad's recklessness with his health, Mom's grief was amplified.

"Mrs. Koenigsmann, your husband is in critical condition," the doctor said. He was around thirty-five years old with an East European accent. Mandy and I stood next to mom, and I held her shoulders from behind in case she collapsed.

"Your husband had a massive heart attack, but we think he will be okay if he does not have another one in the next few hours."

"He can have another heart attack?" My mom asked. She inhaled deeply and placed her hand on her chest.

"It is possible. They are like aftershocks, if you will. Tomorrow we'll find out if he needs surgery. But he's getting the best available care now. We've given him medicine, he's on a monitor, and he's awake and alert. That's good news."

I watched Mom's face turn ashen, the color seeping out of her body with her tears. The cardiologist's words bounced off my eardrums, and all I kept thinking was that if he died, I'd have to tell Judith.

The doctor left us. Ray went home to eat dinner with the intent of coming back for evening visiting hours. Cindy took Mom home first, so she could change her clothes and eat dinner. Then Cindy checked in with her son. Mandy and I planned to leave as soon as Ray returned.

Dad waved for Mandy to come to him. Each room had a large, waist-high window, as if the patients were in a storefront on display so the nurses could keep an eye on them. I watched Mandy lean in close as Dad whispered to her, as if revealing the location of hidden treasure.

When Dad finished talking, he turned his head away from her and closed his eyes. Mandy straightened up. She stretched the corners of her mouth in what was supposed to be a smile. Yet I could tell that she was not happy. She came over to me.

"Honey, may I talk to you for a second?" Mandy held the same expression as she took me by the arm and guided me down the hall, out of earshot of my father and the nurses. We stopped by a window at the end of the corridor. Mandy tilted her head and smacked her lips. Then she straightened her neck and looked up at me, as I was about a foot taller than her.

"Your father just told me he's having chest pains."

"What? He said this? Why the hell didn't he tell the nurses?" I felt the familiar tingle of adrenaline roiling within me. I didn't have to ask the question, because the answer was obvious.

"I asked him why he didn't press the button for the nurse. He told me that if he did all sort of people would come running in and start doing things to him, and he didn't want that."

"That's just like him," I said. "I swear to God, if he survives this, I'm going to murder him."

I marched down the hall to his room and paused outside. By then, Cindy had returned with Mom. I saw Dad poised on an incline as the nurses raised the bed for him. His eyes were closed, and his hands were folded over his chest, as if he were laying in repose. Mom sat next to him, dabbing the corners of her eyes with a tissue. Cindy saw me and waved at me to come inside.

"Where's Ray when I need him?" I asked for no reason.

Mandy caught up with me. She stood at my side and placed her hand on my shoulder.

"Mike, we have to tell someone," said Mandy.

"I know, I know. He's going to hate me, but it won't be the first time."

I walked to the nurse's station and waited patiently, trying to make eye contact with one of the many medical personnel roving behind the chest-high desk area. I coughed, cleared my throat, and still, no one bothered to acknowledge me. Finally, I said, "My father's in room two-oh-four, and he's having chest pain."

In moments, nurses ran into his room, doing all sorts of things to him. As expected, Dad didn't like that—or me for that matter.

I called Ray. He dropped his fork on the kitchen table, grabbed his car keys, and rushed to his car while still on the phone with me. I calmed him down and told him not to get into an accident while racing to the hospital.

In his room, I stood at the foot of his bed and watched my parents hold hands. Dad was heavily medicated and asleep. Mom looked up and sighed.

"That's what I expect from him," she said. "He is so thick-headed. I love him, but I could kill him." Mom leaned over and kissed Dad's cheek. Maybe I imagined this, but I could swear I saw Dad smile.

Chapter 14

August 30th, 2006

For over a decade Mom battled two devastating illnesses, Systemic Lupus and colon cancer. Gradually, she lost the ability to walk. Dad wheeled her around, stooped over and winded, wherever they went. Years earlier, I gave my father a light-blue Toyota Corolla. It was three years old and in perfect shape. Dad was retired, and I did not want him to spend money on a new car, so this was the perfect gift for my parents.

They would visit us whenever Mom was feeling strong enough. I'd stand at the front door and wait for them to arrive. As soon as they pulled into the driveway, I would go outside and help Dad get Mom's wheelchair out of the trunk. Mandy and I insisted on driving to their house instead of them making the trip to see us. However, my parents always asked that they come to our home. I suppose that they wanted to keep their independence for as long they could. Also, Ray and I offered to drive Mom to all her doctors' appointments. Dad's response was a resounding *no* each time.

It was no different when the nurses from the local hospice became involved. Our mom was stoic, and together our parents were models of perseverance. One could only imagine what they shared in their private moments. Yet when we were around, or especially their grandchildren, they were all smiles.

Though the days of pushing his wife up and down wheelchair ramps were over, caring for Mom was no less of a strain. At that time, Dad was eighty-one years old. Aside from his heart attack almost five years earlier, the other ailments creeping up on him were emphysema, chronic obstructive pulmonary disease, and diabetes. The health aides would arrive for their stay, and Dad would take over their duties. When it was time to clean her, change her clothes, or give her medicine, he was in charge.

Knowing that Mom did not have much time left, Ray, Cindy, and I stood vigil at her bedside. Mandy came by when she could, and so did Ray's wife, Linda, and Cindy's son, Jeffrey. On this day, it was just Ray, Cindy, and I visiting Mom and Dad. Cindy joined Ray and me in the sunroom at the back of the house. We were seated at a small table where Mom and Dad always liked to have their coffee in the morning. This room was an add-on at the rear of the house, and the bay window in the living room opened into this addition. We placed the hospital bed next to the bay window, and Mom was able to look through the all-glass sunroom and enjoy the blooming flowers in her garden while she withered away.

"Look at him," Cindy said. She was facing the window, watching as Dad sat beside mom, holding her hand. "He won't leave her side. It's amazing."

A tear trickled down her cheek, and she dabbed it with a tissue.

Our mother had slipped into unconsciousness the night before. If you saw her, you'd cringe. Her mouth was open, and she breathed raspy breaths. Her thin, gray hair was cut short and pushed back on her head, her ever-present smile was replaced by a grimace, her lips stretched out and parted slightly. Occasionally she moved or twitched. There were moments when we each took turns speaking to her, offering our finals words. It was possible she heard us, I thought. Dad was aware of this likelihood better than any of us. I saw him lean close, brush her hair with his hand, and whisper in her ear. He was calm, his eyes placid, and he did not have the distraught expression that he had held for the nearly ten years while Mom fought for her life.

"It's like he's accepted it, you know? I mean, they've been married for fifty-three years. It must be so hard for him to watch her die like this. It's hard enough for me," Cindy said. She stood and walked out the side door and into the backyard. We made a conscious effort in those days to hide our grief from our parents.

I sat there with Ray and watched Cindy. She walked to a corner of the yard and cried. Ray went back inside the house to get more iced tea. I welcomed the silence offered by their absence. My attention focused on my father. He appeared mesmerized by Mom's face. They raised a family together, paid off a home, worked their entire lives, and the two of them never had much of a retirement. I wondered if my father felt cheated in any way, if he blamed his wife for getting sick and needing constant medical care for her all-consuming diseases. He tended to her every need, provided her with dignity by washing her and changing her as her body deteriorated. He comforted her and never complained. The answer was obvious. Of course, he didn't. What made me feel guilty was that I could not be so sure that I'd be as attentive and devoted if—God forbid—Mandy became ill and needed constant care. Despite Dad's example, there was a possibility that I'd fail the love of my life.

"Michael, come in here." Ray appeared in the doorway, his face stricken with panic. In all the time I'd been watching my father hold Mom's hand, I had missed the fact that her breathing had slowed dramatically.

"Cindy!" I called out. She turned. Her face told me that she understood what was happening. I breathed in deep and walked inside. Cindy ran in behind me. In the living room, Ray stood behind my father. Dad held her hand, and he brushed her cheeks with his fingers.

"Goodbye, love. Goodbye," he whispered. Cindy came inside and stood next to me. Mom groaned, gasped for air, and then her breathing stopped. Dad kissed her on the forehead. Ray covered his mouth with his hand. Cindy touched Mom's shoulder and wept. I took a step backward and watched my mother slip away from us with my mouth open. Then she was gone.

At that moment, any doubt I had about my own abilities to be there for my wife vanished. My mind reverberated with the instant replay of my father gently guiding his wife into the next world as only he knew how. My spine tingled, because it became clear. He had died before—long ago his heart stopped—but his journey continued. There was no fear in his eyes, but relief. He would see his beloved wife again, and of that fact he was confident.

Chapter 15

October 12th, 2006

In the weeks since August 30th, when Mom passed away, I had been taking Dad to church. Going to mass on Sunday was mandatory in our family for as long as I could remember. Our parents would take us three kids in the station wagon for the nine o'clock service, and then we'd head over to the bakery for jelly doughnuts and pastries afterward. As an adult, I no longer went to church. Mandy wasn't religious, and I was a closet atheist.

While no single reason caused me to not believe in God, I could no longer wrap my head around the concept of a supreme, anthropomorphic being who judged us continually, gave us both free will and original sin, and we could never do enough good. What disgusted me most about the idea of religion was the never-ending worshipping that the devout were required to do.

Depending on my work schedule, either Mandy or I would bring Dad to our house for the weekend. When I could, I took him to the five o'clock mass on Saturday night, since it was never as crowded as Sunday morning mass. It was on those days that I missed going to church. I still remembered many of the prayers and hymns. What I admired most was my father's faith. Why I did not share his devotion was a mystery to me.

Judith remained a devout Catholic, a result of growing up under Theresa's parenting. Theresa had Judith baptized, made sure she received her first holy communion, and ultimately had her confirmed. When Judith came to New York, she would ask me to go to mass with her. I always declined. Before Mom died, Judith went to church with my parents when she visited. Looking back, I wish I would have gone with them. If going to Sunday service did not help me find God, at least I would have spent more time with my daughter.

That Saturday evening, Dad and I arrived early to the church, as we always did. Dad could not walk very far, and I needed to find a spot up close. During mass, I killed time reading the weekly parish newsletter. When the collection plate came around, I had to fish in my wallet for a few spare singles to donate. Dad had his envelope at the ready. Father Tim came by and stopped next to us. Dad was seated at the end of the pew in the center aisle. For some reason, Father Tim always recognized me. When Mandy and I moved into town, I decided to give attending mass one final shot to see if I could renew my faith. The parish is a mere few blocks from our home, and that made my decision easier. After about a year, I admitted to myself that I was wasting my time and I gave up. Somehow, Father Tim remembered me, and he never missed an opportunity to say hello. He was an affable man in his early seventies, and he had a gentle voice that one would imagine a spiritual person would have, as if he were always in prayer.

"Hello Michael. Is this your father?" Father Tim smiled with his hands clasped together in front of him.

"Hello Father. Yes, this is my dad, Eugene," I said. Dad looked at me from the corner of his eye, then at Father Tim.

"I'm Gene. Nice to meet, you," he said in his deepest voice.

"Hello Gene. I think I saw you here with your son last week." Father Tim smiled. Then he turned his attention to me. "Where has your wife been? Her name is Mandy, right?" Father Tim said. I could sense what he was getting at.

"Mandy is at home. We're lapsed Catholics, Father. I've been bringing my father here since my mother passed away a few weeks ago." Father Tim's mouth opened. I didn't have to be so forthright with him, but I hated being made to feel guilty for not attending regular services. My father was good at shaming me. Ironically, one of the many reasons I did not believe in God was that I found it difficult to understand that a supreme being would be like a homeroom teacher and take attendance on Sundays.

"I am so sorry about your wife, Gene. How are you doing?" Father Tim laid his hand on Dad's shoulder.

"She's no longer in pain, Father. I miss her though. I always will." Dad wiped the corner of his eye.

"What was her name, Gene?"

"Ann. Her name was Ann," Dad said. Tears rolled down his cheeks.

"I will pray for Ann. She is with Jesus now. I will also pray for your health and comfort in your time of mourning." Father Tim held his hands together.

"Thank you, Father." Dad took a handkerchief from his pocket and wiped his face.

"Michael, if your father needs anything, we have an outreach program," Father Tim said.

"Thanks Father, but he lives in Copiague. He goes to Our Lady of Peace."

"I know he doesn't live here. Just call me. It's okay." Father Tim nodded his head at me.

"I will Father. That's kind of you," I said.

"It's the least I can do," he said. He looked down at Dad. "Gene, I am here for you. I will see you after mass." Father Tim touched Dad's shoulder again and then waved to me. Then he walked out of the church and into the vestibule. It was all I could do to keep from tearing up.

"Why did you stop going to church?" Dad looked at me.

"Come on, Dad. We're here now. Isn't that good enough for you?" I snapped at him and immediately regretted doing so. I turned my head to see if the family behind us had heard. If they did, they did not seem to react.

"You should go to mass. I raised you in the Church," Dad whispered.

"Dad, if you must know, and I'm going to let you have it with both barrels here, I'm an atheist." I folded my arms and pursed my lips.

Dad laughed softly. "An atheist, huh? Are you so sure that there is no God?" Dad turned toward me and raised an eyebrow.

"Yup," I said. I folded my arms and stared ahead. Dad let out a long sigh.

"Are you disappointed in me?" I turned my head towards him.

"No, I'm not. You'll have to either believe or not based on your own experiences." Dad tapped his thigh with his envelope.

I swallowed hard. "Well, I guess I haven't had any experiences with God yet," I said, my voice tinged with sarcasm.

"You don't always know when He's helped you," Dad whispered. He turned his head back and forth to check if anyone was listening. The murmur among the congregants grew. In minutes, Father Tim would lead the procession, and I had just revealed myself as an atheist to my profoundly religious father.

"That's reassuring," I said. "Tell me, Dad. Where was God when people were getting slaughtered on the battlefield when you were in the war?" I knew the second I uttered that sentence that I had crossed a line. If there was a God, I thought, I should run to the confessional and beg forgiveness because I had not honored my father with that remark.

"Don't be such a smartass." Dad tapped my arm with his envelope. Twenty years earlier I would have gotten smacked.

"I can't tell you exactly what I saw to make me believe in God. I know that He is there. I saw and felt things. Look, you asked where God was during combat on that day. He was there—with me." Dad turned away and took his handkerchief from his pocket. I could tell that he was crying. I didn't know whether I should put my arms around him or walk out of the church. In another universe, I may have believed in God, and we would never have had that conversation. Yet in the one that I did live in, I sat with my head down, unable to look at my father.

A small band of musicians took up their spots next to the altar. They picked up their instruments and played. The parish was one of those that eschewed a traditional organist for a young, hip, folksy, singing group. I could not help but enjoy the music. A young woman with a pretty voice sang with deep conviction. The keyboardist was an older man in his fifties with a jazzy flair. Also, there was a middle-aged woman on acoustic guitar who backed on vocals and a drummer who appeared to rock out if the opportunity arose. His restraint was palpable, and I got a kick out of watching him as he tried not to add complicated fills before each chorus. For a moment, my mind drifted away from the angst I had created between my father and me. The procession entered, and the congregation stood.

The mass seemed as eternal as the promised afterlife. I knelt, sat, and stood with the crowd; while focusing on Father Tim, the altar boy, and the musicians. Then the most dreadful portion of the mass came. The priest commanded the worshipers to offer each other a sign of peace. That necessitated shaking hands with the folks around you. Dad faced me. The moment I saw his eyes, I began to tear up. Then I hugged him.

"I'm sorry, Dad. I am so sorry," I whispered. Dad put his arms around me and held me tight.

"Me too," he said.

I wiped my face with my hand, then faced front. A woman next to me offered me her hand. I forced a grin and shook her hand. She smiled and then let go. After a few more awkward handshakes, we sat again. Dad tapped my leg. I looked down. In his hand was his handkerchief. I laughed quietly and took it. The idea of wiping my eyes with his used hanky wasn't appealing, but it was such a *dad* gesture that I could not resist the offer. When I finished dabbing my face, I handed it back, and he smiled.

After mass, we did not go straight home.

"Isn't this your block?" Dad asked. He looked out of the passenger window as I drove past my street.

"Yes, but I have a surprise for you. Don't get your expectations up, but I thought of it as we were leaving the church."

"You're the one driving. Do what you want." Dad grinned.

We pulled into the parking lot of the strip mall down the road from the church. The bakery was still open, and I hoped they had what I wanted. By evening, all the breakfast pastries were typically sold out. I went inside, and as luck would have it, there were still some choices left. A young girl helped me with my selections. After I paid, I left the store with a white box tied closed with red and white string. I got in the car with a big smile on my face.

"What's that?" Dad took the box from me and put it on his lap.

"Jelly doughnuts, crullers, and some corn muffins." I started the car and looked at him to gauge his reaction.

"You bought them at this time of night?" Dad looked at the box as if spiders might suddenly crawl out of it.

"Yeah, after church. You took us to the bakery every Sunday after church was over. You bought us doughnuts and big cookies and all that fun stuff." I checked my mirrors and backed out of the spot. Dad sat still and placed his hands on top of the box.

"We did that, didn't we? We enjoyed Sundays together." Dad stared ahead.

"It's not Sunday, but we got an early start," I said. We pulled out of the lot and made the short drive home. Dad carried the carton into the house. Inside, Mandy met us at the door.

"What's that?" Mandy asked. She took the box from my father.

"Ask Dad," I said. "He's the one who made me buy these." I patted Dad on the back and went upstairs. From the kitchen, I could hear Dad and Mandy talking. Words like *church* and *kids* and *bakery* infiltrated the room and made it to my ears. I changed into my comfy clothes and had the silly idea that I would try to convince Mandy that we eat jelly doughnuts for dinner.

Chapter 16

December 1st, 2008

Ron and I were scheduled to report to the precinct for a midnight tour on Wednesday. That meant we had to go in Tuesday night. To those who never work overnights, it is confusing. But cops who work overnights are familiar with the routine. Mandy and Larissa could never figure our schedules out.

Ron was the one who thought of police work as a career. I took the job because I did not want to be a mailman, and I needed steady employment that paid well. When I took the New York City Police Department exam, I was unsure if I would be able to handle all the depressing and dangerous situations police officers face. Yet as I often did, I thought of my father charging into battle as a teenager, and I figured that if he could survive combat, I could lock up bad guys. Dad never wanted me to join the military because, he did not want me to die or get maimed in battle. When he heard that I wanted to become a cop, he expressed the same level of concern for my safety. However, when I graduated the Police Academy back in December of 1981, I saw him smile. He was proud of me, regardless of his objections.

On the midnight shifts, the regulars had an unwritten rule that if you heard shots fired and there was no accompanying nine-one-one call, you didn't announce it over the radio, you investigated first. The reasoning behind this was that you did not want to put another cop's life in danger, making them rush to the scene for what could only be a drug dealer testing a new firearm.

Ron and I rounded the corner onto Frederick Douglass Boulevard after patrolling the area on the western side. We heard three shots, in rapid succession, coming from Bradhurst Avenue. Ron slowed to a crawl. He peeked into the rearview mirror and squinted.

"It's that guy. He's running behind us. Turn around."

I turned around and peered through the rear windshield. Ron had already started a three-point turn. A young man dressed in blue jeans and a white tee shirt jogged with his head down toward us, clutching something in his waistband. He was out in the open, and in my mind, I figured he did not expect to see any cops around. Considering that Ron and I had just heard gunfire, if this young man was not involved, he would at least be escaping from the danger or alerting us to it.

Ron completed the turn and drove at a slow pace toward the man. At that moment, I noted that he wore a dark-colored baseball cap. With his head down, the bill covered his face. It was difficult to tell if he was white, black, Hispanic, or whatever. I took my portable radio off my belt to notify the central dispatcher of our location and that we were about to stop a suspicious person, possibly armed.

"Get down!" Ron swerved the car over the curb. The car straddled the walkway with the driver's side on the road and the passenger side over the curb. I looked up and noticed the young man with his arms outstretched, pointing a handgun at us.

The first round he fired hit the center of the windshield. Because we were on an angle, the shot penetrated the glass and exited through the rear passenger window. Shattered glass struck my face. The young man fired more rounds in rapid succession, hitting our vehicle's front grill and hood. Ron threw the car into reverse, cut the wheel to the left, and backed onto the street, exposing his side. Then he slammed on the brakes. My head jerked back and forth. The gunman fired two more times. From the corner of my eye, I saw Ron grab his chest.

"Ron!" I reached across to touch his shoulder, but another gunshot sprayed more glass inside our vehicle. I held the radio in my left hand and put it to my mouth.

"10-13, one-four-three and eighth, officer shot!"

The gunman seemed cool, unfazed by his attack on a couple of cops. I watched him reach into his pocket and produce a spare magazine while simultaneously dropping the empty one from the gun. Then he slapped the loaded magazine into his handgun. I grabbed the door handle and jumped out. I saw the perp when I looked over the roof of our vehicle. With my pistol in my right hand, I rested my arm on the top of the car and took aim.

"Drop the gun. Drop it now…"

He raised his weapon and aimed at me.

My first shot came as a surprise. It was as if I had never fired a gun, and I was shocked it worked at all. I leveled my sights at him to squeeze the trigger again, but he was no longer in view. I stepped from around the passenger side with my weapon thrust out before me. The gunman was sprawled face-first on the street. His pistol was still in his hand. I ran over while aiming my service pistol at him. From the corner of my eye, I caught sight of Ron with his weapon drawn, covering me from my left. He held his gun in his hand. Our radios crackled with the voices of the other units responding to our call and the central dispatcher pleading for an update. Another squad car screeched to stop next to us. Two officers emerged with their firearms drawn.

I hooked my radio on my belt and leaned over. Immediately, I removed the gun from the young man's hand. One of the other officers approached me. I handed the perp's gun to him. I held the gunman's wrist. He was limp. There was no pulse.

"Is he dead?" I looked up and recognized the officer as one of the new guys in my squad. He wasn't a rookie but still a year or two younger than me at the time.

It was evident that the man I had shot was dead. Why he fired his gun at us, I did not know. Perhaps he was on drugs, maybe it was suicide by police, or maybe he was angry with cops because he believed they had done him an injustice. Still, my partner Ron had been hit, and for no good reason. I was forced to shoot him because of that.

"Call for a bus," I said. *Bus* is the police radio term for an ambulance. It is easier to say and takes less time.

"We already did."

I straightened up and saw Ron sitting on the passenger side of the other patrol car. The door was open, and the dome light was on. Ron grimaced as he held his hand over his chest. The other cop, a female officer who typically worked the four-to-twelve tour, stood next to him with the radio to her mouth. She was updating the other units and advising the central dispatcher of the situation.

News spread across the airwaves of the shooting and the dead suspect. It dawned on me as the scene unfolded that I was a killer. It would not matter to many civilians that Ron and I were attacked. The young man who pulled the trigger on us had no apparent motive, yet I was sure one would be made clear after the investigation began. My stomach churned, and my face felt flush. In moments, I'd be asked a lot of questions by captains and department brass. I needed a union delegate to represent me. Cops from my squad escorted me to one of the ambulances on the scene.

The rest of the night passed by in a blur. My firearm was taken from me for ballistics testing. I was briefly questioned by the duty captain with a union delegate present, and my visit to the hospital resulted in me being released after a cursory examination.

Thank God Ron didn't receive a life-threatening injury. Ron was hit by a nine-millimeter round that had been slowed considerably by the windshield. His bullet-resistant vest stopped the bullet and saved his life. The doctors were going to treat him for blunt force trauma, and it was likely he would be released from the hospital. For some reason, I reflected on how my father had been shot during the war. A bulletproof vest would not have helped him, due to the location of his wounds. Though Ron was comparatively lucky, I became angry and frightened at the same time.

I stopped to see Ron before he was wheeled away for an x-ray to ensure that he did not have any broken ribs. However, I was too late. His parents were escorted to a waiting area near radiology. I saw Ron's wife, Larissa, enter the emergency room. She looked around until her eyes settled on me.

Ronnie, Larissa, Mandy, and I often socialized on our days off. It was no surprise she recognized me so readily in uniform. Larissa ran to me with her arms open. Both Mandy and Larissa called and texted each other frequently. They went to lunch, shopped together, and were as close as Ronnie and I were.

"Mike…" Larissa covered he mouth and rushed over to me.

We embraced. The officers and nurses nearby averted their eyes to offer us privacy, such as they were able to in a public setting. Larissa's eyes were red, and she held crumpled tissues in one hand.

"The doctor said Ronnie's going to be fine. He has some bruising on his chest." She stepped back. I looked down at her and tried to smile. She started to cry. "You saved his life. The sergeant told me what happened. Ronnie's alive because of you."

I stared at her and blinked. Then I placed my hand on her shoulder.

"Larissa, Ron saved me. He swerved the car and protected me from getting hit. Listen, don't say anything here. There are all kinds of people listening." I took her by the arm and led her to an empty stall. Once inside, I closed the curtain.

"Ronnie saved *me*," I whispered.

Larissa looked up. Her lips were pursed together, her cheeks wet with tears. She put her arms around my waist and hugged me tightly.

For a moment, I hesitated. Then I placed my arms around her. She was only about five and a half feet tall, and I could rest my chin on her scalp. Her hair smelled like raspberry shampoo. She leaned her head on me. Her sobs were muted by my shirt. She had light brown hair, hazel eyes, and a complexion that always looked like she was tanned. Her cheeks showed dimples when she smiled, and she had a slight cleft in her chin. Larissa wore a black leather jacket and tight jeans. Although I was in love with Mandy and loyal to my best friend and partner, Ron, Larissa was by any man's estimation, gorgeous.

Since I had shot and killed that young man, I felt detached from myself. It was as though my body was on autopilot, and I was watching my life unfold on a TV screen. But Larissa was so real, so beautiful, and such a comforting presence. I was drawn to her.

She leaned away from me and our eyes met. I reached over, snatched a tissue from a cart against the wall, and wiped her tears.

"Does Mandy know yet?" she asked in a whisper. I nodded. "I called her earlier."

"If you wait, I'll take you home," she said, almost like a question.

I paused. My arms were still around her waist and hers around mine. It was so odd for us to be standing in an embrace. We'd never had more than a moment's physical contact before, except to kiss each other hello or goodbye on the cheek.

"Mandy's going to want to come here. My dad will probably pick her and Ray up, and…" She put her finger to my lips.

"It's okay. I understand." Larissa looked around for a moment, even though we were sequestered in the relative privacy of the curtained stall. She placed her hands on my cheeks, pulled my face close to hers, and kissed me full on the lips. Her tongue found her way into my mouth. Our kissing became passionate. I rubbed my hands up and down her back. Larissa ran her fingers along the nape of my neck. My skin tingled. It was so wrong, what we were doing, yet so pleasurable. I never imagined myself with Larissa, and she had never once given the impression that she had any attraction for me. Yet we continued as though it was the most natural thing we could do. Our arms were tight around each other. I felt her breasts against my body. I don't know how long we kissed, so full of desire, but I loved every guilty moment of it.

Larissa stopped and placed her hand on my chest. My arms fell to my sides. I watched her drop her head, then look back up at me.

"You saved Ronnie," she said.

"I…"

"Shh, you did." She took her cell phone out of her pocket and left the stall. I was confused, unable to comprehend what had just happened, and completely unable to focus. I watched her walk away from the wide space of the open curtain. Finally, my sergeant appeared.

"There you are, Koenigsmann. Your wife and your father are here."

Mandy. If she had arrived a minute earlier, she would have walked in on Larissa and I making out. We would have been hard-pressed to explain that we were both scared and the kiss we had shared came from nowhere. Though Larissa didn't say so, I knew she loved Ronnie with all her heart. In confusion, she lost herself. I admit, so did I.

I killed someone. A young man was dead. My partner survived, and I shared an intimate moment with his frightened wife. There most likely will be no consequences for our slight transgression. In that moment of attraction and lust, we comforted each other. In my mind, I could justify our sin—if it stayed between us.

Dad insisted on driving. I sat in the passenger seat. Mandy sat in the back. Dad, Ray, and Mandy drove to the precinct first. Ray stayed behind to drive my car home using the spare set of keys Mandy kept with her. Dad and Mandy were escorted to the hospital. I could only imagine my father trying to keep up with the police car in front of him. More than likely whoever the operator of the squad car was, they made good use of the lights, sirens, and went through several red lights.

At home, Dad accompanied me inside. I went straight to my room and sat at the end of the bed. Dad waited for me downstairs. The only thing I wanted to do at that moment was strip off my clothes and take a long, hot shower. The scent of Larissa's perfume lingered on my shirt, and my conscience weighed heavily on me. Why was it that I had shot and killed a man, and the only thing bothering me was that I kissed my partner's wife? Yes, I should have felt guilty, but the order of emotions was turned upside down. Mandy walked in on me. I stood up and went back downstairs.

It did not matter what my mental state was. Being rude to Mandy was the wrong thing to do. I imagined that Mandy could perceive the heat signature rising from my skin and a hologram of me and Larissa making out would appear next to me. My father stood in the living room. He still wore his blue flannel, button down jacket with the quilted lining, the same one he wore when he walked the dogs. He must have heard me coming back down. He rose up to greet me.

"Do you want to talk?"

"Uh, no. I think I'm fine, Dad. Thanks." I sat on the couch, crossed my legs and rested my hand on the armrest.

Dad sat across from me on the love seat with his hands folded on his lap. He looked at the floor first, then at me. I knew that he wanted to comfort me, but I was confused, light-headed, and hungry. I had not eaten for almost ten hours. My phone vibrated in my pocket. For a moment, I couldn't imagine who would be sending me a text.

"They gave me the BAR because I was the tallest man in my squad," Dad said. I jerked my head up and looked at him. He gazed out the window. In the light of the overhead lamp, I saw that his eyes were red. Knowing my dad, he was tearing up out of concern for me. Yet I was not paying attention to him. I was focused on my own emotions. Also, it was finally sinking in how close Ron and I came to getting murdered.

"The thing was useless as far as I was concerned. It was way too heavy and did not hold enough ammunition to be of any real use. If I fired it fully automatic, the magazine would empty in three seconds, and I would have to reload." My father gripped the armrest with his fingers. I watched him purse his lips and shake his head. "Those soldiers, the Germans, they came charging straight at us. They were bold, no fear."

"Dad, you don't have to say anything. I'm okay, really."

"I'm telling you this for a reason," he said. "I don't want you walking around, feeling like I did for all these years. You did your job, what you were paid to do."

"Dad, look…I'm just going to sit here for a while. You can stay with me. I just want to think."

"I'm sorry. I shouldn't have spoken." He stood. I got up also. Dad paused, and I walked up next to him and placed my hand on his shoulder.

"You know Dad, the irony is I spent my entire life admiring you because you were a soldier once. Every green, plastic army man I had when I was a kid, my G.I. Joes, toy guns, all had an intriguing quality about them. They represented all that you were to me. You're my hero, Dad. But now, since I had this happen to me, you're more of a hero than you ever were. How were you able to come home and look at people that you loved in the eye knowing that they knew what you did? I feel so, so…mortified. Dad, I killed a man." I put my arms around him. My cheek rested against his neck, the very same side a German bullet fragment exited from six decades earlier. Dad hugged me. I could feel his hands tremble.

Dad placed his hands on my shoulders. I sat down, and he took a spot next to me on the love seat. He sat on the edge of the cushion angled towards me.

"I don't have any soothing advice or magic trick that will make you feel better. I pray every morning and night for the souls of the men I had to…kill. I pray for their families, children, wives, mothers, many of whom are no longer living. I feel in my heart God knows I did not murder them. I can see their eyes, feel their pain, hear them calling out loud, calling for help. But I am lucky that I got to come home. Any of the torment and anguish I may have for the acts I committed pales against the family I have now. You're home, Michael. Be happy about that. You did what you had to do." Dad patted my knee and then stood up. He looked down at me, smiled, winked, and then walked into the kitchen.

His words did not sink in. What he did not know and what I could not tell him was that the overwhelming sense of shame that I experienced at that moment was not for saving my own life and Ronnie's by dropping some guy with my service pistol. I felt remorse for kissing Larissa. Worse than that, I wanted to do so again. The thought of it aroused me. Deeper still, when we had parted ways, I could see it in Larissa's eyes that she wanted more herself. Shooting someone was bad enough. Adultery was worse. My God, the regret was killing me.

Chapter 17

March 2009

After my mother passed away on August 30th, 2006, Dad's health declined rapidly. By then, he was eighty-one years old. Caring for Mom all those years took its toll. During that period, he did not allow himself time to rest. Dad tended to Mom's every need, often stepping in to bathe her and change her clothes when there were nurses and aides there to assist him. Not only did diabetes creep up on him, but he also did not follow the dietary restrictions that his doctor ordered or inject his insulin as scheduled. Ray, Cynthia, and I did our best to convince Dad that he should move in with Mandy and me after Mom passed. We had an extra room downstairs that would be perfect for him. Ray and Cindy took him from time to time, but his days of living alone were numbered. But he did not want to sell his house and move out after living there for over a half-century. For almost two years, the three of us visited him as often as we could. Mandy and I would bring him to our house on weekends. Judith flew up from Florida when she was able to and stayed in the bedroom that Ray and I had shared when we were kids. Despite the care and attention we gave him, his health was worsened.

The first Saturday in February 2009, Ray had convinced Dad to spend the weekend at his place. His wife, Linda, made the downstairs bedroom comfortable for him with fresh bedsheets and pillowcases. Ray's house had a full bathroom on the first floor, next to the bedroom where Dad stayed. This was a convenience that my house did not offer. The afternoon went well until Dad became sick. Ray called an ambulance over Dad's objections. He was taken to the hospital and admitted. There, the doctor discovered that he was in renal failure. It took a few days to get his kidneys functioning again, but this trip to the emergency room started a cycle. For weeks, Dad see-sawed back and forth between a rehabilitation center and the hospital. None of the doctors at the hospital were affiliated with Dad's health provider, and he had to settle for whichever physician was available each time he was admitted. Finally, Ray was able to get Dad into a Catholic nursing home located across the parking lot from Good Shepard Hospital where my father's primary care physician was affiliated. Our Lady of Good Counsel was perfect for him. Nuns and priests made regular rounds throughout the day to each room. The nurses and nurse assistants were patient with him, understanding that he was hard of hearing. He stubbornly refused to wear his hearing aids, stating that they buzzed in his ears. At the other hospital, the doctors and nurses had believed he was suffering from dementia, because he would not answer them. Cindy, Ray, and I repeatedly explained that he was sharp as a tack and that he could not hear them.

The nursing home facility was spotless, though sparsely decorated. We decorated his room with framed pictures of our family. Cindy took it upon herself to bring him newspapers. Dad's roommate was in the final stages of Alzheimer's and unresponsive. I felt terrible that Dad had no one to talk to, but he seemed satisfied with his accommodations. Each day, the aides would put Dad in a chair and wheel him into the day room.

On March 15th, 2009, I arrived at the nursing home to spend time with him. Mandy had stopped in during her lunch break, because she worked nearby. Though we all tried to get there daily, the demands of our schedules caused us to miss an afternoon or night with Dad sporadically. However, we made sure that Dad had at least one of us see him each day. Visiting hours for the evening began at five o'clock. I was early, but the guard at the front desk permitted me to go to my father's floor anyway. I checked his room, and he wasn't there. The main hall was at the end of the corridor. I could see Dad seated at a table in a Geri chair, which is a rolling, medical recliner. Dad was sitting upright, and his head rested against the cushioned back of the chair. A young man, an aide, stood next to him, coaxing him to eat dinner. The aide held a forkful of mashed potatoes before Dad's mouth. I stood in the background, careful not to be seen. The staff would not expect a visitor this early, and I wanted to make sure they treated my father with dignity.

"Come on, Gene. Have some potatoes. They're good for you," the aide said.

Dad's head dropped. He breathed with his mouth open and did not respond. The young aide persisted. "Food is like medicine for you, Gene. You need to eat."

The young man stood with his left side facing me. His smile was genuine but practiced and there to put his patient at ease. He was determined and gentle, yet his tone was tinged with concern. After observing for another minute or so, I approached them.

"Hi, you must be Gene's son," he said. The ID card dangling from a lanyard around his neck read *Thomas Manning*. For a moment, I was disappointed that the young man had not been rude or nasty to my father. Perhaps my fear of Dad's eventual death caused me frustration that I needed to take out on someone. Logically, I understood that he could not hang on much longer in his state. There was no improvement. Dad's muscles weakened. He could barely keep his head up, and his breathing was labored. I was confident that Ray and Cindy felt the same way. Yet we did not talk about it to each other.

The aide put the fork down on Dad's plate. He held out his hand for me to shake. Then I felt guilty.

"Yes, I'm his youngest son. You probably met Ray and my sister Cindy already."

"I believe I have," he said. Then he placed his hand on Dad's shoulder. "I just wish I could get him to eat." Thomas shook his head and sucked his teeth.

"I'll give it a try," I said.

"Good luck. I'll come back for the tray later." Thomas nodded and then walked into the hallway.

Dad lifted his head and noticed me. Lacking the wherewithal to smile, Dad motioned for me to sit using his hand. I pulled out a chair and sat across from him. In the background, a man about my father's age rolled himself into the room in a wheelchair. During previous visits, Fred, as I heard the aides call him, would come over to us to say hello. Dad would ignore him. Fred would soon get the hint that Dad did not want to chat. Then he would leave. There was no reason for my father to be so rude to Fred. Then, just as I had anticipated, Fred saw us and immediately approached from my left.

"Hello, young man. I see you are here to visit your father. How sweet of you." Fred had a thick, German accent. I was interested in learning more about him, but my dad's caginess around him prevented me from engaging Fred in conversation. Fred beamed and put out his hand. I shook it and smiled back.

"Hello, sir. How are you today?" I said. I peeked at Dad. He inhaled and then released a long sigh.

"I am well, thank you," Fred answered. "Gene, your son is a gentleman. You must be proud. And he is tall and strong, too." Fred was a lean man with a gaunt face who was much more ambulatory than my father. He appeared to have been a laborer, someone who worked outside, perhaps as a builder; due to his sun-weathered skin.

"Thank you, Fred. We can talk, later," said Dad.

"Yes, yes. We will. Of that I am certain." Fred tapped my shoulder and then wheeled himself across the room to the big screen TV. Others were gathered there, watching the news, and Fred took up a spot next to them.

I watched my father as his head dipped and his watery eyes closed. A nervous feeling gripped my gut. The terse exchanges between Fred and Dad had me wondering.

"Hey Dad, why are you so terse with Fred? Every time he comes over, you blow him off," I said. My father opened his eyes and looked at me.

"I talk to Fred all day long. He's a fascinating man. It's just that when you kids come to visit, I want to speak only to you. Fred's a friendly man, but I don't want to have to entertain him while I have visitors." Dad coughed into a crumpled tissue and then placed it in the top pocket of his pajamas.

"Oh, I didn't know," I said. "I just thought that maybe you didn't like him."

"What's not to like?" Dad raised an eyebrow.

"Well, he's around your age, and he has a German accent. It's possible that he was in the Wehrmacht, or the Luftwaffe, or worse yet, the Waffen-SS during the war. I mean, I wouldn't want you to have a flashback and try to stab him with a plastic fork or something." I instantly felt like a jerk for making that remark. I chuckled to pass off my comment as a lame joke.

"Don't be ridiculous." Dad pursed his lips and shook his head. Then he narrowed his eyes and peered over at Fred.

"I would never ask a man about his experiences in the war. It's too painful to talk about." Dad looked back at me and blinked his heavy eyelids a few times. Then he turned his gaze on the TV. Images of fighting in Iraq played on the news. "Fred told me everything anyway. I didn't have to ask. He has a captivating story. Better than mine. You should ask him about it." Dad grinned. He stared at the ceiling and then moved his lips as if he were trying to form words. Then he focused on me.

"Did you know that Fred lived in Lindenhurst and worked at the Brooklyn Navy Yard when I worked there?" He raised an eyebrow.

"No, I didn't. That's quite a coincidence," I said.

"Not really, if you think about it. The Navy employed thousands of people there. At least once a year, I bump into an old-timer like me who worked at yard who I never met before. It's like the NYPD. How many times do you meet someone who asks if you know their son, or daughter, or uncle who is a city cop and didn't know them?"

"That happens all the time," I said.

Dad coughed and then wiped his lips with a tissue. I watched his shaky hand dab the corners of his mouth. When he finished, he cleared his throat.

"You always bugged me about what I did as a soldier. I suppose you wanted to hear about me shooting Germans since that's what you saw in war movies when you were a kid," he said. Couched again.

"Look, Dad. You don't have to talk about it if you don't want to. Let's talk about anything else." I started to sweat, and I tugged at the collar of my polo shirt.

"You're a police officer. Do you like it when civilians ask if you ever shot anybody?"

"You made your point. I won't ask you about the army anymore." He gave me a taste of what I had been dishing out to him for over twenty years. My mind released a torrent of memories of that night when my partner, Ron, and I encountered a gunman on the street during a midnight tour. Ron and I had been best friends since I was transferred to the 32nd Precinct and we were partnered up together. We worked together for seven years. In all that time, we never had to discharge our service pistols. We were more than buddies, were like brothers. Mandy and his wife, Larissa, were best friends as well. I always felt a bit awkward when we were out together since Ron, Larissa, and Mandy were all around the same age, and I was the old man of the group. Over time, it did not matter anymore. Yet since the shooting, everything had changed.

Dad rubbed his hands together. He did that when he felt uncomfortable.

"I'm sorry. I was harsh. I've been thinking about Italy a lot lately, my time in Rome. I miss Rome. I guess I'll never make it back there. Your mother and I had planned a trip a while ago." Dad's eyes teared up. Yet I could not tell if it was due to emotions or because he was ill. They were always watery of late.

"Also, I've been thinking about my buddies. I remember Sgt. Thames. I put my life in his hands and he—Well, he ended up like a lot of men."

"Dad, we can watch TV," I said.

"No, I want to talk." Dad leaned back and settled his eyes on me. I knew that expression. He was going to speak about an awkward topic. I was reminded of his clumsy attempt to explain the facts of life to me when I was thirteen.

Anticipation rushed through me. It was kind of like the day I received my gun and shield at the police academy, but more like when Theresa said she'd go with me to the senior prom, or when Mandy said *yes* when I asked her to marry me. I had dreamed of becoming a cop when I was a kid and about dating beautiful girls. But when the moment for each came, my mouth became dry and my palms sweaty. My stomach experienced a familiar pang. It is weird to suggest that hearing my father talk about his participation in the war could elicit the same type of reaction, but my dad's role had been a constant loop of imagined battle scenes playing in my head since I was five years old. Since kindergarten I wondered, was my dad a hero? Did he charge with a bayonet fixed on the end of his rifle while pulling the pin of a grenade with his teeth? More importantly, when, where, and how was he wounded? It was these details that had me curious, and damn it, I felt guilty for wanting to learn them. After all, these were memories that he had suppressed for decades and wished to forget. Yet since I could speak, I had been poking him to reveal his secrets. I knew that he had been shot, his buddies had been killed, and that he kept letters sent to him by his family in the bottom drawer of his dresser. Yet I did not possess many of the particulars about what he had seen or what he did. In fact, I only knew that he had fought in Italy. *Where* in Italy and in what battles remained a mystery.

Dad pointed to the television. The news showed footage of fighting in Iraq.

"You see what they're doing to our boys and girls over there in that desert? It's a damn shame. Those kids are brave as any of us who went overseas in my time. Like my generation, they're coming back without arms and legs after all kinds of terrible things happened to them. And our government won't let them fight the way they're supposed to." He coughed again and covered his mouth with his arm.

"Dad, don't talk. It's okay," I said. I got up and stood by his side. He grabbed my hand with both of his and squeezed it.

"I'm fine. Sit... sit down. I feel like I can't clear my throat. Too much phlegm." He let go of my hand. I remained at his side for a moment, waiting for another coughing fit. Finally, I sat back down with my arms on the rests. Dad ran his fingers through his thinning, gray hair, and then straightened himself up as best as he could. He cleared his throat and spoke, slowly in the beginning, and then he picked up the pace. For sixty-six years, he kept his secrets bottled up inside, unable or unwilling to share the horrifying and graphic details of the events that led to him being wounded in action. Yet there was more. Nearly dying and facing his mortality changed him in drastic ways that he had not expected. Perhaps, I thought, his brush with death was the impetus for him not to follow in his father's footsteps and instead lead an honest life? Maybe, I imagined, Dad had a vision of Heaven while facing his mortality? Could he have possibly seen God? From what small amount of information I gleaned from my grandmother about Alphonse, it occurred to me that my father would want to be just like him. After all, I wanted to be just like Dad.

My pre-adolescent visions of my superhero father clad in olive drab, leaping across barbed wire while blasting away at enemy machine gun nests were dispelled. What I pictured then, while sitting across from my father in the day room, was a teenager enlisting in the army because that was what he was supposed to do. I shed my heroic fantasies of him, and I came to know him as a brave man who performed his duties with an earnestness which he later applied to raising his family and at work.

Listening to my father, I lost track of time, ignored Mandy's persistent text messages, and stayed past visiting hours. Finally, Dad finished his tale. I wiped my sweaty palms on my pants and took a deep breath.

That night, after I mitigated Mandy's complaints about my ignoring her messages, I sat in my den with a beer in hand. I ran and reran my visit with Dad in my mind. My father was at once a child, a son, soldier, husband, father, grandfather, widower, and a nursing home resident. There was a larger story here than a narrative of his involvement in the Italian Campaign. Beneath the surface of his account, starting way back in his childhood under my grandfather's roof, was his cry for redemption. My father, the most devout Catholic I ever knew, felt in need of forgiveness. Out of all that I had learned that evening, that left me unsettled.

Mandy entered the room. She motioned for me come to bed. I held up my finger, indicating that I would be there momentarily. I closed my eyes and counted ten heartbeats before I opened them again. Though a part of me was in denial, I sensed that my father did not have much time left. Before this conversation with my dad, everything that I had heard came in bits and pieces. There were vignettes and fragments of Dad's history fed to me out of order over the years. Now that I had learned the details of his role in combat—how he was injured—I felt that I had gained something greater than the sum of its parts. I had intimate facts that remained untold for decades. These provided me insights into a man whom I knew only as a parent and not as an eighteen-year-old boy in a baggy uniform with a helmet dipping forward over his glasses.

I shivered in fear. My gut did a summersault, and I swallowed hard. Dad was letting go. It was apparent, although a part me still denied this. I set my beer down and cradled my head in my hands. When it was time, my father would surrender his final breath in bed, surrounded by those who loved him, not on a battlefield in Italy, where he had once died and was born again.

Chapter 18

June 1st, 1944, 1300 hrs.

Gene lay prone, taking aim with the BAR while hidden among the tangled grape vines on the hillside. The gentle slope drifted down to the village. The Wehrmacht had months to prepare for this encounter. Allied aircraft and artillery had bombarded the location in advance of the Texas 36th Infantry Division's push. The 141st Regiment, Gene's unit, was in position to spearhead the attack while the 142nd bypassed the German line and came up in the rear. The 143rd joined them on their right flank. Beyond Velletri was Rome. The Wehrmacht occupied a hill overlooking Velletri and the town itself. A victory here would mean the Americans could liberate Rome. In the weeks before the push by the Allies, Velletri had been shelled and became a battered landscape like many other Italian towns and cities. Many of Velletri's residents had evacuated to the countryside and Rome. Yet it was hardly a ghost town. There were reports that some of the population took refuge in cellars or remained in their homes. On that summer day, there was one more battle to wage. Young American boys like Gene would risk limbs and blood, not for an idea or to liberate citizens of a town whom they never met, but for each other.

Gene suppressed his fear by emulating his stone-faced father. His buddies were lined up in a row on both sides of him. Their platoon would move in first, or so he assumed since there were no other troops before them. Some of the young GIs murmured prayers, others tried to sleep, because the regiment had spent the night before moving into position. Some chose to stare ahead, watching shells detonate a few hundred yards away.

Gene pushed his helmet back and adjusted his glasses. He reminisced about his father, what he looked like, and the way other men were deferential to him. Those who did business with Alphonse respected him. They also feared him. Gene closed his eyes and savored the memory of his dad, whom he missed.

The barrel of his rifle dipped as his mind drifted away from the battleground. His job was to provide sustained, covering fire as the troops advanced. A soldier was assigned to carry ammo for him, along with his own weapons and gear. Gene hated that others had to haul around heavy ammunition cans for him, so he slung as many bandoliers over his shoulders as he could without toppling over when he ran. His buddy, Harry, on his right, also aimed at the enemy with his rifle. After what they had been through, their bond was strong. The day before, when Sgt. Warren ordered Harry to bear the load of Gene's ammo, Gene insisted that it be someone else. Harry's leg was still bandaged from the bullet that grazed him. Gene wanted another GI to carry the ammo for him not only because Harry was recovering from the wound, but because he was a friend. Sgt. Warren capitulated and ordered one of the new, replacement troops to perform the task. Sgt. Warren pointed to one of the new replacements. "You there. You're elected. Your job is to carry extra ammo for the BAR. Got it?" He did not wait for the young GI to respond. He slapped the kid on the shoulder, winked, and then walked away.

Gene looked at the fresh-faced soldier to his left, whom Sgt. Warren assigned ammo duty to. The young soldier was lean, his helmet was too big for him, and he was loaded with gear. The soldier had blue eyes and a sliver of a blond mustache that was visible when his face was profiled against the sun.

"Hey, are you okay?" Gene asked him. The young soldier turned to Gene.

"Yeah, sure. I'm sweating bullets though."

"Don't say that," Gene said.

"Say what?"

"Bullets. Don't jinx yourself." Gene smiled. Harry laughed and nudged Gene. Gene looked back at Harry and grinned.

"Right, I'll watch my mouth." The kid's helmet slid down over his eyes. Then he straightened it and looked at Gene.

"Am I supposed to run next to you or what?" he asked.

"What's your name, again?" Gene said.

"Baker. Thomas Baker."

"Tom, stay right behind me. I don't want you getting shot, okay? You have enough shit to carry. You can't fire your rifle while hauling those cans around."

"You're going to cover me?" Tom raised his eyebrows.

"Hey Baker, just run as fast as you can and don't get killed. It's that easy," Harry said.

"Sounds simple enough when you're not loaded up like a pack mule." Tom sighed. "If I get hit, I hope it is in the leg or something. I'm too young to die."

"Knock it off. I told you that you're going to jinx yourself," Gene snapped at Tom.

"You sound more like a pack jackass than a pack mule. I carried those cans, and I survived," Harry said.

"Then here you go. Be my guest." Tom pushed one of the heavy ammo cans at Harry, though it moved just a few inches.

"Knock it off, you two. I'm getting a headache." Gene removed his helmet, scratched his head, and then put it back on.

Harry sneered and focused ahead. Tom unwrapped a stick of gum and stuck it in his mouth. The three of them remained silent as they lay still among the vineyard. Gene wiped sweat from his brow with his hand. Then he gazed ahead and contemplated the upcoming battle. This would be more than just a small unit action. A familiar pang of anxiety struck him.

Gene had never considered his own death or how it would happen. He had spent the previous thirty days engaged in skirmishes, ducking artillery, and hiding from the Luftwaffe. But he never actually imagined himself dying. Even when he and Harry were escaping the Germans after Sgt. Thames was killed at the farmhouse, he did not believe that he could die. He became angry and fought back against the pursuing enemy. This time was different. He had plenty of time to stare ahead at the looming battlefield and consider his fate. Gene wanted the fight to be over with, so he could stop thinking about death. It then occurred to him that he had not received Communion in weeks. In his shirt pocket were rosary beads and a small prayer book his mom had given him. He had almost forgotten about them. Momentarily, he would be ordered to charge in the face of German machine guns. Would God forgive him for not praying? Then he had a more chilling notion. Would God hold him accountable for the enemy soldiers he had killed?

No one in the 141st Regiment had gotten any sleep or food since nightfall the evening before. In the Italian countryside, sunset came late during summer. The Germans would stop fighting, as they rarely engaged the enemy in the dark. This time, the Americans took advantage of their vulnerability and moved all three regiments under cover of darkness in a flanking maneuver. That morning, the 143rd Regiment attacked from the front of the German position. The 142nd attacked them from the rear while they sparred with the 143rd. Meanwhile, Gene's regiment was sent ahead to secure the last roadblock to Rome—Velletri.

He was caught off guard as his fellow soldiers sprang from among the vegetation and charged down the knoll, straight at their opponents. Gunfire erupted from the shelled homes and heaps of rubble. He acted on cue, hefting his automatic rifle and jogging forward in a practiced, steady pace. His mouth was dry, and he wished he bothered to sip from his canteen beforehand. Harry and Tom rose from behind the vines and charged forward.

There were plenty of places for the Germans to take cover, Gene thought as he scanned the bombed-out structures. There were still civilians inside those buildings, many not willing to leave their homes. He wondered if they were praying and if God could hear their muted entreaties over the cacophony of combat. Suddenly the idea of death consumed him. His lungs constricted, he wheezed as he ran, and he experienced an overwhelming pang of nausea. He could die. This was as sure as the bets his father placed at the track. He hoped—he prayed—that God was listening to him.

He recalled Sister Josephine, a nun who was one of his teachers from Catholic school. She was younger than most of the other nuns and not as strict. She was fond of Gene. She had learned that Gene was overseas and corresponded with him. In one of her letters to him, she said that God existed in all the places of the Earth and that evil fills in the gaps where love fears to blend in. She advised he must love even his opponents, as Jesus taught, as they too were children of the Lord. He thought such strong faith and devotion came only to the unchallenged. But she was a beloved teacher at his Catholic high school and someone he admired.

When he reached the edge of town, a burst of machine-gun fire ripped across the gravel in front of him. Others in his platoon had fallen, gasping and crying for help. Gene jumped out of the way of the fusillade and landed on his side. He rolled over and hid behind a burned-out car that was on a cobblestone road. The street led into the village. Many of the homes and buildings were still standing, but they were heavily damaged. Others were flattened. Crumbled bricks, shattered glass, and other debris were strewn about the streets and sidewalks.

Gene's heart pounded, and his breaths were short. Harry and Tom took cover behind a pile of rubble to Gene's right.

The Germans were in a nearby home, just to the right of where he lay out in the open. Several men in the regiment had been hit. A Wehrmacht soldier was visible from a second story window. Gene aimed and placed the tip of his finger on the trigger.

He prayed, "Oh my God, I am heartily sorry for having offended thee." Gene squeezed the trigger. He hit his target, and the man hung outside, over the windowsill. "And I detest all my sins, because I dread the loss of Heaven and the pains of Hell."

Members of the platoon charged into the building. German soldiers shouted in defiance as they realized their situation was hopeless. Shots were fired, screams were stifled, and moments later, there was silence. The GIs returned to the street, and the house-to-house hunt for the enemy began.

"Move it out, move it now!"

Gene looked to his left at Sgt. Warren. The sergeant urged those who were unharmed to attack. Sgt. Warren was in his mid-twenties. To young eighteen-year-old GIs like Gene, he was like an old man. Sgt. Warren carried an M1 Carbine and a Colt, Model 1911, .45 caliber pistol in a hip holster. Even without weapons, Sgt. Warren was a commanding presence. With a physique of a football player and a straight razor posture, he didn't need an ostentatious display of firearms to inspire his men. His appearance was carefully constructed to boost morale. Sgt. Warren pointed to him. "Koenigsmann," he said. Then he stepped forward and grabbed Gene's collar. "You take point."

"Yes, Sergeant!" Gene pushed himself off the ground and paused long enough to catch a glimpse of the German soldier he had shot. The body still dangled from the second story. Gene thought it indecent to dash off and leave him there. When someone died back home, there was a wake and then a funeral. Everyone experienced grief. He remembered his father laid out in their living room for two days. Men from the neighborhood, many of whom had been intimidated by his father when he was alive but worked for him while plying their nefarious trade, paid their respects. They gave his mother thick envelopes and the promise to help out of she needed it. In the weeks since the start of the May offensive, Gene had been party to enough killing. Fatigue had set in and begun to wear him down mentally.

"Come on, soldier. This is a fight!" The sergeant grabbed his sleeve and pushed him forward. Together, they reached a broad point between ruined buildings. The cobblestone street was littered with bricks, household items, and abandoned vehicles. The Allied bombardment had stopped. The gunfire was heavy, and it was coming from their right and left flanks. Gene's platoon was poised to move into the town first.

They crouched by a waist-high wall. It was made of white-washed brick, and it offered solid cover against rifle fire. Gene crawled on his stomach, using his elbows to propel himself forward. He cradled his BAR in his arms. Gene peeked around the corner and pointed his weapon down the thoroughfare.

Through wisps of smoke, he couldn't make out any movement. The war seemed like it was going on everywhere except their immediate vicinity, despite the clash he had been just involved in. Just as he was about to give Sgt. Warren the *all-clear* signal, a man dashed into the road from a nearby building.

Rifle fire erupted around him. The man, a civilian dressed in a dark suit, yelled while running at them with his hands over his head.

"Cease fire, cease fire!" Sgt. Warren stood and waved at the other soldiers. It took a few seconds, but they heeded the command. The man paused about twenty yards from Gene's location. He gasped for air and kept his arms high above his head. The man wore a bowler hat, and he had a thick, dark mustache. Gene made eye contact with him, and the man lowered his arms.

"Io sono un medico. Io sono un medico. Ho appena partorito un bambino."

Sgt. Warren held his weapon at his hip and raised his hand indicating to the man to slow his speech.

"I don't know what you're saying," Sgt. Warren said. "Do you speak English?"

"L'inglese, non in inglese. Parli italiano?"

Gene rolled off his stomach and kneeled behind the wall. Using his left arm, he held on to the top of the partition and pulled himself up.

"He said he's a doctor, and he just delivered a baby boy," Gene said.

Sgt. Warren looked at him with his eyebrows raised and his head cocked to one side.

"You speak *Italian*, Koenigsmann?"

Gene eyeballed him as if he couldn't be bothered to answer the obvious.

"Yes, I can speak it. I just don't write in Italian," Gene said.

Sgt. Warren shook his head and pushed his helmet back.

"Only in America can a German kid from Brooklyn go to Italy and speak Italian." Sgt. Warren laughed. "Then talk to the man. Find out who he is and where the mother and the baby are. We have to get them out of here before all hell breaks loose," Sgt. Warren said.

Gene turned to the doctor. *"Dove si trova la madre e il bambino?"* The doctor hesitated and then pointed to the building he emerged from.

"È la madre in grado di camminare?"

"Sì, ma lei avrà bisogno di aiuto."

"What is he saying?" Sgt. Warren asked.

"I asked where the mother and the baby are. They are in that brick building right there. He says the mother can walk, but she needs help."

Sgt. Warren scratched his chin. Then he looked at Gene. "Do you think this could be a trap?" he whispered.

"No, this isn't a trap. Look at him." Gene pointed at the man. The doctor removed his hat and held it in his hands.

"Ask him where the father is." Sgt. Warren focused on the physician and squinted as if his careful scrutiny would reveal a ruse.

"Dove si trova il padre del bambino?"

"Egli è morto."

Gene turned toward the sergeant.

"Well?" asked Sgt. Warren.

"He's dead." Gene stretched the corner of his mouth and made a *tsk* sound to express sympathy.

"I don't want to do this, it's a distraction. Damn it. Those Germans ran away when we first hit, but they'll regroup. Then they'll be back." Sgt. Warren sighed as he looked past the doctor and up the road. Finally, he slapped his thigh. "All right. We're doing this. I can't risk this baby getting killed, not on his birthday, not on my watch." He turned and pointed to Tom and Harry. "You two, cover us. We're going in."

Gene and Sgt. Warren left the wall and hurried, crouched over, into the middle of the street. They approached the doctor with a quick step. Sgt. Warren grabbed him by the arm. "Take us to the baby," he said. The doctor didn't need a translation. The three of them headed over to the building. Enemy small arms fire erupted from among a shelled-out house about a hundred yards further north. Gene, Sgt. Warren, and the doctor were in plain sight. The sergeant and Gene ran for the structures on the side of the street where the baby and the mother were. Others in their platoon provided covering fire.

They made it to the entrance of the brick building where the mother and the newborn had taken refuge. There was no door, and Gene could see inside. The mother sat at the edge of the bed with the baby cradled in her arms. She jumped up when she saw Sgt. Warren and Gene enter. She wore a long, blue dress, had dark hair down past her shoulders, and brown eyes that were open wide. She breathed through parted lips, and her lower jaw quivered.

"Sono Americani, sono qui per aiutarci." The doctor edged past them and walked over to her. He picked up his black, leather, medical bag and escorted her to the door.

"Tell them to follow us," Sgt. Warren said to Gene. Then the sergeant smiled at the young woman.

"Esegui il più velocemente possibile. Noi non lasceremo alle spalle," Gene said. He told them to run as fast as possible and that he and the sergeant would not leave them behind. The doctor put his arm around the new mother. She crossed herself and then held her baby close to her chest with both hands.

"Let's move," Sgt. Warren said.

The group scurried back to the spot where Gene and the sergeant had come from.

Soldiers from their platoon provided substantial covering fire for them as they headed for the point from which they had left. Sgt. Warren jogged next to the mother. She cradled the shrieking infant and ran hunched forward. The doctor trotted on the opposite side of Sgt. Warren and the young mother. Gene urged everyone forward. Sgt. Warren and the mother were unable to move quickly. Bullets struck the shops and cars all around.

"Correre più veloce, correre!" Gene yelled for the doctor and the mother to run faster. He kept himself between Sgt. Warren and the woman, who was behind him, and the doctor, who was just ahead of all of them. Gene kept checking over his shoulder to see if they were keeping up with him.

"Don't worry about us. Get that doctor out of here," Sgt. Warren called out.

They hustled along the shadows of the lurching facades of damaged buildings. In less than a minute, which seemed much longer to Gene, they arrived at the spot by the corner they had held before rescuing the mother and baby. The doctor ducked behind the wall along with the mother and her newborn. Sgt. Warren pointed with his finger at two soldiers and a medic who waited nearby along the side of the nearest building, which was out of sight from the enemy's stronghold. The two GIs had a stretcher and held their spot.

Meanwhile, the medic ran to the corner of the building and called for the mother and the doctor. From where they hid behind the short wall, they remained exposed to snipers. The doctor took the baby from the mother and told her to crawl to the medic. She hesitated at first, and then she kissed her newborn and crawled the roughly ten yards behind the crumbling, stone fence to the waiting arms of the medic. She stood when she reached safety. Then she watched the doctor prepare himself for his run. She placed her hands over her mouth while gasping. Gene reached for the baby, but the doctor held tight.

"No, no, giovanotto. Io proteggerò questo bambino. Si combatte quelli fascists." Gene held his weapon as he nodded a reluctant acquiescence to the doctor. *"Essere sicuri, medico. Dio vi benedica,"* he said. And then he smiled. The doctor turned and looked to where he needed to crawl and then back at Gene.

"Questo bambino,   è   nato quando gli americani arrivarono. Porterai il bambino in America così sarà al sicuro dalla guerra?"

Gene blinked, thought for a moment, and then he answered. *"Lo porteremo a Brooklyn, dove è Ilive. Si adatterà perfettamente."*

The doctor seemed pleased as he nodded and studied Gene.

"Dimmi giovane, sei italiano?" he asked.

"Io? No, sono Tedesco." A smile grew on the physician's face, and then he laughed out loud. He smacked Gene on the shoulder.

"Bene, il mio amico tedesco-americano di Brooklyn che parla come un vero uomo italiano, ah! Ti vedrò nella tua città natale quando questa guerra sarà vinta! Che Dio sia con te." Immediately, the doctor clutched the newborn and crawled using one arm for support. He reached the mother and

awaiting soldiers. Together, they were escorted to the rear of the line.

"What was that all about?" asked Sgt. Warren.

Gene grinned. "He wanted to know if we can take the boy to America where he will be safe from the war."

"No kidding?" Sgt. Warren rested his back against the wall and took a deep breath. He pushed his helmet back and looked at Gene. "What'd you tell him?"

"I said bring him to Brooklyn, and he will fit right in."

"You're a funny guy, Koenigsmann." Sgt. Warren turned and peeked over the wall at the situation behind them. "And that was a beautiful bit of diplomacy. Still, we have some fighting to do."

Gene watched in the distance as the doctor, mother, baby, and the three soldiers in attendance headed up the road. Gene thought about the men he had killed and the baby they had just saved. He wondered if God balanced his sins against the good deeds he performed during a war. If God did that, he thought, would the rescue of a mother, her baby, and a doctor outweigh the murder of men who would kill him if he did not shoot them first? Gene reached into his shirt pocket, taking out his rosary beads. He opened his mouth to pray, but he could not find the words. He turned his head in the direction of the house where he had shot the German soldier earlier. Gene swallowed hard. He could not see the body through his tears. He shoved the beads back into his pocket, removed his glasses, and wiped his eyes with a handkerchief. After taking a deep breath, he cleared his throat.

"What's wrong, Koenigsmann?" asked Sgt. Warren.

Gene sat forward and looked at the sergeant. He moved so he was in a crouched position with his BAR upright.

"I was just wondering if I'd ever see them again, that's all."

"Well, I think it's just as likely they're thinking the same about us." Sgt. Warren stood up and yelled, "Move out!"

In moments, the men formed two columns and moved into town. They marched, ran, took cover, and fired at their unseen enemy. Soon, artillery rained upon them.

Chapter 19

March 30th, 2009

Regardless of our plan to take turns visiting Dad, we still saw him as much as we could. Ray used much of his vacation time to tend to him. Cindy showed signs of stress. She wept after each visit, and she had trouble sleeping. The plan she came up with made sense.

The nurses liked to put Dad in the sunroom. If it were up to him, he'd lay in bed all day. How he could stand the pain from his open bed sores was anyone's guess. However, since his health declined even further over the past few weeks, he lost his will to live. He was unable to sit up in bed or have the strength to move his arms.

One half of me could see the decline in his health, the other half believed he was a hardened, old warhorse and that nothing could kill him, especially Wehrmacht bullets. Our mom fought a heroic battle against her diseases, both Lupus and colon cancer, and her struggles were lessons in perseverance and bravery. Dad's gift was stamina. Plus, he never complained. If he did experience discomfort or soreness, he never let on. The nurses had to guess.

I was on the way to visit dad on the way home from work, and I decided to give Ray a call. Ray answered with a tinge of dread in his voice, as if he expected to hear bad news. I managed to use a pleasant tone, although I was concerned.

"Dad won't read anymore. I brought him one of his favorite books, and it just sits there. He won't even look at a newspaper." Ray spoke rapid-fire into the phone. I had my cell on speaker and kept it on my lap while driving.

"Maybe he's just tired?"

"No Mike, he's giving up. You know how much mom and dad loved to read. Their entire house is crammed with books. I took one of his Civil War books over there today, and he won't even glance at the cover."

"Not for nothing, Ray, Dad knows more about the Civil War than most historians. I think he's bored with it already." I picked up my cell and held it in front of me.

"Don't be naïve, Mike. You know he's dying. I don't think he has much time."

"Come on, we've been burying Dad for almost six months now. He fights back each time," I said. Ray cut me off.

"He doesn't have another six months, let alone six weeks. His lungs are filling with fluid, he has an arrhythmia, his legs are turning black, and his kidneys are malfunctioning. The doctors can't even control his diabetes." I heard Ray's heavy breathing on the line. Yet his words and their urgency would not sink in.

"I'm not…not ready to say goodbye," I said.

"I know."

"We just lost Mom. How can Dad go too?"

"He's old, Mike. He's been sick for a long time, and I think he wants to die. He misses Mom."

It was true. Ever since our mother's death in August, Dad had gone on a steady decline. He stopped taking care of himself; ate whatever he wanted, despite his diabetes; and he gradually had lost the circulation in his legs.

"Dad doesn't want to die. He loves us, and he does not want to leave his family. Yeah, he misses Mom, but he is not ready to give up the ghost." I felt myself getting choked up.

"Mike, the pain he is in, I wouldn't want to live like that. I can tell that he's given up." I could hear Ray moving around on the other end of the line.

"Why are you in such a hurry to let him go?" I asked. My throat tightened, and my voice cracked.

"And why are you making it so hard for him to leave?"

Neither of us talked for a few moments. Finally, I cleared my throat and spoke.

"Ray, I don't want to fight. None of us know what is going to happen in the next few hours, let alone tomorrow. We're all under a lot of stress. I remember Dad telling me a long while ago that he was not afraid to die because he almost did when he was in the war. But a lot of time has passed since then. You're right about one thing. I must let him go. We must let him die without feeling guilty for leaving his family."

The nearest gate for the nursing home parking lot was open, and I turned into it. Though it was about two-hundred yards from the building, I decided to park there because the lot wasn't crowded. I found a spot and parked facing the building. I heard Ray sigh.

"We need to stop telling Dad to fight and hold on. If he talks about dying, just tell him it is okay. I read that in one of those pamphlets in the waiting room at the nursing home."

"They have pamphlets for that?" I opened the car door and stepped outside. The air was brisk, and the briny scent of the bay immediately caught my attention. Having grown up on the south shore, I was not only used to the smell, but I also cherished it. I never feel quite at home until I could fill my lungs with sea air.

"Yeah, you walk past them each time you walk in." Ray chuckled.

"I'm in the parking lot waiting to go in to see Dad now. I'll have to pick one up." I crossed the lot, stopping for a second to let a minivan pass. The driver was an apparently confused old man who gazed at the building while moving at a walker's pace.

"Call me after you leave. I want to hear how Dad's doing."

"Sure. Oh and Ray, I have a question. Do you know where Dad's discharge papers are?"

"Yeah, he keeps them in a briefcase under his bed. Why?"

I laughed. "A briefcase, huh? That sounds like Dad."

"Why do you want them?" Ray asked again.

"Because while I was talking to him, he said they gave him his Purple Heart, but he can't find it anywhere. Also, he never got his campaign ribbons. I think we should get them for him."

"No kidding. I still don't get why he tells you all of this and never says anything to me."

"Maybe because you don't ask him, Ray. I could have used your help for the past twenty years or so while I harassed him for information."

"Funny." Ray chuckled. "I'll tell you what. I'll swing by his house tomorrow and get the papers. I think it is a single document. Anyway, we'll call his congressman and see what we can do."

"I'll call." I cut him off.

"Of course, you get all the glory," Ray said.

"Ray, I didn't mean it like that. You call. Go ahead."

There was silence.

"Go ahead, Mike. Call the congressman. You're the one who's been interested in Dad's service all along."

"Thank you," I said.

"I'll talk to you tomorrow." Ray hung up before I had the chance to say goodbye. Inside, the guard at the front desk waved to me. I nodded to him and stopped at the elevator. After I pressed the button, I looked around the waiting room. There were residents in wheelchairs looking at the TV, others sat in the chairs and stared into the distance at nothing. A few others had visitors, sons, daughters, and grandchildren. I wondered how many of the old people had children as anxious as my siblings and me about their parent's impending death. Did any of them feel the need to learn their parent's story like me? I was sure that they did.

Chapter 20

April 2nd - April 15th, 2009

R ay located Dad's discharge papers exactly where he said they would be. It was a funny place to keep such vital documents, under the bed in a suitcase. My father had many quirks, and this was a prime example. I called my congressman first for information on how to obtain medals for a veteran. An aide, Amanda, was happy to assist me.

"Where does your father live?" Amanda asked. Her voice was enthusiastic, and she sounded young.

"Copiague," I answered. I hoped that she did not hear me gulp. Since I lived in a different district, I suddenly realized that I needed to call Dad's representative.

"Oh, I'm sorry. Your father lives in Congressman Horvath's district," Amanda said.

I knew that, but for some dumb reason, I had called Congressman Timlin's office first.

"I'm sorry," I said. "I should have known that. I shouldn't have bothered you."

"You're not bothering me at all. Anything that Congressman Timlin can do for a veteran, he will go out of his way to do."

"Thanks. I'll call over there," I said.

"Do you have Congressman Horvath's number? There's a young man named Kevin who handles veteran affairs at his office. I am confident he'll treat your request as a high priority, as we would here. If he doesn't, which I am sure won't be a problem, call me back and I will see what I can do," Amanda said.

"Thank you. You're very nice," I said. I could hear the disappointment in her voice. Politicians like to not only assist veterans, they also enjoy the publicity that surrounds such events. In my case, I was seeking my father's Purple Heart for wounds received at the uncelebrated Battle of Velletri. Amanda provided me with Kevin's direct line at Congressman Horvath's office, and she assured me that she would phone ahead to apprise him of my application to the Veterans' Administration.

About thirty minutes after I spoke with Amanda, I called Congressman Horvath's office. I wanted to give Amanda some time to phone ahead as she had promised. Visions of my family standing around Dad, smiling and with tears in our eyes as he was awarded his Purple Heart and his campaign ribbons, filled my imagination. Kevin answered the phone on the first ring. I explained to him what my wishes were, and Kevin filled me in on the process with the same enthusiasm that Amanda had. I thanked him profusely and ended the call.

I completed the form and then faxed it to the VA, and then Congressman Horvath made the request. Two weeks later Kevin called me on my cell phone. I was at work during a four-to-twelve tour. Ronnie was the operator. I was free to answer the call.

"Hello, Mike? This is Kevin at Congressman Horvath's Office." His voice had his typical cheerfulness.

"Hey Kevin, how are you?

"I'm great. Everything's in order, and I have good news. Your father's medals are here."

While it had been a dream of mine to uncover the story behind my father's wartime service, arranging for his official recognition was beyond anything I had imagined. My eyes welled up.

"What's the matter?" Ron tapped my arm. I raised my hand and mouthed the word *nothing.*

"That's great," I said. "So, what do I do? Do I go there and get them?"

"Michael, it would be a great honor for Congressman Horvath to present your father with his Purple Heart. I understand he is in a nursing home, and the Congressman wishes to visit him in person. We can call the newspapers and the local news channel if you wish."

I took the phone away from my ear and covered my mouth with my hand. My overwhelming emotion was pride. Also, I was happy. My only regret was that mom wasn't alive to see this come to its fruition.

"Mike, what's going on?" Ronnie pulled the cruiser to the curb. We sat in front of a seedy building with some young men idling around in front. They watched us park. One by one they casually walked away.

"I'm sorry. Kevin, could you hold on for a second? I'm at work. I'll be right back."

"Sure thing, take your time."

Ronnie watched me and waited for an explanation. I used a paper napkin to wipe my eyes.

"My Dad's Purple Heart arrived. Congressman Horvath wants to have a ceremony of sorts and give it to him personally," I said.

Ronnie's eyes opened wide.

"Dude, that's awesome. When is this happening?" Ronnie was fully acquainted with my endeavors. As my partner and best friend, I told him everything. He and Larissa had known both of my parents since we were in the academy. Larissa. Since the night of the shooting, I could not get her out of my head. She texted me often, leading with some query about whether Mandy and I wanted to hang out with her and Ronnie. Then she would gently lead the conversation into something sexual. Or I did. Whoever started the dirty texts did not matter. It was wrong. What made matters worse was that Ronnie, not knowing my and Larissa's attraction for each other, often made wisecracks about Larissa and me having some sort of affair. Worse than that, when the four of us went out, Mandy would join him in teasing the two of us when she had a few drinks in her. "You two make a cute couple," she would always comment. I imagined how Mandy would have reacted if she had caught Larissa and I kissing behind the curtain in the emergency room. She would have shot me with my own gun.

"I'm going to arrange that now," I said. Then I put the phone back to my ear.

"Kevin? Sorry for the wait. My partner wanted to know what is going on."

"No problem. This is an important event. Why don't you talk to your father and the rest of your family and find out when and how we should do this. The Congressman made it clear to me that he is here on Long Island all week, and he will drop everything to recognize a veteran."

"Thank you. I'll have this all figured out by tomorrow night. I think I want to surprise him. I know my father. If I tell him there's going to be any pomp and circumstance, he'll hide in his room."

"I understand. Tomorrow is fine. I look forward to your call," he said.

"Thanks again, Kevin."

He hung up before I did. I sat with my cell phone in my hand, examining it as if it were some sort of enchanted contraption. What I had fantasized about for so long was about to come to fruition. A scene where my father stood proudly next to the Congressman filled my head. The Congressman would pin Dad's Purple Heart on his chest and perhaps remark on his bravery. Ray, Cindy, their kids, and I would stand before them with Mandy, Ron, and Larissa at our sides. We would all beam with pride. The awe and mystery surrounding my Dad's service came bubbling back to the surface. I got goosebumps.

"Mike, you better tell your father. He'll freak out," Ronnie said.

"I know. I'll call him in the morning. Right now, he's probably in the sunroom watching the news with Fred."

"What about Ray and Cindy? How will they react?" Ronnie looked around, making sure that the group of men we scared off with our presence did not return. The radio crackled with chatter from other units, but we had no calls.

"They'll be on board with the Congressman's visit. I somehow think Dad won't complain. It's not like he'll be enthusiastic. He's always been tight-lipped about his service, but I think he needs closure." I looked at Ronnie. Ron nodded and placed both hands on the steering wheel.

"You should tell him in person. Don't call him. This is huge for him and your family," Ron said.

"You're right." I took a deep breath and held it in for a moment. Butterflies replaced my earlier anticipation. The uncertainty of Dad's reaction scared me. Since Ronnie and I were off for the next three days after our tour ended, it would be convenient for me to visit Dad instead of calling him. Yet I did not want to tell him by myself.

"I would love to have some company. Want to tag along?"

"Sorry man. I have a side job." Ronnie had worked in construction before he was on the job. He often took side jobs for extra money.

"Are you going in the morning or at night?" Ronnie asked.

"I want to go as early as possible. Mandy can't miss work. Ray and Cindy are at their jobs also. I kind of wanted you to come along. Dad likes you. He won't make a scene with you around."

"Take Larissa. She's been bugging me to go shopping, and you can take her after you visit your dad." Ronnie raised his palms and put them back on the steering wheel.

"Take Larissa? She's not going to want to hang around with me all day. Doesn't she have any friends who can take her to the mall?" My stomach felt like I had taken a dive down a roller coaster. I already knew that Larissa wanted to go shopping, because she had texted me earlier and suggested, playfully as it was, that I take her to buy lingerie after Ronnie left for his second job. The barely concealed suggestion was that we fool around. On the surface, she had merely made a joke. At least, I had hoped she was kidding. The temptation was killing me.

"Larissa doesn't have friends. She only wants me," he said. "Oh, and she digs you in a major way." Ronnie reached over and slapped my arm.

"Funny," I said.

"Come by tomorrow. I'm leaving at eight. Meet me at my place at seven. The three of us will have coffee. Larissa will spend two hours getting dressed and ready. By that time, you can follow her to the shop so she can drop off her car, and then the two of you will have the day together." Ronnie smiled.

"Sure. I'll run it past Mandy," I said. My voice cracked, and my heart beat fast.

"Run it by her? You know she'll be cool with that. Now, if it were the other way around, you'd have to worry about me spending time alone with Mandy, if you know what I mean." Ronnie chuckled.

"She's all yours, my man." I laughed also.

"So, are we set? Come by in the morning."

"Yeah, it's a date." I wished I didn't say that.

Later that night when Ronnie and I took our meal break, I phoned Mandy. I sat in the sector car, parked in front of the precinct for privacy. Just as I explained that I needed to tell my dad in person about receiving his Purple Heart, Mandy chimed in.

"You're going with Larissa, right?"

My heart beat rapidly, and my palms became wet.

"I was just about to tell you," I said.

"News travels fast. Ronnie phoned Larissa, and then she called me a little while ago. I was going to text you, but you called me first," Mandy said.

"So, you're okay with this?" I gulped.

"Why not? Larissa wants us to all to go to dinner. I'm thinking steaks or something like that. So you two go back to their place, and I'll meet the three of you there. Sound good?"

My head spun.

"Yeah sure. We'll talk tonight. I don't think we'll be late. The rookies will make any arrest that comes up." I bit my lower lip. Larissa was just a friend. Kissing her was a mistake. I was sure she felt the same way and that all of her teasing and sexual innuendo was her way of dealing with the awkwardness.

"I'll probably be asleep when you get home, so don't wake me," she said.

"When do I bother you when you're asleep?"

"When you want to have sex. That's when. I'm not available tonight. Maybe you'll get lucky with Larissa tomorrow." Mandy giggled. I managed a quiet laugh. Larissa's Dolce and Gabanna perfume, her eyes, lips, and her passionate kiss rushed to the forefront of my mind. Awash in guilt, I ended the conversation and went back into the precinct. Ronnie and I finished our tour, tired and sweaty, and changed into our civilian clothes in the locker room. Our lockers were next to each other, and we carpooled to and from work. One day Ronnie would drive and the other day I would. That night was Ronnie's turn. I could not look at him. When I did, I imagined Larissa at his side, wearing her usual black leather jacket, tight jeans, lipstick, and low-cut top. When I was alone, I fantasized about her. My hormones raged, and the devil on my left shoulder muted the angel on my right.

I would envision Larissa and I alone, either in the tiny, upstairs apartment she shared with Ronnie at his parent's house. Or we would be in my and Mandy's house. Most of the time, I used our living room as a setting for my imaginary affair. My fantasy began innocently, with Larissa coming over to our place to return borrowed clothing to Mandy. Of course, Mandy would be at work. We would talk, laugh a bit, and then we sit on the couch next to each other. Our arms would touch. I would offer her wine. We'd sip from our glasses, feeling the dizzying effects of the alcohol. Then we would kiss, just like we did in the emergency room.

"Are you coming over tomorrow or what?" Ronnie unlocked the doors with his key fob. I stopped with my hand on the passenger door handle and blinked several times.

"Yeah, I'll come by early. I spoke to Mandy already."

Ronnie smiled. "I know. She texted me."

"She did, huh? What else did she say?"

"She said you better get to bed right away when you get home so you're not late picking up Larissa. No nookie for you tonight, Romeo." Ronnie opened the door and got in the car. I entered the car also.

"She said that to you? That she wasn't going to have sex with me?" I strapped myself in and looked at Ronnie.

"Sure. She wants you to get some sleep." Ronnie started the car and backed out of the precinct lot. Suddenly making out with Larissa didn't seem like such a bad thing. Many cops joked about sleeping with other guys' wives. Ronnie was one of them. I was aware that Mandy texted him often, and he would message her back. The four of us were friends on Facebook. Mandy and Ron shared a lot of memes and commented on each other's posts. Larissa had told me that Mandy had forwarded them a porn video she had been sent by a coworker. I saw the same clip involving two women and a young delivery man, because Mandy had lured me into bed by playing it for me on her iPad. Still, while Ronnie and Mandy being chummy with each other made me a tad uncomfortable, neither Ron nor Mandy seemed bothered by Larissa and me being friendly.

We did not speak from the moment Ronnie merged onto the expressway until we pulled into his driveway. Since we had worked together all night, we had nothing else to talk about. I stared out the window and mulled over my situation with

Larissa. The most significant way I would help myself was to do nothing. If Larissa made an advance, became suggestive in a sexual manner, I would laugh it off. If Mandy could text dirty jokes and send porn links to Ronnie, then I was safe when it came to flirting with Larissa, I reasoned.

Out of the blue, I thought of my father in the nursing home, sharing a room with a mentally challenged man he could not communicate with. Dad was faithful to our mother for fifty-three years. He bathed her and changed her clothes as she lay dying from colon cancer. The way Dad cared for her during her illness made him a model husband. Still, my parents had gotten into loud and angry disputes that frightened me when I was young. Yet the love they shared was undeniable. There was no scenario I could conjure where I could see my father kissing another woman. For that matter, I could not believe that my mother would have ever had an affair with another man. Larissa, and my desire for her, vanished. The void was replaced with shame.

"Are you asleep?" Ronnie nudged my arm. I turned my head and faced him.

"No. I was just deep in thought." I yawned and unbuckled the seat belt.

"What was it that had you in a trance the whole ride home?"

I paused and stretched the corner of my mouth. "I was thinking about my parents and how much they loved each other. I was also trying to come up with a way to tell my father about Congressman Horvath and the Purple Heart that he has for him. Dad doesn't want to think about the war, much less be rewarded for being wounded." I opened the door and put my leg outside.

"He'll be okay. He'll want you to be proud of him. All parents want their kids to look up to them. My dad was in Korea, and he goes to the VFW and hangs out with all of his friends. The vets talk about what they did overseas. My dad told me that he loves the camaraderie and the support he finds there. He used to take me with him to the hall before I was on the job. I sat and listened and learned about history. Plus, I drank free beer." Ronnie got out, and I followed. He locked the door. We walked down to the end of the driveway where my car was parked. I unlocked the doors and turned to Ron.

"I wish my dad had some sort of outlet like that. He never joined any veterans' groups. All he has now is some old German man who was in the Wehrmacht to sit and talk to all day. I'm fascinated by the irony in that." I opened my door and stood with my arm resting on it.

"Stop thinking about it. Have the ceremony for your father. He'll appreciate the gesture, whether he says so or not. I wish I could be there with you tomorrow, buddy." Ronnie stood next to me with his hands in his pockets.

"Thanks. I'm overthinking this. It'll work out, I'm sure." I tapped Ron's arm and nodded. After I started the car, I rolled down the window. Ron bent over to see me.

"Why don't you spend the night? You have to be here in like five hours?" Ron pointed to the house. I slumped behind the wheel and tilted my head back. The four-to-twelve shift ended at eleven-thirty-five. We left the precinct after midnight. It took us almost ninety minutes to drive home from the city. By then, it was nearly two AM. By the time I arrived at my house, fell asleep, woke up, showered, shaved, and then drove to Ron's again, I would have only had about three hours of sleep. His offer was enticing.

"Is that okay with Larissa?" I scratched my neck and rested my hand on the steering wheel.

"Are you kidding? She won't give a shit. If we're lucky, she'll make us breakfast." Ron straightened up. "Come on man. Cut the engine."

I did as I was told. The dilemma I had was whether to call Mandy or to text her. I called her.

"What? Yeah, sure. Spend the night. I told you not to wake me," Mandy said.

"Great. I'll see you tomorrow. I love you," I said. Mandy mumbled what sounded like *I love you*, then ended the call.

Inside, we walked as quietly as we could upstairs, so as not to wake Ron's parents who were downstairs. Larissa was unemployed, and according to Ron, she wasn't looking for a job. We entered the apartment. Larissa was on the couch watching TV.

"Hi honey," she said to Ron. He walked to the couch, leaned over, and kissed her. She saw me and smiled.

"Are you spending the night?" Larissa sat upright. She wore a white tank top with no bra and pink panties.

"Yes. Ron thought it would be a good idea." I cleared my throat and stared at the TV. Larissa was watching an action flick with exploding cars and men shooting at each other. Ron walked into the kitchen area, which was separated by a waist-high wall. He opened the fridge and looked inside.

"Any leftovers, babe?" he asked.

"There's some spaghetti you can both have," she said.

Larissa stood and walked over to me. Her undergarments were skimpier than I had initially thought, and her breasts almost spilled out of her shirt. She stopped in front of me, hugged my waist, and kissed me on the cheek. I could feel myself blush.

"I didn't ruin any plans, did I?" I grinned at Larissa.

"Nah. She always walks around like that in the house," Ron said. He entered the living area holding a plate with pasta and a fork. "Help yourself, Mike. There's plenty in the fridge," Ron said.

I had been at their house numerous times, and never had I seen Larissa in her underwear before. Then again, I had never spent the night or dropped in at two o'clock in the morning either.

"No thanks. I had that burger before. I'm good," I said.

"You can sleep on the couch. I'll get some sheets, a pillow, and stuff," Ron said. He put the plate on the coffee table and went into the bedroom. In moments, he returned with linens, a pillow, and a blanket. Larissa took them from him.

"Go to bed, honey. I'll fix up the couch. I'm gonna watch the end of this movie, anyway," she said. Larissa kissed him on the lips and smiled.

"Thanks, babe. I'll turn in after I eat." Ron picked up his plate, sat in a chair on the opposite side of the room, and ate. Larissa spread out the sheet for me and left the pillow and blanket on the coffee table. She motioned for me to sit and I did. The couch wasn't very wide, and Larissa stretched out with her legs across my lap.

"Do you sleep in your undies or in the nude?" Larissa asked. She chuckled and tapped my thigh with her foot.

"Undies," I said. My voice cracked.

"You might as well get comfortable," she said. "We have to get up early."

"She's right. Make yourself at home. You know where the bathroom is, and we have extra toothbrushes." Ron stood and placed the empty plate and fork in the sink. He went into the bathroom and shut the door. The water ran, and I could hear him urinate. After he cleaned up, he opened the door and motioned for me to follow him in.

A toothbrush that was still in its package was left on the vanity for me. I relieved myself and brushed my teeth. When I was done, I went back into the living room area, hoping that Larissa had gone to bed also. She had not.

Larissa was on her feet. She spread the blanket out and placed the pillow on an armrest. She turned when she heard me come in.

"You're still dressed. Don't be embarrassed. I'm not gonna rape you," she said with a giggle. I gulped. From the bedroom, I could hear Ronnie rolling over in bed. I walked to the chair and faced the wall. After removing my cargo shorts, I took off my Polo shirt. While I had no tee-shirt on, I did not want to sleep in a clean shirt and get it all sweaty. Larissa went into the kitchen and got a bottle of water. I made it to the couch, sat on my end, and put the blanket over my legs.

"Oh, shirtless, huh? You're a sexy man." Larissa purred like a kitten.

"I'm trying to sleep in here, you guys," Ron called out.

Larissa sipped from her water bottle and picked up a small pillow from the other end of the sofa. She placed the pillow against my thigh and lay down with her head on it. I sat still and said nothing, hoping that I would not get aroused. I concentrated on the movie. During commercials, I sneaked a peek at her chest. It was all I could do to restrain myself and not caress her. I sat with my feet on the floor and my head leaning sideways against the back of the couch until I dozed off. I woke up towards the morning because I was chilly, and I needed a blanket to cover my torso. Larissa was gone. I stretched out on my back and covered myself up to my shoulders. It took longer than I had expected, but I finally fell back to sleep. Before long, Ron woke me up.

Chapter 21

June 2nd, 1944

It was their second day in Velletri. Thirst and fatigue plagued the regiment, as well as the enemy. Yet the fighting continued. Gene and Harry barely slept throughout the evening. They bunked down with others in their platoon in a clothing boutique that was relatively unscathed save for a shattered, plate glass window in front. The soldiers took turns standing guard. Yet Harry and Gene remained awake all night. Neither of them talked much. Gene held his rosary beads, and Harry read a pulp novel by moonlight.

By morning, a distant explosion woke up the rest of the squad. Gunfire erupted on both sides. Gene imagined that an unseen referee had blown a whistle, and the war game continued. For the entire day, they worked their way up the avenue towards the other side of town. They faced scattered resistance. As they cleared each building, silencing German soldiers with their M1 Garands and Gene's BAR, their exhaustion grew more intense. At four o'clock in the afternoon, Gene and Harry agreed to find a place to rest. They entered an abandoned apartment building that had been cleared. They rested in the living room of a flat on the second floor so they could spy on the street below for activity. Also, if they had to exit through the window, it was not too high to jump from. Tom was still with them. He plopped down on the sofa and placed his gear and the ammo cans on the floor in front of him. Harry sat next to the broken window with his back to the wall and glanced out occasionally. Gene smoked a cigarette while lounging in a comfy chair. They had not seen Sgt. Warren since the night before. His last orders to them before they were separated had been to continue their advance. The three of them were grateful for a bit of respite. They sipped water, ate k-rations, and smoked cigarettes. They were too tired to carry on a conversation.

By 1530 hours, the gunfire had ceased. Harry checked outside, poking his head out just for a second.

"I can see our platoon coming up the road. We had better get out there to meet them," Harry said.

"You're right. I'm tired of us battling the Germans all by ourselves." Gene chuckled.

"I agree," said Tom. "Harry, you wanna grab one of these?" Tom picked up an ammo can and offered it to him. Harry stood up, sighed, and took it from him.

"Thanks, buddy," Tom said. Harry did not answer. He walked to the door, poked his head out, and went into the hallway. Gene picked up his weapon and followed. Tom walked out after Gene with a grin on his face. Out in the street, they caught up with the platoon. The three walked a line on the side of the boulevard, near the point. The column of American soldiers moved forward until gunfire erupted from a building a few blocks ahead. They ran for cover.

Gene trotted with his head down over to a pile of rubble, all bricks and stone, about four feet high on their side of the road. Harry and Tom reached him and kneeled. Gene climbed midway up the pile and rested the muzzle of his BAR on the heap. He peered at a derelict vehicle up the block.

"Gene, get down. You're going to get hit," Harry said. He grabbed Gene's sleeve and tugged on it. Gene pulled away from him.

"I see one of them. He's got his back to me. I think he's calling out to others." Gene took aim with his weapon.

"You're exposed. There's a sniper out there, man. Get down," Harry said.

"I can get him. He's about thirty, maybe forty, feet from us, next to that burned out car," Gene said. He peered down the barrel, placed his front sight on the enemy soldier, then lined it up with the rear sight. He put his finger on the trigger. The soldier spun around and fired a burst of rounds at Gene, aiming from the hip. Gene did not hear anything, but he saw the muzzle flare. Then he fell over backward.

The soldier had shot Gene with two rounds from his Sturmgewehr. Gene felt like he had been struck twice with a baseball bat. At once, he recognized that his mouth was full of blood. A bullet had penetrated his clenched teeth, shattering most of them, and pierced the roof of his mouth. Gene felt a stinging sensation on the right side of his neck where one-half of the bullet had exited after splitting in two. Blood poured from between his parted lips. His right armed seared with pain. Another round had penetrated his elbow.

"Son of a bitch!" Harry popped up and took aim at the German soldier. He emptied his rifle at the man. One of Harry's shots caught him in his chest. The enemy's knees buckled. He dropped his gun and fell face-forward onto the pavement. Harry looked at Tom and Gene. Tom had already turned Gene onto his side, allowing his mouth to drain so he could breathe. Harry opened his first aid kit and ripped open a pack of bandages. He scrambled over to Gene and pressed one against his mouth.

"Breathe through your nose, Gene. You're gonna be all right." Harry panted and moved fast.

"Medic! We need a medic!" he called out to the others behind them.

"Tom, open another bandage and wrap up his arm. You have to stop the bleeding," Harry said. Tom nodded. He removed a bandage from Harry's kit and wrapped Gene's arm.

"You tend to him. I'll hold them off, you got it?" Harry said. He placed his hand on Tom's shoulder.

"Yeah, I got it. Count on it," Tom said. He held the bandages against Gene's mouth and elbow. Harry took a deep breath, then removed a morphine capsule from the kit.

"Gene. This is for the pain, buddy. You're gonna make it," he said. Then he injected the drug into Gene's right thigh. The rush went to Gene's head first, then to his stomach, and then to the rest of his body. Gene listened to Harry firing away at the enemy. Harry had picked up Gene's BAR and sprayed short bursts at the Germans. Gene's head felt light, his pain drained from his body. He believed he was floating upward, above the fracas and towards the beckoning clouds in the crystal-blue sky.

Gene was no longer encumbered by the heft of his backpack. He did not have his weighty Browning Automatic Rifle cradled in his arms. He felt adrift, like he was on his father's boat, tossing about in the waves of the Atlantic Ocean. The commotion around him had ceased. Gene wondered if he was on his way to Heaven. Perhaps this was Purgatory, the ethereal plane between earth and the afterlife, which he heard so much about from Sister Helen in school. With his mind awash in pulsing white noise, he relaxed and become rapt in the drifting motion he experienced as he lay still. There was no pain. A warmth overtook him. His eyes were closed. Yet he witnessed a shimmering vista of golden-yellow light surrounding him. Gene did not breathe and did not feel the desire to inhale. He heard Harry's voice, then Tom's, and then the light vanished.

Two GI's carried his body on a stretcher. They paused and lined themselves up next to the row of others who had given their lives. They steadied themselves before they placed him on the ground. Gene opened his eyes and raised his head.

"Hey, I'm awake," he tried to say. But words did not come from his mouth. Blood and teeth spewed from between his lips. That's when he realized that his right arm was bandaged, dark and moist with blood, useless.

"Oh my God. He's alive," the lead soldier yelped. The handles of the litter slipped from his fingers, and Gene fell off and landed on the ground.

"Medic, medic!" one of them yelled. Gene grasped a handful of dirt as he looked upward again and wondered if God could understand him through a mouthful of blood and torn flesh. Once again, he lost consciousness. A gentle shroud of peace and warmth enveloped him.

Gene awoke to the murmuring of prayers. This time, a chaplain hovered over him. The slacking canvass of the stretcher no longer supported his weight. Shredded foliage among the debris from the battle tickled his ear; an odd feeling to single out from the miasma of pain, thirst, fear, and bewilderment overcoming him.

"By the sacred mysteries of man's redemption may almighty God remit to you all penalties of the present life and of the life to come. May He open to you the gates of paradise and lead you to joys everlasting."

The chaplain held the book in an open palm resting on his knees. With his other hand, he blessed Gene and continued to recite the prayers. Gene remained in the moment, unable to perceive any activity beyond his immediate surroundings. There was an eerie familiarity about the man above his face, the gray hair protruding from beneath his helmet at the temples, the Roman collar around his neck. He was clothed in standard-issue, olive green fatigues. Yet his face resembled a person from long ago. All priests had a comforting demeanor. That made Gene feel at ease in the presence of the chaplain. He held onto that idea. This allowed him to settle into a dream as he once again closed his eyes to stave off the stinging, fierce pain.

At once, he believed he had been transported away from the battlefield. He was on the streets of Bay Ridge again. Gene circled his head around, eyeing the familiar shops and brownstones as if he were a tourist. To return to the neighborhood seemed as natural as fetching a glass of water. He felt refreshed, bereft of his uniform or weapon. His wounds had disappeared, and he wore his everyday slacks and shirt.

Down his block, he recognized a man on the front steps of his home. Alphonse turned and noticed him. His father smiled and nodded. Gene walked toward his father, his arms swinging at his sides. A surge of delight filled him. His dad was not dead after all. This was happening. Maybe he never went to war, fought in Italy, or saw so many of his buddies get killed. Gene quickened his pace.

Alphonse leaned on the wrought iron rail at the top of the stoop. He admired the fingernails on his right hand and polished them against the lapel of his suit jacket. Alphonse welcomed his boy with his typical aplomb. He smiled, reached out, and patted Gene's crew cut. Alphonse's grin seemed perceptive, like he had been let in on a secret. Gene blushed with the slight embarrassment of having ever been afraid. His father was a model of courage and confidence.

Gene wanted to hold his father's hand as he did when he was a boy and accompany him to his places of business. Gene would take secret pleasure, watching other men squirm in his father's presence. He remembered Sundays at Mr. Molfetta's home. Gene craved the aroma of sauce, stirred and nurtured since dawn in a massive pot on the stove. Then he recalled his mother, who encouraged him to be the man of the family after his father's passing. But his father was not dead. Alphonse was standing in front of him.

"Gene, what are you doing home? You have so much to do." Alphonse raised an eyebrow and put his hands in his pockets. There was a glint in his eye. Alphonse stretched the corner of his mouth.

"I wanted to go home," Gene said, careful to keep his chin up, just as his father taught him to do. Alphonse shook his head.

"I can't let you do that, Gene. You have responsibilities."

"The war?"

Alphonse chuckled. Then he sighed, and his shoulders sagged. It was the kind of signal a dad gives to his son after all the lessons had been taught and some reinforcement was necessary. He moved down a step. At his full height, he was shorter than Gene, whom he last saw years before. This vantage point gave him a paternal edge—higher ground.

"Think of your mother. You need to be strong for her. I can't do any more for you. I have to leave, Gene. You go back now." Alphonse turned to walk away.

"Is Mom here?" Gene glared at him. Noise filled his ears, not much different from the revving of a truck's engine.

Alphonse looked back.

"Go home, Gene. You will be fine. I love you. I don't think I ever told you that before. I wish I did while I was alive." Alphonse put his head down and swallowed. Then he faced his son again. "I'm happy that you found me. Go and live your life."

"Dad, come back. Don't leave me again. Let's go on the boat. We'll go fishing. I'll tell you about Africa, Italy, and everything I saw over there," Gene pleaded with him. He gulped hard. There was a pressing sensation in his ears, a cacophony of voices, moaning, and the whirring of a motor stirred him. He felt like he was tipping over the edge of a cliff while dreaming.

Inside the covered truck, he raised his head as best he could and looked outside through the open, canvas flap. Rome was a few miles away. Gene figured that by then Germans were retreating from the advancing Texas 36th Division, including the 141st Regiment. He coughed and spewed blood on his shirt. His jaw could not open wide, and he became vaguely aware of a bandage and a splint on his right arm. The dreamy state he had been in lifted in stages. Soon, his name, rank, and serial number returned to the forefront of his mind. There were other wounded men in the truck with him. Some were injured more seriously than he was. He did not recognize anyone, and he suddenly worried about his friends. They were safe if they had not been injured. Before he had been shot, he had never thought he would get hurt, even though he had seen others die.

His mother was at home, unaware of what had happened to him. In days, she would receive a dreaded telegram with a scant few lines informing her that he had been wounded in action. Worry and grief would overcome her. Gene tried to squelch the image her, alone and frightened on the doorstep of their home, clutching a yellow slip of paper that bore terrible news. He needed to write to her as soon as possible, he told himself. He could not let her know that he was in pain, and that he had nearly been left to die. Suddenly, he had a comforting thought, as if an angel had touched his shoulder. A memory calmed him down.

"Dad," he said. Though he could not form intelligible words, he mumbled again, thinking of the man who had given him strength and guidance even in the face of death. He closed his eyes and envisioned Alphonse, his fedora square on his head, leaning on the rail of their front stoop, his right hand in the pocket of his jacket. Gene inhaled through his nostrils, let his breath out slowly, and calmed himself down. His father would have brushed off the pain. Gene grimaced and tried to do the same.

Chapter 22

April 16th, 2009, 8:00 AM

Ron shook my shoulder. I woke up thinking I was in bed with Mandy. Yet I was still on the same couch where I had leered at Larissa hours earlier. With my partner hovering over me, it was all I could do not to appear guilty. I wished I could rinse out the memory of kissing Larissa with a strong mouthwash. Better yet, I wanted to figure out a way to see my father without having to drag her around with me all day. I did not know if I could resist Larissa's charms without Ron snoozing in the next room.

"I have to get going, buddy. Larissa's in the shower. She told me to tell you that you're next. Go fry yourself an egg or something." Ron scratched his chin and looked down at me. I sat up, looked around, and cleared my throat.

"Thanks, but you know I don't eat breakfast. Is there coffee?"

"Sure, at 7-Eleven or at one of your finer hotels. This place definitely ain't either." Ron chuckled and walked to the door. He carried a brown bag with his lunch inside. It was still odd for me to see him in work boots, jeans, and a tee-shirt with the name of a construction company on it when we both worked side-by-side in police uniforms.

"See you tonight, Mike. Say hi to your father." Ron nodded, stepped out, and shut the door behind him. Despite his morning gruffness, which I had experienced many times over, there seemed to be a caginess about Ron that I could not put a finger on. If I were paranoid, which I hoped I was not, I would say that he was reading my mind, and he knew that I had kissed his wife and that I lusted after her. If that were true, I was liable to be shot, beaten severely, or both. Guilt. Damn it. I could never imagine my dad in such a predicament.

Images of my father standing by my mom while she was in her hospital bed after surgery ran through my head like a silent movie. For fifty-three years they stayed together, through the hard times and the best of days. I had everything going for me, and I was about to blow my marriage apart for a mere temptation of the flesh. Thinking about it for a second, I laughed to myself. When Larissa and I were alone on the rare occasions in the past, we had almost nothing to say to each other. We had very little in common, and I always believed she lacked class. She chewed with her mouth open, talked too loudly, and she was hooked on reality television. There was nothing about me that was high society, but I had my standards. I fell in love with Mandy because she read books, followed the news, could name two or three prominent scientists, and she was smarter than I was.

"You can hop in. I left some hot water for you." Larissa emerged from the bathroom with an oversized towel wrapped around her bosom. The cloth draped down to her knees. Her wet hair fell straight, just past her shoulders. She smiled at me and walked into the bedroom. I must admit, I was a bit disappointed when she closed the door behind her. I hated myself for feeling that way.

She had left a towel for me folded on the toilet seat. I took care of my personal business, showered, and used the same toothbrush I had been given the night before. While I dressed, my lustful thoughts about Larissa faded. I concentrated on my father, wondered what he was up to that morning, and figured that he might be in discomfort. I renewed my purpose and focused on getting to my dad soon. I wanted him to know about his Purple Heart.

I opened the bathroom door and saw Larissa. She was poised with her hand raised, about to knock.

"You startled me," she giggled and placed her hand over her mouth.

"You surprised me too," I said.

"I guess you're ready," Larissa said. She eyed me up and down, noticing that I was dressed.

"Follow me to the shop. It's around the corner. The guy said it won't take more than a few hours. After we visit your dad, can you bring me back to pick it up?" She raised her eyebrows and held her hands together in front of her.

"Of course," I said. "We won't be at the nursing home too long anyway." I cleared my throat. For some reason, I was still a bit uneasy around her.

Larissa went to the kitchen table and picked up her pocketbook and car keys. She wore a floral print sundress that came down about mid-thigh and sandals. One of the straps of her dress had slipped and showed a black strap of her bra beneath. I averted my eyes and opened the door.

Larissa drove her Honda Civic ahead of me at a snail's pace. Luckily, the garage was nearby, as she had stated. She parked in front and went inside. I waited at the curb with my engine idling. I watched her through the shop's plate glass window. She spoke to the manager and gave him her car keys. When she came out, I watched her approach with the morning sunlight shining through her hair and dress. She opened the door and hopped in. The sweet scent of her perfume filled the car. Yet I had not noticed the aroma at her apartment.

"You had some shopping to do?" I asked.

"Yeah, I have to go to the mall and get a few things. Do you mind?" Larissa put her pocketbook on the floor in front of her and buckled her seatbelt.

"No problem. But the first order of business is coffee or maybe something to eat?" I looked at her and stretched the corners of my mouth.

"I'm not hungry. Let's just get coffee. I'm barely awake. I got like two hours of sleep," she said.

"Me too," I said as I put the car in gear and drove away.

"You spent half the night asleep sitting straight up. I don't know how you can do that," Larissa said. Her voice was scratchy. She grinned at me and cocked her head.

"Well, you were laying with your head practically in my lap. What was I supposed to do?" My mouth became dry. I looked straight ahead.

"You had no problem with where my head was," she said. Then she leaned over and turned on the radio. She found a morning sports talk program and left it on. We did not speak again until we stopped for coffee. After that, we went to the mall. It was near my and Mandy's house, and I felt a bit better on home turf.

We entered the mall. Larissa paused.

"I have to buy a bunch of girlie things like eyeliner, lipstick, makeup, and stuff. You're welcome to tag along, but I don't want you to be bored."

I eyed her for a moment and then blinked. Initially, I did not know what to make of her wanting to go off alone. But since I disliked shopping for *girlie things* with Mandy, I considered this as Larissa doing me a favor.

"I can find something to do. Maybe I'll buy a CD or something." I shrugged my shoulders.

"You're okay with that? I won't be long, I promise."

"Take your time," I said. "I'll find some way to amuse myself."

"I'll text you when I'm ready. We'll meet back here." She raised an eyebrow and tilted her head.

"Sounds like a plan," I said. I did not like the way I was reacting. Larissa was nothing short of cagey, and I suspected that I was being blown off. Finally, I took her word that she merely did not want me to become bored as she chose a shade of lipstick, and I shrugged it off. Lipstick, I thought to myself. I had already kissed her while she wore lip balm.

"See you in a bit," she said. Then she put her hand around my neck and gave me a peck on my cheek. A thrill went through me. My heart pumped faster. I breathed shallow breaths. I wanted her to hold me longer.

I watched Larissa walk away and make a left around the corner. With no actual agenda, I strolled the length of the mall with my hands in my pockets. The music store had nothing that I was interested in. I had a streaming music subscription through an app on my phone, and I had no use for a CD. Back out in the mall, I stayed close to the storefronts and avoided the men and women operating the kiosks hawking their wares. After about an hour or more, my cell phone chimed. Larissa had sent me a text as promised. I turned around and headed to the food court.

I saw her first. She had a small bag and a larger one. She clutched both in her left hand and had her pocketbook slung over her right shoulder. The larger one was from Victoria's Secret. Seeing that, I felt relieved. No wonder she wanted privacy. I felt the muscles in my face relax. Larissa looked uncomfortable, as if something was on her mind.

"Are you ready?" she asked. She smiled when she saw me.

"Sure," I said. "Did you get what you came for?" I asked.

"Just about," she said. Larissa tucked the bags under her arm and walked beside me. At the car, she placed everything in the back seat.

While we drove to the nursing home, Larissa talked about her father and how much she loved her parents. She also remarked how much she admired me for being so dedicated to my father. At one point, I took a call from Mandy. We spoke on the speaker connected by Bluetooth.

"What are you guys doing now?" Mandy asked. "Are you gonna visit your dad first or hang out for a while?"

"We're going to see Dad. I don't know how long we'll be there. It depends on how he feels. Also, I don't know how he's going to react when I tell him that Congressman Horvath wants to present him with his medal and campaign ribbons personally. He doesn't want the attention."

"He'll do it. He has no choice. You know how he'll react. Just let him rant. I'm sure when he has time to think about it, he'll be happy, because all of you will be there to visit him at the same time."

"I guess you're right," I said.

"It'll all work out," Mandy said. "Did you call Judith? Do you think she wants to come up to see this?"

"I'll call her later. This is short notice, and I don't think she'll be able to make it in time," I said. I caught a glimpse of Larissa from the corner of my eye. Her head snapped toward me when Mandy mentioned my daughter's name. It was as though she had forgotten that I was a father. There were days when I did not think so either.

"Too bad. Your dad would want to see her," Mandy said. I didn't respond as I fought back an unexpected surge of emotion. My conscience was plagued by the fact that I was an awful father. Despite my best efforts to be involved in her upbringing, she was raised by her mother and her maternal grandparents. I wiped the corner of my eye with my fingers. My body jerked a little when Larissa leaned over and rubbed my arm to comfort me. I looked at her and smiled.

"Mandy, Mike and I are going back to my place to wait for you and Ron when we get back. You two can meet us there, and we'll all go out together," Larissa said.

"Yeah, I'm pretty sure that was the plan all along. Ron and I talked about it yesterday."

"Okay, we're all set then?" I said.

"Sure thing, hon," Mandy said. "Say hi to Dad for me."

"I will."

"You two have fun," Mandy said.

"Don't worry. We will," Larissa said.

"Hey Larissa, if you jump my husband's bones, try not to make it too hot. I want him to come home to me after," Mandy said with a giggle.

"No promises there, girl," Larissa said. "I'm all over him right now." She rubbed her hand on my chest as she spoke. I almost drove into a tree due to being so stirred. Mandy laughed.

"I have to get back to work. See you tonight, Mike. I love you," Mandy said. She hung up before I could respond. Larissa sat back in her seat and crossed her legs. She smiled wide. My mind raced. Did I marry a swinger? Did Ron and Mandy have a thing going on? They texted and chatted all the time. They shared links to stuff they found online of the *not safe for work* variety. They joked about sex right in front of us. If Ron was not my partner and I did not trust him with my life, I would not tolerate him flirting with my wife. Yet somehow their banter was natural. They both had similar personalities. They clicked. If Mandy had met Ron before she met me, they would have made a perfect couple. Around Larissa, I was uncomfortable. Since the night of the shooting and our passionate kiss, I felt like a lewd old man enticing a suggestive girl.

As we drove to the nursing home, Larissa anticipated the fun we would all have at the restaurant later that evening. She mentioned Mandy's suggestion that she should jump my bones. As scintillating as that idea was, I was fraught with guilt and misperception. I was confused by Mandy's seemingly tacit endorsement of a sexual encounter between Larissa and me. And I was guilty of making out with my partner's wife, especially on the night of the shooting. I needed a stiff drink.

We pulled into the parking lot of the nursing home. Larissa got out first. I pulled my shirt down over my crotch to hide my noticeable erection. I had hoped it would have dissipated by the time we got there, but Larissa kept putting her hand on my arm or my thigh when she talked. She would say, "Oh, I want to try the flank steak. I hear it cuts like butter." She would grab my leg, almost touching my crotch when she said the word *oh*. Of course, she was teasing me. All I could think of when I got out of the car was my sick dad, cooped up in the day room of Our Lady of Good Counsel,

211

slowly dying of diabetes and the frailty of aging. Much like how one forgets all of the bad qualities of a person after their demise, I had begun the process of sanctifying my father's life and canonizing him as the *world's greatest dad and hero soldier* months ago, when we learned that he did not have much more time on this planet. He was a good father, better than I was, but he had a temper and was prone to be distant and cold. But he loved us all. One thing he would never do, and never did do as far as I was aware, was cheat on my mother. More shame washed over me. Larissa bounced just ahead of me, her charms barely concealed beneath her summer dress. I caught up with her, our arms brushed against each other, and I experienced a tuning fork-like vibration of regretful pleasure that I had come to expect whenever I was alone with her. Larissa. My God, Larissa.

Chapter 23

April 16th, 2009, 1:00 PM

Visiting hours began at nine o'clock, and we arrived just before one o'clock in the afternoon. Part of me chided myself for not getting there earlier and spending valuable time with Dad and galivanting around with Larissa instead. Fred encountered us in the hallway. He wheeled himself towards the day room. He stopped and turned his wheelchair to greet us. We waited next to him.

"Hello, Michael," he said. "And good afternoon, young lady. We have met before, but I have forgotten your name. I am sorry." Fred smiled in his typically charming way. His German accent was mellowed by years of living in America.

"I'm Larissa. My husband, Ron, and I are friends with Michael and Mandy," she said.

"Ah yes. Now I remember. The other policeman's wife. His name is Ronald, yes?" Fred turned again and headed for the day room. He motioned with his head for us to follow. I walked next to him, and Larissa followed close behind. The hallway was not wide enough for three people to walk next to each other.

"I'm afraid that your father is not doing so well today, Michael. He is weaker than most days. The nurse increased his

213

oxygen." Fred stopped by the door. Larissa and I did as well. I could see my father seated in a Geri chair in front of the TV with his back to us.

"Great," I said. "I was hoping he was in a good mood. I have some news for him, and I don't know how he's going to take it."

"Then perhaps you wait until another day to tell him?" Fred looked up at me and raised his eyebrows. My eyes met his. Fred had been a powerful man in his day. I could see that from his broad shoulders and chest. Regardless of his advanced age, his upper arms and forearms were still thick. Considering that he used a wheelchair, Fred was in good shape for a man of his age. Both he and my father were in their early eighties, and my dad was far worse for the wear. I wondered why Fred was in the facility in the first place.

"No, I have to tell him. For anyone else, this would be happy news. But for my father, it's just opening old wounds, so to speak."

"Oh? I should think that news such as this should be frankly told to him. It is better to tear off the bandage than to peel it slowly, as they say," Fred said with a hint of a smile.

I turned to Larissa. She looked back at me with a blank expression. I could not be sure if she was paying full attention.

"You see, my dad was wounded in Italy during the war. World War II," I said. I did not want to assume that Fred would automatically know which conflict I was referring to. "And he left the army hospital to go home without receiving his campaign ribbons. Also, he lost his Purple Heart. That's what he told me…"

"So, your dad is a hero?" Fred grinned.

"He wouldn't say that, but I think he is. Besides, you get the Purple Heart for getting wounded in battle. It's not awarded for valor." I shifted my weight from one foot to the other.

"I know this, Michael. Your father and I have talked much about the war. He was young like I was. A fearless man, your father was in combat. That is not what he told me. It is was I

214

believe. To fight such as he did, one must have courage. He is a humble man. That is certain." Fred turned and looked at Dad, then back at us. From my peripheral vision, I could see that Larissa was becoming bored. She leaned against me and then stood straight again. I guessed that she did not want to seem too familiar with me in front of either Fred or my father.

I cleared my throat. "You were in the war also?" I said, trying to act surprised. Dad had told me all about Fred's service in the Wehrmacht. Yet I did not mention this to Fred because I did not want to risk betraying any sort of trust that Fred may have had with my father. While Dad did not say that what Fred had told him was confidential, I decided to keep my father's mention of Fred's days as a POW to myself. I put my hands in my pockets and took a deep breath. As uncomfortable as it was to speak to my dad about the war, I was treading on uncertain ground with Fred—a German man—and a former enemy.

"Oh yes, like I said, I am the same age as your father. We both fought at the same time. In fact, I was taken prisoner about seven days after your dad was wounded." Fred leaned back and placed both of his forearms on the armrests. I expected him to take on a solemn expression and perhaps fold his hands in front of him or maybe look off into the distance as he recalled his involvement in the conflict.

"I was captured by American troops at the French port of Cherbourg after the landings at Normandy. I was a member of the Wehrmacht, the German Army, under the command of Field Marshal Erwin Rommel."

"The Desert Fox?" I said. I had heard of Erwin Rommel, and I knew for sure who he was, but to talk to someone who had been under his command was captivating.

"Yes, that is who he was. We were all proud to fight for him."

"You said you were captured. Were you... shot?" I gulped.

"No, I was forced to surrender. My platoon commander said we were surrounded. We had no choice. But that was okay. We were tired and hungry. The Americans treated us well. They did not shoot us." Fred laughed. I chuckled as well. Larissa folded her arms.

"I'm gonna say hello to your father," she said. "It was nice talking to you, Fred." Larissa tapped my arm and motioned for me to hurry with a tilt of her head. I smiled at her and then turned my attention back to Fred.

"I will see you later, miss," Fred said. He waved at her as she walked past him.

"So you were saying?" I said.

"Ah, yes. The Americans detained us. I was taken to a POW camp upstate here in New York, one of only a few, in fact. Camp Natural Bridge, it was called, just outside West Point."

"I didn't know that New York had a POW camp. How interesting," I said.

"Beautiful countryside up there. So naturally, after the war, I was released and sent back home. Many members of my family were killed during the bombings, so I decided to return here, and I came to work in America. I moved to Brooklyn, and I spent twenty years working at the Brooklyn Navy Yard."

"Where my father worked," I said. I nearly yelled that out like the winning answer on game show. This was an overreaction caused since I had already learned this information from my father. Hearing the story from Fred was more stimulating though.

"Such a coincidence, yes? We were both surprised. Yet if one thinks about it, not so much so. There are many veterans of the war living on Long Island. I just happened to be from the other side." Fred chuckled and looked away for a moment. Then he turned his attention back to me. "And for some reason, your father and I did not meet each other at the Navy Yard. We both started working there around the same time, moved to Long Island within a year of each other. Your family lived in Copiague, I raised my family in Lindenhurst. Our wives both died." Fred stopped suddenly. I watched a tear roll down his cheek.

"Fred, I am so sorry." I touched his shoulder.

"You must not feel bad for me. I was so lucky to have my sweetheart, Ellen, for a wife. I just miss her so," he said. He cast his eyes down. I kept my hand on his shoulder and rubbed it.

"Thank you, Fred."

"For what?" He looked at me and wiped his eye with a tissue that he had removed from his pocket.

"For looking after my father. I know you're there for him. He has given up on life. I'm glad that you're his friend. I mean that. You're a good man."

Fred placed his hand on mine.

"You are a good son. Now, go to him. Like I said, he is not doing well today. He needs you. I will return later." Fred tapped my hand and pushed himself away, toward his room. I watched him for a moment and turned my attention to the day room. Larissa was seated next to Dad, talking. She took her cell phone from her pocketbook and checked her messages. She typed in a reply and then placed her phone back. I saw her smile. After taking a deep breath, I went inside and greeted my father. I sat next to him, opposite from Larissa.

Fred had not exaggerated my father's condition. He also responded to the news of Congressman Horvath's impending visit with a casual nod.

"Just don't videotape me," Dad said. His head drooped, and he breathed through his mouth.

"No videotape, Dad. We record using cell phones now. Camcorders are out of date."

"Ha," said Dad. In the past, he would have lashed out at my smart aleck response.

"I'm gonna talk to a nurse," I said.

"Good idea," Larissa said.

There were two nurses at the station. One of them greeted me with a smile as I approached. She was a young, eager, blond woman in her early thirties, and I appreciated her enthusiasm. I told her my concerns, and she said that the doctor had been in to see him, and they had taken some blood for some tests. His insulin needed to be adjusted, and he needed to eat more. She said that had eaten breakfast, and they were encouraged by that. He needed to rest. We agreed that he should be put back into bed. The nurse called for two assistants to collect my father and put him back in his room. I returned to Dad and Larissa.

"The nurse wants you to take a nap, Dad," I said.

"Okay," he said, his head still drooped.

"I'm gonna call the congressman's office, okay?" I said.

"Yes, okay. I'll see you tomorrow. Ray is coming and so is Cindy." Dad sounded like a drone. No emotion.

At that moment, a young man and woman arrived. They both wore light blue scrubs.

"Hi Mr. Koenigsmann, we're here to take you back to your room. Is that okay?"

Dad picked up his hand and let it drop.

"It's fine. I spoke to him," I said. The young man pushed my dad in his chair, and the woman followed.

"Should I come along?" Larissa asked. She pointed down the hall to where the orderlies were wheeling my father.

"Yeah, of course. We'll say goodbye to him after they put him in bed, and then we'll go." I took a deep breath and watched as the young man and woman made a left turn into Dad's room.

"He doesn't look too good. I have to tell Ray. This thing with the congressman is going to have to happen, like, tomorrow." I wiped my eye with my hand. Larissa held my hand. I gripped hers tightly.

"Your dad is a strong man. He's not going anywhere soon. He's just tired." Larissa took my other hand and stood close to me. I could smell her, feel the warmth of her skin, and see down her neckline. I shivered.

"You're right. He's not ready to go anyway. The Mets are playing well."

Larissa laughed. I managed to chuckle as well.

"They probably have him in bed already. Let's say goodbye."

I walked ahead of Larissa. She tailed me close behind. I stopped at the door and peeked in before I stepped inside. The young man and woman had gone. Dad was propped up in bed and watching the news on TV. I was sure he was not actually paying attention to the program but merely facing the screen. He turned his head toward me.

"Hi Dad," I said. I stepped into the room and walked over to his bed. Larissa stood in the doorway.

"I'm going to call Ray and Cindy, and we're going to come by tomorrow. I'm going to try to arrange Congressman Horvath's visit for tomorrow morning." I figured it was a longshot that the congressman would have so much slack in his schedule that he could be anywhere on a moment's notice. However, Kevin did tell me that Representative Horvath was in town and ready to pin my dad's Purple Heart on him whenever the time was right.

"Just don't take any pictures," Dad said. He tried to laugh but coughed instead.

"I can't make any promises, Dad. But I'll fend off the media if need be." I smiled at him and placed my hand on his forearm. His skin felt like crepe paper. His muscles, once mighty and thick, had atrophied from age and illness. Dad's eyelids closed. I could tell that he wanted to sleep. I leaned forward and kissed his forehead. How many times had he bent over and kissed me before I fell asleep at night, I wondered? I pressed the buttons on the imaginary calculator in my head. I utilized an ad-hoc mathematical equation to determine the number of times my father came home from work during the week from the time I was born until I too old to be tucked in. Dad would take a knee beside me and press his lips against my cheek to say goodnight. The world instantly became safe then. I was inoculated against monsters and demons and all the wicked people who might steal me away, like those kids on the milk cartons.

A sudden thought troubled me. No matter how many times I kissed my father or how tightly I held onto his arm or whatever words I used to console him, I could not stave off the looming specter of death. My father was aware that his time was near. I choked on tears and turned away. Larissa placed her hand over her mouth. After I composed myself, I turned back and observed him. He breathed the silent breaths of temporary respite from his pain and sad thoughts of dying. I laid my hand on his shoulder, rubbed it, and whispered goodbye. Then I hurried past Larissa and into the corridor.

"I have some calls to make. If you don't mind, I'll make them in the car. I don't want to do anything else when I get home." I walked ahead of Larissa.

"Aren't we going to my place?" Larissa caught up with me and walked at my side.

"Oh yeah. I forgot. No problem."

We stopped at the elevator, and I pressed the button. The doors opened, and we stepped into the empty car. I faced the closing doors. Larissa stood at my side and watched me, unsure of what to do. I then faced her. With both hands, I grabbed her around her waist and pulled her close to me. She embraced me and buried her face in my chest. We remained like that until the doors opened again. We walked past other visitors and exited the building through the lobby. We didn't talk to each other for the better part of the ride because of the much-needed calls I had to make. Larissa drove while I used my cell phone. I called Ray, then Cindy, and then Kevin at the congressman's office. Kevin put me on hold for nearly five minutes. When he returned, he told me emphatically that tomorrow morning at nine o'clock Congressman Horvath would be there to present my father with his Purple Heart. My heart raced, and I got goosebumps. I thanked him and then hung up.

"It's done," I said.

"I heard. Tomorrow morning. Ron and I will be there. That's so great," she said. I could only smile as I texted Mandy. She called me right away.

"Honey, that's great news. I'm so happy. How did Dad react?" Mandy asked.

"I'm not sure how he feels about it. He's so tired. All he wanted to do is sleep. He's so sick." I choked up. Mandy sighed.

"Hon, he's a strong man," she said. I cut her off.

"Yeah, I know. But he's not immortal. Mandy, sweetheart, I know you love him. I do too, but it's time. I mean, he doesn't have much time. I doubt he's going to last the week."

"Don't say that," she said.

I ran my free hand through my hair and squeezed my eyes shut. Then I shook my head, as if I wanted to expel evil thoughts.

"You're right. I shouldn't write him off. He's just tired. Besides, the doctor hasn't called or anything. If something were happening, he would have called, right?"

"That's true," she said.

I looked at Larissa, and she nodded in agreement. Then she turned her attention back to the road.

"Is Larissa driving?" Mandy asked.

"Yeah, she's been very supportive," I said.

"Put her on speaker," Mandy said. I pressed the icon on the screen and held the handset between us.

"Hi sweetie," Mandy said. "Thanks for escorting Mike all morning. I owe you one." Mandy giggled.

"No problem. I owe you. I get to be seen in public with this handsome guy." Larissa winked at me.

"Where are you two off to now?" Mandy asked.

"Back to my place. We're going to relax a bit, then maybe get some lunch before you and Ron get home."

"Don't eat too late. You'll spoil dinner. Ron texted me and said he wants to try that new steak place in town."

"I'm wearing shorts," I said.

"Then we'll stop at our place on the way there, and you can change," Mandy said. I could imagine that she rolled her eyes when she said that.

"He can wear shorts. That place is casual. It's like the Outback," Larissa said.

"Fine, I'll wear shorts," I said.

"So you two are just going to watch TV or hump each other?" Mandy laughed. Her comment made me wonder just how explicit the phone calls and texts between her and Ron got.

"I got some new lingerie I want to model for him, Mandy. Is that okay?" Larissa rubbed my arm.

"Whoa, slow down girls," I said.

"What's the matter, honey? Are you all embarrassed?"

"His face is bright red," Larissa said.

"I know just how to get to him," Mandy said.

"You two are cruel," I said. My face felt flush, and my heart rate quickened.

"We went from lamenting my father's bad health to you guys teasing me. Nice," I said.

"Are you upset, sweetie?" Mandy asked.

"Nah, I'm fine. You guys were joking. It was funny." I stretched the corners of my mouth and looked at Larissa.

"He'll be fine once he sees me in the sheer, red, lace Teddy I bought," Larissa said.

"Ooh, put it on for me too when I get there," Mandy said.

"Of course," Larissa said.

"Okay, that's enough, girls. We're not swingers," I said. I swallowed hard.

"We're just goofing around, sweetheart," Mandy said. She laughed out loud.

"Lighten up a bit, Mike," Larissa said. She tapped my arm and smiled.

"I have to get back to work. You two kids have fun. See ya later," Mandy said.

"Bye," said Larissa. I did not get a chance to speak before Mandy ended the call.

Larissa and I did not speak much the rest of the ride. My mind focused on my father, who was withering away in the nursing home. As his life was ending, it became apparent how much he meant to me, let alone Ray and Cindy. I thought about Judith. We had a friendly relationship. However, I would never be nominated for any *Father of the Year* awards. As I mulled over my failures as a father, I remembered that I should call her later that night. Yet I did not want to wait. It was sad enough that most of our communication was through Facebook. My calls to her were infrequent and usually just a brief hello on the holidays. I took out my phone and texted her.

Hey sweetie, how are you? I just saw grandpa. He's getting his Purple Heart tomorrow from the congressman. I wish you could be there.

A few minutes later she wrote back.

That's awesome! I wish I could be there too. I'll call you tomorrow night. Send pics. She ended the message with a smiley face emoticon.

Talk to you tomorrow, sweetie.

"Are you coming in?" Larissa asked.

"Oh, I was just texting Judith. I miss her." I did not realize that we had parked in front of their place.

"Aw, you're a good dad." Larissa tilted her head and pushed out her lower lip.

"No, I'm not. I'm a lousy father who was barely involved in her upbringing." I stuffed my phone back into my pocket and stared out the windshield.

"Don't be so hard on yourself, Mike. You were so young when you had her. It's not like you and Theresa were married, and you were some sort of deadbeat. You did all that you could do." Larissa rubbed my knee.

"I have been telling myself that for her entire life. She deserved—no she deserves better than me," I said. Tears fell from my eyes. "My dad was there for everything."

"Mike, your dad is great, I get it. But you two are different people who had two very different experiences. I know you think you're a disappointment to him, but you're not. I know your father well enough, and he loves you very much. Judith loves you too." Larissa held my hand. "If you want to be closer to her, then make an effort. Go see her more often. Call her out of the blue. Buy her gifts online and have them sent to her. Damn it, just don't beat yourself up." She squeezed my hand.

I wiped my eyes with my hand. "You're right. I need to get closer to her and stop pitying myself. I'll call her more and do all those things that you suggested." I looked at her and managed to smile.

"I'm glad. You're a good father, like I said. But you're going to be an even more awesome dad. Now, let's go inside." She leaned forward and kissed my cheek. Then she got out of the car, holding her little bag. I followed her a few steps behind.

Once inside her apartment, I sat on the couch and sank into the plush cushions.

"I'll be right out," Larissa said. Then she went into her bedroom. I was still feeling glum from ruminating about my failures as a parent. I propped my elbow on the arm of the couch and rested my cheek on my palm. Ahead, my reflection showed on the flat-screen TV. My cell phone vibrated, and I guessed that it was either Ray or Cindy with questions about tomorrow's big day with Dad and the congressman. Instead of reaching for it and answering, I decided to ignore them for a while.

"Close your eyes," Larissa called out to me. Her voice startled me. I had almost forgotten about her, since I was wrapped up in my thoughts. I took a deep breath and did as I was told.

"Go ahead and open them," she said.

"Wow," I said. She was wearing a red, lace Teddy, which she had purchased during our visit to the mall. The top was a sheer fabric, which left little to the imagination. Beneath, she wore skimpy, red, lace panties. Larissa shifted from side to side, posing like a fashion model. She tilted her head and rubbed her hands slowly up and down the front of her body. Then she turned, stuck out her bottom, then faced me again.

"Do you like it?" she said. Her voice was low, almost a whisper.

"Yeah," I said. I breathed through my mouth, and my heart raced. She walked over to me and then straddled my lap. Then she leaned forward and pushed her breasts into my face and rubbed them back and forth.

"Larissa," I whispered.

"Do you remember our kiss in the emergency room that night?" she asked. Then she rubbed her fingers in my hair. Larissa leaned forward and touched her lips to mine. We kissed. I wrapped my arms around her and pulled her close. She held onto my shoulders. My hands caressed her body. Larissa lowered the straps on her Teddy and allowed them to slide down her arms. The front of her lingerie sagged, exposing her breasts. Then she laid on the couch next to me. My mind raced with images of Mandy sitting at her desk at work, unaware what the two of us were doing, and perhaps not caring. Her text messages and phone calls with Ron were hardly innocent, but I did not think, nor could I stomach, if Mandy were cheating on me. I knelt before Larissa. She unbuttoned my shorts and pulled them down, along with my boxer briefs. I stood up quickly, kicked off my sneakers, and then dropped my shorts and underwear to the rug. I climbed on the couch and knelt over Larissa. She noticed my erection.

"Come to me. I want you. I need you," she gasped. If there were an imaginary angel on one shoulder and a devil on the other, each attempting to persuade me to either make the right choice or the wrong one, the devil won the debate. The angel flew away in disgust.

I lowered myself to her, and in moments we were engaged in heavy foreplay. Larissa pulled the Teddy over her head and tossed it aside. Then she slid out of her panties and threw them on the rug next to her lingerie. She lay below me, naked, and beckoning me with her beauty. What had before only played out in my imagination was happening. It was wrong, so wrong, and I could not stop myself.

"I need protection," I whispered, careful not to ruin the mood.

"It's okay," she said.

I entered her and was immediately enchanted by the illicit pleasure. Then I paused.

"Are you… protected?" I whispered.

"What, sweetie? Don't need it. I'm good." Larissa pulled my head down and kissed me. We continued our lovemaking. As we approached climax, she revealed secrets that only lovers shared. Her moans and reactions to intimate touching enthralled me. Suddenly, I froze.

"What's the matter, honey?" Larissa asked.

"You're using birth control, right?" I looked into her eyes.

"Mike, it's going to be okay. Like I said, you're going to be an even more awesome dad." Larissa smiled.

"Oh God," I said. I got up and walked to the other side of the room.

"Mike, Mike, listen to me." Larissa stood and picked up her lingerie from the carpet. She held it against her breasts and reached out to me with her other hand.

"I am so stupid. I'm such a shitty husband," I muttered as I paced back and forth.

"No, no Mike. I need you. You're helping me. You're helping us," she said. Larissa's voice quavered. She walked over and held my arm. I looked down and shook my head.

"You need me? You want my sperm, that's it? And you wanted to me to cheat on Mandy to get it? Oh, my God." I brushed off her hand and walked back to the sofa. I picked up my clothes and sneakers and headed to the bathroom.

"I chose you, Mike, over some stranger. Just listen to me. Listen, Mike. I'm not some sort of slut." Larissa stood in the doorway of the bathroom and glared at me. She crossed her arms, still clutching her red lingerie. I wanted to vomit. Guilt and humiliation overcame me. I glanced at Larissa. She looked so young, and indeed she was, compared to me.

"I love Ron. I really do. But we can't have children. If it was me and I couldn't produce eggs or didn't have ovaries or some other bullshit that would keep me from having a baby, I could process that. It would still be horrible. I would be miserable, but I would be able to handle questions about adoption and sperm donation a lot better. But Ron is the one who is sterile. It's a genetic thing. The doctor told us he has Y chromosome infertility, and he produces no sperm." She breathed hard and grimaced. "Who fucking knew that when we got married that he couldn't become a father?" She dropped her hands and bent forward while she spoke. "Like I said, I love him. But it is frustrating as hell to see girls younger than me pushing around strollers, and I can't have a baby because my husband is shooting blanks."

"Larissa, I… I… don't know what to say. I'm not going to pretend I didn't want to… to… have sex with you. That night in the emergency room when we kissed, it was exciting. I wanted you. I was flattered that you found me attractive, and you were interested in me." I placed my clothes on the vanity and dropped my sneakers. "Larissa, I felt guilty after that, but I still lusted after you. That makes me a cheater. And I cannot be so cruel and unfaithful to Mandy, and I can't be an absentee father to yet another child."

"If you didn't ask for a condom, we'd still be having sex. Why can't that still happen? Why are you so worried about Mandy when you're in my house naked, and you were just inside me? Why? Just a few more minutes, Mike. Help me, please." Larissa broke down and cried. She covered her mouth and walked, hunched over, to the couch. She sat with her knees up in front of her and her face her hands. Her muffled sobs reached me inside the bathroom. I shook my head and sighed. After a moment, I got dressed and walked into the living room with my sneakers in my hand. I sat next to her and placed my hand on her shoulder. She looked up at me, tears streaming down her cheeks.

"I'm sorry, Larissa. That's all I can say." I wiped my eyes with my hand.

"Don't be. It's all my fault. I planned this whole… affair. I want to be a mother so much, Mike. You don't know how that feels. She put her feet down and wiped her eyes with her lingerie.

"You're right, I don't." I rubbed her shoulder for a while and then took my hand away. Larissa leaned forward and calmed down.

"I have all the working parts. The factory is open for business, and I need one, microscopic cell. One in about one-hundred-million sperm, and my husband can't produce any at all. That makes me so angry, Mike. And I know Mandy doesn't want kids, and you're okay with that. And you have Judith, and she's wonderful." She stopped talking and looked at me.

"It's unfair, Mike. It's not goddamned fair." Her lower lip trembled, and she blinked several times. I hugged her and pulled her close. She rested her head against my chest.

"I… I would do it, Larissa, if I did not have Mandy, and if I didn't have Judith. I watched my baby girl grow up from afar. Her mother and grandparents liked me well enough, but I was an outsider who came to see my kid on weekends and holidays. I was the part-time dad who showed up with a gift-wrapped box on Christmas and her birthday. But I never changed a diaper, put a bandage on a scraped knee, or stayed up with her all night when she had a fever. I feel even worse because my dad did all of that for me, and I couldn't do that for my daughter, because I wasn't married to her mother. Yes, I am proud to be her father, and I love her with all my heart. But I have nothing but regret for one, irresponsible act I committed as a young man which led to Judith being raised by a single mom. I can't do that again, Larissa."

"I'm sorry," she said. "I'm sorry I lured you here and tried to steal your sperm."

I could not stop myself, but I laughed hard. Larissa's head bounced up and down on my chest. She looked at me with her mouth open.

"What's so funny?" She raised her eyebrows and tilted her head to one side.

"I apologize. It's just, I can't help it. The way you said, 'I'm sorry I tried to steal your sperm.' It sounded... I dunno, funny." I covered my mouth and continued to giggle.

"You jerk." Larissa smiled and tapped my shoulder. Then she laughed also.

"I suppose that did sound kind of weird," she said.

"I'm sorry. I shouldn't have laughed. I should be supportive." I placed my hands on my lap and gazed into her eyes.

"You are here for me, Mike. Thank you." She kissed me on the forehead. She got up and went into her bedroom. Moments later, she emerged wearing a white, terrycloth bathrobe. She sat next to me and crossed her legs. I placed my hand on her knee.

"Does Ron know about... *this*?" I asked.

She looked down at the floor, sighed, then faced me.

"Yeah, he does. That's why he's at work today."

"And he's okay with me, his best friend and partner, being the father of his child?"

"Yeah, we talked about it. We decided to try it this way since artificial insemination is so expensive. I mean, we're almost broke from all the testing and other stuff. There was a small amount of hope we had from experimental therapy, then that didn't work. He can't produce sperm. That's it. So we decided that you should be the father." Larissa sniffed and wiped her nose with a tissue she had removed from her pocket.

"You guys could have asked me," I said.

"And you would have said yes?" Larissa leaned back and rested her arm on the back of the sofa.

I exhaled sharply and rubbed my palms on my shorts.

"No, I guess not. Just like now. Although I'll admit that if I did want to be the—How do you say it, donor?—I would prefer to do it like this rather than in a doctor's office." I chuckled.

The Heart of Velletri

"I wouldn't have asked for it any other way," Larissa said. Then she leaned over and kissed my cheek. We sat silent for a while. Finally, Larissa spoke.

"Are you going to tell Mandy about this?" she asked.

"No way. I mean, she and Ron chit-chat all the time. I know that she teases you and me about having sex together, and Ron jokes about screwing Mandy. That's just their personalities. But if I know my wife, she'd be furious if she found we actually had sex."

Larissa shrugged her shoulders.

"I suppose we married a couple of perverts." I grinned at her.

"Yes. And what are we?" Larissa pulled her feet up and sat cross-legged.

"Friends? Can we be friends?" I swallowed and felt my adam's apple bob up and down.

"We can be close friends, *without* benefits," she said.

We laughed. Larissa cuddled next to me. I placed my arm around her and kissed the top of her head.

"What do we do now?" Larissa asked.

I scratched my chin and sucked my teeth. "We can look into a real sperm donor, if you want," I said.

"No, I mean, we have some time to kill before Mandy and Ron come home. Do you want to watch some TV or something?" Larissa looked at me and smiled.

"Why don't you get dressed, and we'll go get some coffee. I would love to sit across from you and talk. I have to admit, as long as Ron and I have been partners, I never learned much about you, your life, or your family for that matter."

"Are you asking me on a date, Mike?"

"A coffee date between close friends, and one Ron and Mandy don't have to know about."

Larissa hugged me tightly. Then she got up. "I'll be right back. Let me get dressed. After coffee, we can pick up my car from the mechanic," she said. Then she went into the bedroom.

"What are you going to tell Ron when you guys are alone later? I mean, he's going to ask, right?"

Larissa came to the door with her robe untied, her body exposed.

"I'm going to tell him the truth. He deserves that much," she said.

I opened my mouth, but I remained silent. So, I nodded instead.

While I waited for Larissa to get changed, I checked my phone. Messages from Mandy, Ray, and Cindy awaited my attention regarding tomorrow's ceremony. Another wave of shame came over me. The burn filled my cheeks and then settled in my stomach. I closed my mind and forced the images of my dad out of my head. I was done comparing myself to him. He did what he had to do to provide for his family and to raise us properly. Nevertheless, my life was my own, and I could no longer compare myself to him. Over the years, I had idolized him, placed him on a pedestal, and tore myself down each time I did not measure up to him. It had to stop. The moment I backed away from Larissa, the moment I resolved to remain loyal to my wife and to be a better father to my daughter, I took control of who I was. Soon my father was no longer going to be there for me, and it was time I stood on my own and was a man.

Chapter 24

September 8th, 1944

After fourteen months in the army, Gene finally rode in a jeep. After so many miles of hiking through the Italian countryside, a lift from one of these vehicles would have been nice occasionally. Mostly, officers traveled in Jeeps with a private as the driver. Gene wondered why he was never chosen for that detail.

The driver took a sharp turn. Gene held tight and watched as if he were in a theater back home at the latest feature. His uniform had been bloodied after he was wounded. What was left of it had been removed from his body and disposed of while he recovered at the field hospital in Rome. The Allied forces were moving quickly now, and the Germans were being chased to France. He traded his pajamas for a pair of dungarees and a light blue, button-down shirt.

At the quartermaster, a sergeant stood behind the counter and listened to Gene's request for new battle fatigues. He shook his head.

"They're only sending us ammunition and bombs, private. We don't have much call for new uniforms. You're going home now. You don't need one anyway," said the sergeant.

The sergeant grinned. Gene sensed the man was glad for him. Even with his protests to join his old unit at the front lines, Gene was denied, because he could not handle a rifle.

The rest of his buddies had moved on to France. Harry had made a brief visit before he left. Gene waited for him in the lobby of the hospital. By then, he was able to speak, and he had been issued false teeth. Gene had the foresight to write his address on a slip of paper for his pal. Gene saw Harry first. Harry carried his helmet in his hand and his rifle slung over his shoulder.

"Harry, over here!" Gene called out. Harry stopped. He spotted Gene from across the lobby, through the mob of personnel moving about.

Gene walked towards him. Harry hurried through the crowd. They met in the middle. They embraced for a moment. Then they let go.

"Hi Gene. I'm glad to see you up and walking around again. I'm surprised to find you down here," Harry said.

"I can't stand sitting in my bed all day. Besides, I didn't want you to get lost trying to find me in this place."

"Gene, I don't have a lot of time. The convoy is leaving in ten minutes. I stopped by to give you my address." Harry took a piece of paper from his pocket and handed it to him.

"Thanks. Here's mine. I figured you'd want to mail me a letter or something," Gene said.

"You're still going to work on my family's ranch with me after the war, aren't you?" Harry fumbled with his helmet.

"Of course. First you come to Brooklyn and see the sights. Then I'll go home with you and become a cowboy." Gene laughed.

"Sure. We'll be cowboys. We're already good with guns," Harry said.

"Harry, thanks for saving me, buddy. I would have died if it weren't for you." Gene put his hand on Harry's shoulder.

"No, don't thank me. Besides, you saved me back at that farmhouse. I would have been either killed or captured if you didn't fight the way you did. I was scared out of my wits."

Gene took his hand from Harry's shoulder. "I have news for you. I was scared too. That's why I ran so fast." They both laughed. Harry looked down for a moment. Then he put his helmet on.

"Gene, I have to go. I don't want to get left behind." Harry pointed to the entrance with his thumb.

"Of course. I'm glad you dropped by," Gene said. They shook hands.

"Harry, be safe my friend. Keep your head down. Let someone else take point."

"I will. I want to live to be a cowboy." Gene threw his arms around him. Harry hugged him back.

"I asked to stay. They would not let me. The doctors say I can't fight. I'm sorry, Harry. I don't want to leave you behind."

Harry let go. "No, Gene. Don't be sorry. I'm happy you're going home. I want you to. I'll be okay. I'm going to make it through this. I should have died along with Sgt. Thames. I lived through Velletri. I can make it through France. The Germans are beaten anyway. This war will be over soon."

Gene wiped his eyes with his sleeve.

"Just be careful. Write to me and let me know how you're doing," Gene said.

"I sure will, Gene. Goodbye." Harry smiled and walked away. When he reached the door, he waved to his friend one more time. Gene waved back. He put Harry's address in his shirt pocket and returned to his ward. He sat on his bed, closed his eyes, and prayed for his buddy's safe return.

The jeep rounded another turn, and Gene became anxious. He didn't want to die in a car accident after nearly getting killed in battle. When they finally arrived at the port, he took his duffel bag, stood outside the vehicle, and looked at the ship. He did not pack a lot to bring home; just some mementos, letters, k-rations in case he wanted to snack on the ship, and underwear. Before he left the ward, Gene crammed his Purple Heart into his duffel bag. Each time he looked at it, he was reminded of the near-fatal wounds he suffered. He would just as soon have thrown it away. Unit loyalty and a commitment to his country aside, he wouldn't admit out loud that he was glad to be headed back to his family, let alone that he was lucky to be breathing.

Gene waved to the driver. The young driver behind the wheel wished him luck. Gene picked up his bag and walked up the gangplank. Although he was dressed in civilian clothes and boarded a ship for the United States, it seemed unreal to him that he was heading back to Brooklyn. Gene recalled the vision he had seen after he had been shot of his father on the steps of their home in Bay Ridge. If it was a dream, it was more lucid than any he had ever had. Gene found spiritual meaning in the visit from his father. Being able to speak to him and see him as he was before diabetes struck him down was a blessing. From then on, Gene vowed to be more faithful.

On board, he settled into his bunk and surveyed his surroundings. Others came through, tossed their bags on their beds, and nodded hello. They would be his bunk-mates for the nearly two-week journey home.

By late afternoon, his ship and the rest of the convoy were well out to sea in the Mediterranean. He and the other wounded GIs who were ambulatory awaited permission to go on deck. Then the alarm sounded.

There was commotion topside. Gene and his new buddies sat still and wondered aloud if they would be torpedoed.

"Damn U-boats. I thought we got every one of them?" one of the soldiers said. He was a lanky kid with his arm in a sling. Gene sized him up and tried to guess how he hurt his arm. The last fighting in Italy had taken place a month or so before. He looked at his own arm, scarred and stiff, unable to extend fully, yet he did not need a sling. Gene figured that he had probably fallen out of a truck or something unrelated to combat.

"Nah, it's the Luftwaffe," said another young man.

"There's no German air force left, not around here anyway," Gene said after clearing his throat. For too long,

Gene was unable to speak because his jaw had been wired shut, and his mouth had dozens of stitches. Now that he was able to, he talked as much as he could.

A loud thump jolted them. Then another. The ship rocked back and forth, and then there were more explosions. The entire group, all combat veterans, looked around at each other. Gene saw at least one other of his bunkmates praying with his hands together and his eyes closed. Gene reached into his pocket and took out his rosary beads. Then he recited a Hail Mary in his head.

From his days in Our Lady of Angels learning Catechism, he was raised to be devout. None of the teachings seemed tangible though. Jesus, God, priests, nuns, they were all part of some hierarchical world with the Lord at the top, Jesus as a second-in-command, and the clergy as some sort of theocratic police force. The Holy Ghost was inserted in there somewhere, and Gene had never fully understood His role. However, Gene understood God more than ever after what he had seen and experienced.

Soon the *all clear* was sounded. There was a palpable sigh of relief from everyone in the room. Gene collapsed on his bunk and could only think of the next ten days at sea. "U-boats," he said out loud to no one in particular. "I joined the army so I wouldn't die in some tin can at sea, getting sunk by some damned German submarine."

"Hey, we made it. You should be happy, buddy," said the lanky kid.

"Yeah, today we did. We have two more weeks to go," said Gene.

"Someone didn't make it." One of the nearby soldiers stepped up to him and looked down, crouching to see below the top bunk.

"You hear those explosions outside?"

"So, what about them?" Gene asked.

"We must have sunk something," offered another young man.

"Any of you want to go topside and look?" another soldier said. The men moved about the cabin. Many headed out to survey the damage themselves. There were no sailors about.

Gene fell into the back of the queue that had formed. GIs waited their turn to go topside. He was halfway upstairs when they came across a sailor rushing down past them.

"What happened. Did we get a U-boat?" several of the soldiers asked at the same time.

The sailor paused, looked each of them in the eye, and shook his head.

"What?" Gene asked him. "Tell us more."

"When you boys get home, thank the Lord you're still alive. While you're doing that, pray for the souls of the sailors who died for you today."

The line stopped moving, and there was silence.

"Who died for us? Just say what happened," asked Gene as he gulped.

"That U-boat shot two torpedoes at us. One of our frigates moved right in front and took the hits. Sailors are being picked up out of the sea at this moment. A lot of others went down trying to save their ship."

The seaman held his head high and pursed his lips together.

"What about the U-boat? Did we get it?" Gene asked.

"Yeah, we sure did. Our blimps caught sight of it right away. This water is so clear, you can see them coming." The sailor stood straight and excused himself. No one thought to comment further, and after they made way for the young sailor, the line slowly resumed its now mournful march to the top deck.

"I'm sure glad I joined the army," someone whispered behind Gene. He looked back, and it was the kid with his arm in a sling.

"Me too," said Gene in a low voice. Though, he wasn't quite sure why they were whispering.

The Heart of Velletri

Gene went back to his bunk and laid down. The sound of soldiers and sailors alike could be heard from the top deck. Outside, a massive rescue operation was underway. Gene envisioned dozens of sailors fighting to keep their heads above water. The sea would be slick with oil, which spewed from their sinking ship, he imagined. Others had been killed outright from the explosion. They could have been his age or only a few years older. To die in the sea, drowning so helplessly revolted him. He became nauseated.

Gene rolled onto his side, held his stomach, and closed his eyes. Flashbacks of the assault on Velletri filled his mind. Memories of the skirmish in the woods, being chased by German soldiers tormented him. Gene saw the bodies of the men he killed. Boys his age were slain by grenades and bullets spit out by his rifle. None of them would return home as he would. Gene thought about his mother. He imagined her reaction when she saw him again. Gene was certain that she would be surprised. Knowing her, she would cry. Gene would move back home, maybe go to school, and he would find a job. Mr. Molfetta would give him one for sure. The idea made him even more sick. The type of work Mr. Molfetta offered involved hurting others. Gene's mind filled with images of dead Wehrmacht soldiers and the gunman his father had shot when Gene was small. Mr. Molfetta's world was not for him, Gene concluded.

"Hey, look at this."

Gene opened his eyes. A soldier sat on the bunk next to him, holding a pistol in his hands. Gene had met him before but had not spoken to him much. But Gene had learned his name. He remembered it because when the kid had introduced himself he had said his name was Theodore, but everyone called him Ted. Gene sat upright.

"Jesus, Ted. You startled me." Gene leaned over and peered at what was in Ted's hand. "You have a gun? So what?" He brushed his hair back and sat on the side of the bed facing the Ted.

"It's a Luger."

"Big deal. There are millions of them all over Europe."
Gene sucked his teeth and shook his head.

"Yeah? Well, I got five more in my duffel bag and about a dozen bayonets. If that does not impress you, I have Nazi belt buckles, a Hitler Youth Knife, an officer's hat, and a bunch of other things. I already shipped a lot of stuff home." Ted smiled and placed the Luger at his side. Then he leaned back on his hands. Gene focused on the pistol.

Gene remembered what his father told him about his exploits in the Great War. He thought about his dad looting homes and soldier's bodies while cruising around France on his motorcycle. His ill-gotten gains were sent home and used to finance his nefarious lifestyle alongside the notorious Mr. Molfetta. Gene's stomach became more unsettled. He looked at Ted. The kid was so full of himself. Gene considered him to be a less clever, underachieving version of his father. While Ted had some handguns and other trinkets from the enemy, his father was a war profiteer by comparison. Yet Gene no longer felt proud of his father's plundering. Yes, he missed his dad, and he still loved him. Gene wished he had kept the radio store and never met Mr. Molfetta.

"Hey Ted. Do me a favor?"

"What is it, Gene?"

"Put that away, will you?"

"Put what away?" Ted stretched the corner of his mouth, looking confused.

"The Luger. Put it back in your pack, okay?" Gene wiped sweat from his forehead with his bare hand.

"Why should I do that?" Ted asked.

"Because I'm sick of guns. That's why." Gene glared at him.

Ted locked eyes with Gene for a moment. Finally, he blinked.

"Fine, I'll put it away." Ted reached under his bunk and took out his duffel bag, opened it, and stuffed the handgun inside. Gene laid back down and closed his eyes.

Outside, seamen Gene's age floated in the Mediterranean Sea. Some were alive, others dead, and still others trying to rescue them. Further away, in the town of Velletri, bodies of German troops, many of them Gene's age as well, were rotting away with their families wondering if their sons would ever come home again.

I killed people. My rifle, my bullets, my grenades. I did it. I killed other men. Tears fell from his eyes, and he hoped that Ted and others could not hear him cry. He had one final thought before he was finally able to fall asleep. He never wanted to see another gun again in his life.

Chapter 25

April 17th, 2009, 9:00 AM

When Mandy and I stepped off the elevator, we sensed a
tinge of excitement among the staff. Two young nurses,
both women, looked up at us from their seats behind their
station and smiled. I recognized them, and I smiled back and
waved. From where we stood, we could see into the day room
further down the long hall. Thomas, an aid who I had met
before, walked up to me. I recalled his gentle nature and
patience with my father as he had helped him eat his dinner.

"This is quite an honor for your father, Mike. You must
be proud," he said.

"Yes, I am," I answered. Thomas shook my hand. A slight
veil of apprehension draped over me.

"I didn't know your dad was a hero. It makes sense
considering how strong he is and the fight he is putting up,"
said Thomas. He held hands together in front of him, and he
smiled with his mouth closed.

"Don't say that around my father. He'll be the first one to
say that he didn't do anything courageous. Besides, he's just
getting his Purple Heart and the campaign ribbons that he
somehow never received. He lost his Purple Heart a long time
ago."

"You have to get wounded to receive a Purple Heart, Mike. That means you had to fight the enemy. I served two tours in Iraq. That's brave enough for me. He's my hero."

"Thank you for your service," I said.

"It was my honor," said Thomas.

The exchange made me uncomfortable. I looked at Mandy, hoping that she would interrupt or lead me away by the hand. She didn't. Mandy was on her cell phone, texting someone using her thumb.

"Will you be there for the ceremony?" I asked.

"I'll be there in a few minutes. I have a patient to tend to first. I'll see you there, Mike." Thomas tapped my upper arm and walked away. My shoulders sagged, and I exhaled. This was an event that I had been planning in my head for almost two decades, and I grew more apprehensive each minute. Mandy finished tapping out her message and then put her phone back in her pocketbook.

"Don't worry. It's on vibrate," she said. She walked past me to the day room.

I raised my finger and opened my mouth, ready to ask why she had an attitude. But I paused for about a dozen reasons, including that I did not want to talk about my fling with Larissa and Mandy's relationship with Ron. I let it drop. The day was about my father. Honestly, it was also about me, since Dad never asked for any recognition. All along, my efforts to elevate my father into a living saint and super-warrior were designed to make me appear not so bad in comparison. I figured that if I was supposed to be as virtuous and honorable as he was, then my failure to do so was because Dad's accomplishments were too noteworthy for an ordinary man to meet. However, I would not admit that.

After walking about fifty feet, we stopped at the next nurse's station. Another hall intersected at the point where we stood. From that spot, I could see through the windows into the vast day room. Red, white, and blue streamers decorated the doorway. A banner, roughly six feet long, hung from the ceiling above the TV and read, *In Honor of Our Hero,*

Eugene. The sign was printed out on several sheets of paper and fastened together. There were more aides and nurses on hand than usual. Men and women wearing business attire milled around, chatting with the elderly residents. I guessed they were administrators and other bigwigs from the facility. However, much of the attention surrounded my father. Ray, Cindy, and Congressman Horvath stood together, chatting. It looked like Ray was doing most of the talking. Larissa and Ron stood near them. Larissa held onto the straps of her handbag slung over her shoulder. Ron was on his phone, apparently sending a text. He stopped what he was doing and slipped his phone into his pocket. Seconds later, Mandy's phone vibrated in her pocketbook. I looked at her. Mandy gazed ahead and did not budge. I decided to remain silent.

I focused on my dad. He was slumped in his Geri chair. His chin was on his chest, and his shoulders were slumped. For no apparent reason, tears welled in my eyes. Mandy held my hand.

"Mike, it's okay," she said.

I patted her hand. "I know, thanks. It's just that I had hoped to do this for him for years. Now he gets to have his moment when he's withering away. I waited too long." I walked over to the hall desk and took a tissue from a small, red box on the counter. A young nurse grinned at me. I recognized her from previous visits.

"Good morning, Mr. Koenigsmann. You must be so excited. Congressman Horvath is inside with your father already. So are your brother, sister, and your friends. They're all waiting for you."

"Thank you," I said. "You all have been so good to my father. It means more to me than you will ever know." I wiped my eyes and turned away. Mandy stood next to me and placed her hand on my shoulder.

"You can let it out, Mike. It's fine. But we should go in. They're waiting for us like she said." She took my hand and accompanied me inside.

"I hope my father didn't grind his dentures too hard when he saw that they printed *Eugene* instead of *Gene* on the banner," I said.

Mandy laughed. "I'm sure he's okay with it," she said.

At the entrance, I paused and took a deep breath. Mandy walked in before I did and met Cindy; her son, Jeffrey; Ray; his wife and kids; Ron; and Larissa. She hugged each of them. At the center of the great room, among the folding chairs, residents, visitors, and the staff was a long table. On top of the table was a large, padded shipping envelope. My dad was seated facing the door. The nurses had dressed him in his best blue pajamas with a bathrobe. He did not have a need for pants or shirts since he was in bed most of the time. He saw me when Mandy and I entered. I waved, but he did not respond. I figured he was either in discomfort, was overwhelmed, or both. Fred was nowhere to be seen. The Congressman stood next to my father. I went to him first. He held out his hand, and I shook it firmly.

"Hello Congressman. Thank you for coming," I said.

"It is my pleasure Michael," Congressman Horvath said. The congressman was a tall man in his early sixties. He had dark hair with gray at the temples and a deep voice like my father's. Congressman Horvath looked at Mandy. She approached him, wearing a genial smile.

"This is my wife Mandy," I said. Then I stepped aside. Mandy leaned past me and shook the congressman's hand.

"It's nice to meet you. You both must be so proud. I spoke with your brother, Raymond, and your sister, Cindy. They are delighted as well." The Congressman stood with his arms at his sides. "I have been in office for over twenty years, and I never had the honor that I have today in handing a veteran his Purple Heart. I must say that I am deeply humbled."

"I can speak for my family, Congressman Horvath, when I say that we are grateful to you for helping make this happen. I have tried for most of my adult life to help my dad receive his recognition but to no avail. Partly because he is so stubborn and partly because I had no idea how to proceed." I pressed my lips together to keep from weeping.

"Well, I did nothing really. But I am privileged, as I said, to have played any role here." The congressman placed his hand on my shoulder.

"I think it is time to make the presentation. Those people over there are motioning to you Congressman," Mandy said.

I went to my father and stood at his right side. Dad did his best to smile. I bent forward and kissed his head. Ray, Cindy, Ron, Larissa, and Mandy took up a position on the other side of the table. Congressman Horvath opened the envelope and pulled out an ornate, blue case and some smaller ones. My heart skipped a beat. Dad's eyes teared up. From nowhere, Fred rolled up next to Ray. He wore a plaid shirt, dress pants, and had shaved. Fred's expression was somber. He saw me and nodded. I did the same. Others in the room, including the medical staff and administrators gathered around Ray, Cindy, and the others. Mandy bent over my father and kissed his cheek. He stretched the corner of his mouth and patted her hand. Then Mandy stood at my right side. Congressman Horvath spoke.

"Good afternoon everyone. I am so happy to see all of you on this special occasion. I was saying to Gene's son, Michael, that in over twenty years in office I never had the honor that I am given today. That is to give an American hero, a combat veteran, wounded in battle in defense of our country his Purple Heart. Our veterans are so important to all of us because they fought for our freedoms, protected us against the enemy, and we cannot do enough for them." Congressman Horvath then picked up the large, blue case and opened it. Inside I could see the purple ribbon and the heart shape with a miniature bust of George Washington. Dad took the opened case containing the medal, looked at it, and then placed it down in front of himself.

"I am also pleased to present to you, Gene, the European—African—Middle Eastern Campaign Ribbon, the World War II Victory Medal, and the Good Conduct Medal."

The congressman placed three cases, all opened, in front of my father next to the Purple Heart. For some reason, I watched Fred. He folded his hands in his lap and stared at the floor. I gave him a lot of credit for coming to the event instead of sitting in his room.

"Say something, Dad," Ray said.

Cindy held her cell phone in front of her and captured the event on video. Other members of the staff and some visitors did as well. Larissa and Mandy took pictures and a video with their phones.

Dad touched the blue case, then took his hand away. He produced a tissue from his robe pocket and wiped his eyes.

"When I was in Italy, I lost my friends. A good sergeant of mine died trying to save us. I miss him and the others every day." He paused and hung his head. I placed my hand on his shoulder. "I told myself for all these years that I did what I had to do. They were trying to kill us so I..." Dad stopped talking and placed his hand over his mouth.

"It's okay, Dad. You don't have to talk," I said. Dad raised his hand and motioned to me. I understood that the gesture meant for me to shut up.

"I joined the army. I decided to go over there. I was a kid, I keep telling myself. I would have been drafted anyway. But we were eager to defend our country. We were soldiers." Dad paused and looked down. Then he picked his head up again. "The Germans. They attacked Harry, Sgt. Thames, and me. Most of our squad was killed by artillery. Sgt. Thames, he did what he could. Harry and I... we ran. We shot Germans, we hid in the woods, we shot more of them, I kept shooting, and we were so tired and scared. We didn't know if we were going to make it. We killed soldiers our age. German soldiers." Dad looked up and faced the group. "Fred," he whispered.

Fred pushed himself around the table. I moved out of the way to make room for him. Mandy went over to the other side and stood next to Larissa.

Fred positioned himself next to my father on his right side. Dad grabbed Fred's hands. Then they embraced. After a moment, they let go but held onto each other's hands.

"Fred, what have I done?" Dad said. Tears streamed down his cheeks.

"Gene, we were young boys. And we were soldiers, indeed. But you have no reason to be ashamed, Gene. I feel your pain. I have it too. That is what war does to us." Fred stroked Dad's arm as he spoke in a soothing tone. Fred's lips quivered, and his hands shook. I saw the redness in his eyes. Finally, tears fell from his face. Dad handed him a tissue. Fred took it and wiped his cheeks. I could hear muffled weeping all around the room. Ray, Cindy, and even Larissa all sobbed as they watched the two veterans from opposite sides come to terms with their roles in the war.

"Our countries were at war, Gene. But we are friends, yes? We are friends. I am your friend." Fred placed his hand on Dad's shoulder and looked him in the eye.

"Yes, we are. We are. Thank you, my friend," Dad said.

Fred reached for the table and picked up the Purple Heart. He handed it to my father.

"Take this, Gene. It is yours. Take this for your own good, for the sake of your children, and for your friends who have died in battle. This is yours. You earned it." Fred placed the Purple Heart on Dad's lap and then sat back in his wheelchair. Dad looked at the case. The medal was resplendent in its polish and modest elegance. He picked it up and then examined it carefully.

"Thank you for your service, Gene," said Congressman Horvath. Larissa clapped her hands, and then the room erupted in applause. I stepped away from the group and hurried outside into the hall. I found the bathroom and went inside. At the sink, I placed my hands on the vanity, hung my head, and cried. All those years I waited for my dad to receive his honors, and I always thought it would be a proud occasion. I never considered the pain and reconciliation he would experience when this occurred. I did this for me. But then again, my father had to visit his past once more. Though I did not want to acknowledge it, Dad was close to the end. The spirits of his long-lost buddies would be waiting for him, and he needed to find peace.

Chapter 26

May 6, 2009

Ray's words were *get here now*. My new partner, George, and I were on patrol near Frederick Douglass Boulevard and 152nd St. when I answered my cell phone. Even though George was a rookie with a fresh, academy crew cut, I allowed him to be the vehicle operator. Although we had only been working together for a month, he understood what this phone call meant. He drove, lights and sirens on, back to the station house. Dad was a fighter, a stubborn man, and I refused to believe that this was an emergency.

"Who told you Dad was dying?" I demanded.

"The doctor."

"His doctor? Dr. Burns?"

"No, the emergency room doctor. He said that they're handing Dad over to palliative care."

"What the hell does that mean?"

I knew precisely what palliative care meant, but I was in denial. We had experienced this with our mother not three years earlier. Dad had been her primary caregiver. At the time, he was eighty years old, diabetic and with heart disease, and entirely devoted to her after fifty-three years of marriage. With mom ravaged by cancer and systemic lupus, we were in awe of Dad's loyalty and gentleness.

Ray wavered on the other end of the phone. Partly, he was unnerved by my incredulity, and partly because he had just seen Dad, weakened and in agony, mere moments earlier. Ray was near tears. There was no need for me to argue with him. In my mind, it was not possible that Dad could have deteriorated so rapidly in just a few days. It was Wednesday. I had visited him on Monday. During my time that night with him, we had speculated that he could visit Mandy and I if he could tolerate a trip in my car. Dad was cheerful and had a positive outlook. He finished his dinner and ate dessert too. Now, out of the blue, Ray was calling me and proclaiming that our father is dying. I could not process that information.

"Michael, he's dying. You have to come now."

"I'll leave. I'm coming. It's about an hour's drive."

"Hurry up. I don't know how long he can hang on," Ray said.

"All right already. You hear the sirens? I'll be there as fast as I can."

Ray hung up. I put my cell phone in my shirt pocket and shifted my weight.

"Is your father dead?" George asked. He kept his eyes on the road while he maneuvered in and around traffic.

"No. My brother said he does not have long though. Just drive normally. I don't want to get us both killed." I shut off the lights and sirens.

"Okay, I just thought you'd want to be there when, you know."

"Don't worry, George. My dad is tough as nails. He ain't going anywhere. I'm sure my brother is overreacting." I shrugged and shook my head.

"I hope you're right, man."

George pulled in front of the precinct and shut off the engine. We both got out. I'll admit that I took my time. I still believed that Dad would live for more months, if not years. Not surprisingly, I had also been in denial with my mother when she was dying. As the nurses and caretakers from hospice came and left my parent's house each day, I still envisioned holidays where my folks dropped by with a cake from the bakery.

At the top of the steps leading into the precinct, I paused and took out my phone. I called Mandy and told her the news. By then, Cindy had already phoned her, knowing that Ray would contact me. Both were on the way to the hospital. I thought about calling Ron, but I sent a text instead. Larissa deserved a phone call, but I sent her a text message as well. Within a few seconds, my phone beeped with responses, but I did not look at them. The desk sergeant did not bat an eye when I asked to leave early. He was aware of my family situation. In the locker room, I dressed like it was a lazy Saturday, and I had nothing to do and all day to do it. After securing my locker, I holstered my off-duty revolver on my belt and kept my tee shirt untucked to conceal it. After taking a deep breath, I walked to the parking lot.

As I drove, I turned on the radio as a distraction. There was no way my father was dying. He seemed too robust, too stubborn to go. Yet as much as I tried to convince myself of the same when my mother was failing, in my heart, I understood that I was kidding myself.

The emergency room was full of activity. I entered through the sliding, automatic doors. I stopped in the vestibule. For a humid afternoon in May, I was surprised to see so many people lining up to get in. The desk was besieged with patients waiting to be triaged. Since the place was so busy, I expected the nurses and the security guards to be a bit hurried or perhaps impolite.

"Hi, my father was brought here. His name is Eugene Koenigsmann." The nurse pursed her lips and asked me how to spell my last name. I rattled off four letters as she keyed them into her computer. Once she found the name, her eyes softened. The nurse pointed to the guard who was behind the desk with her. She said something, but I could not hear what it was. There was a strict rule about allowing only two visitors at a time. Ray was inside already since he was the one who called everyone. Cindy undoubtedly had arrived already. So I was confused as to why I was being escorted inside the emergency room.

"Come this way, sir," he said. "Your family is waiting for you."

He nodded and pushed the button.

My stomach became unsettled, and I found it difficult to inhale. When I entered the emergency room, I saw my father laying on a gurney across from the vast, bustling unit. By his side were Ray, Cindy, and a nurse who was tending to him.

Dad gasped for breath. His false teeth had come loose and dangled inside his mouth. His skin appeared gray, and he was damp with sweat. His eyes were closed. To me, he seemed frail and vulnerable.

Ray waved to me. Then he approached.

"Mike, this is bad. They brought him here a little while ago. Dr. Burns signed off his case. He's going into that palliative care unit," he whispered. We were in the aisle about five or six feet from his curtained stall. Dad could not hear us, as he wasn't wearing his hearing aids.

There was no arguing or disbelieving anymore. After witnessing too many grisly scenes as a cop and after being present when my mom had breathed her last breath, it was evident that Dad did not have long.

Since it was a Catholic hospital, a nun was there to aid us. Sister Agnes was a slim woman in her early sixties. She had a determined smile—in the face of her grim tasks—that could only come from rigorous faith. A priest accompanied her. Father Paul was about ten years younger than me. He had the look of a floor manager in a busy department store—haggard, yet focused, and ready to serve. I admired the ability professionals had to keep calm in times of calamity. Yet there I was, an NYPD officer trained to handle emergencies in a quiet, professional manner, and I was losing my composure. However, that was to be expected. My father was struggling

252

to breathe before my eyes. I remained silent and fought back the urge to cry.

Dad chose Ray to be his health-care proxy. Though Dad had signed a *do not resuscitate* order months earlier, the doctors had asked Ray before my arrival if he would allow them to take heroic measures to save Dad's life or let him die naturally. The DNR was on file with another hospital. The doctors wanted a new one for their own records. Ray argued that the choice had been already made by Dad earlier that year. But they insisted that he reaffirm Dad's wishes.

Ray explained the situation to me. He looked at me with his eyebrows raised and his head tilted to one side. "Mike, am I doing the right thing? Am I letting him die for no reason?" Ray looked down, his chin touched his chest.

We stood next to the nurse's station where no one was seated. Cindy was talking to Sister Agnes and Father Paul at Dad's bedside. They could not hear us talking.

"Listen," I said. "The doctors are putting him in the unit. That could only mean… you know." I shrugged and looked at him. A physician who recognized Ray walked over on our side of the desk.

"Ray," he said. Then he put his hand on his shoulder. "I'm so sorry. Listen, we're going to make him comfortable. He's not going to be in pain. Sister Agnes is going to walk with you and your family, show you his room, and explain everything. The charge nurse will also be there to answer questions."

"He's being admitted?" Ray stood back and raised his eyebrows.

"Yes, that's the plan. We're going to make your father comfortable." The doctor narrowed his eyes and nodded. Years of informing people that their loved ones were dying created that countenance.

"You mean he's not going back to the nursing home? He's going to *die*…here?" Ray choked on the word *die*. I could feel myself welling up.

"Ray, we can't move him. Your father can't ride in an ambulance. The nurse is putting an IV in, and we'll give him meds to calm him down and ease his pain." The doctor pursed his lips.

Most doctors don't intend to come off as patronizing even when they're as respectful and compassionate as he was. It's just that physicians are educated about death and dying and ordinary folks are not. They are regular witnesses to the cosmic joke about the end stages of life, and it aggravates the rest of us who cannot see the punchline coming.

The physician patted Ray on the shoulder and sighed. When we walked back to the curtained area where Dad was, Father Paul was there, and he was speaking to Cindy and Sister Agnes. Father Paul acknowledged us with a nod. Dad's breath was rasping and slow. A nurse was finally able to remove Dad's dentures, exposing the almost toothless mouth he'd had for over sixty years.

"Father, may I speak to you over there?" Ray asked him.

"Sure, we can talk by the desk."

The pair of them walked off. Then Ray looked back and waved me along. I caught up with them and stood next to Ray with my arms folded.

"Father, the doctors want to know if they should attempt to save his life, but I already signed a DNR in the nursing home. They say they don't have it on file."

"What? How are they going to save him? His lungs are shot, and his heart is failing," I said. I could not believe what I was hearing. "Didn't the doctor just tell you they're moving him to that unit back there?" Just stating the words *palliative care unit* made me queasy, so I did not mention them.

"They still want the paperwork," said Ray.

"What are your father's wishes?" Father Paul asked.

"He doesn't want to suffer. He talked to a priest about it in the nursing home. He's very religious."

"Then, it seems to me that you know what decision you should make." He leaned in as he spoke, careful that no one walking by would overhear our conversation.

Ray wept, and his face turned bright red. "It's just that. If I make this decision—all over again—it's like I'm the one killing him. Am I doing something wrong? Is this a sin?"

Father Paul reached over the nurse's desk and pulled a tissue out of a small box next to a keyboard. He handed it to my brother. Ray wiped his eyes.

"No, Ray. Not at all. You're a dedicated, loving son helping his father. You're following his wishes. This is what he wants." Father Paul placed his hand on Ray's shoulder. Ray sniffed and took a deep breath.

"Thank you, Father. I needed to hear that."

"Of course, Ray." He removed his hand from Ray's shoulder.

An image of my dad as a young soldier on the battlefield in Italy entered my head. In his recollections to me, he had said that after he was wounded in battle his buddies thought he was dead, and then he woke up just as he was about to be buried. This time, he was going to die for real. There would be no miracle resuscitation. His lungs were filling with fluid, and his heart too weak. Between my nerves affecting my stomach and emotions overwhelming me, I was not sure if I was going to vomit, cry, or both.

"You know Father. They thought he was dead in the war. The army had almost buried him. A priest gave him Last Rites," I said. "My father wasn't able to speak because his mouth was bloody and the roof of his mouth was damaged. But he saw the same priest again when he was in Rome in the army hospital. When he could finally talk, Dad spoke to him. The priest checked on him every day after that."

"Remarkable," the priest said. "And it was a miracle, if you will, that he regained consciousness and wasn't buried."

"Yeah," I said. "That's why he's so dedicated to the Franciscans and their charities. It's because that priest was a Franciscan."

"That's quite a story," Father Paul said. He stretched his lips and nodded.

I looked back at Cindy and Dad. Sister Agnes had left. A nurse was giving him an injection intravenously. Dad lay still, staring at the ceiling.

"He's awake," I said and walked over to him. Father Paul went ahead of me. As he passed by, he paused and asked, "What name does your dad prefer to be called, Eugene or Mr. Koenigsmann?"

"Gene. Never call him Eugene," I answered.

Father Paul stood next to Dad's gurney. Cindy, Ray, and I stood at the other side.

"Hello Gene," said Father Paul.

Dad glanced at him but did not respond.

"You're here in the hospital. The nurses are getting a room ready for you. The doctors are going to make you comfortable."

Dad shrugged and looked around at all of us, then back at the priest.

"The doctors and nurses are here for you Gene. They're going to help you rest."

"Okay," said Dad.

"Your family is here for you too."

Dad glared at Father Paul.

"I'm here for *them*," he said with a shrug.

Dad would not let go. He remained the proud parent, still the head of the family. If he was frightened, he did not let on.

Soon everyone else arrived, including my Mandy. As we were led away to the room where we would watch our father fade away. I sensed within his life a string of themes emerging which took root over sixty years ago in a bombed-out, dusty village just outside of Rome.

There was no reason for me to know anything about Dad's time spent in Italy other than to satisfy my curiosity. There were dreadful details hidden behind his stoic veneer, and all of it had to do with bloodshed, his own and that of his enemies.

My father had been a soldier, and that defined much of his existence. On the surface, it appeared that his duty was performed with honor, and we were spared the gory details. All my life, from childhood to the time I spent in uniform on the busy, crack-infested New York City streets as a cop, I could only refer back to my then eighteen-year-old father with a rifle slung over his shoulder. He survived so much more than I did. That was enough to empower me to endure my own bouts of fatigue and stress.

That day in the emergency room as my father realized that he was about to spend the last few hours with his family, I witnessed him grasping onto his role as a father. I felt at the edge of a precipice, on the verge of a profound commencement. In a few hours, I would inherit his wisdom as my own.

My father was dying, and I was not prepared to live without him.

Chapter 27

May 7th, 2009, 10:00 a.m.

Ray stopped me at the door of Dad's hospital room. I had taken the day off due to Dad's worsening condition. Considering the circumstances of my early departure the day before, the desk sergeant did not hesitate to grant me leave when I called out for the tour.

"Listen, last night he went to sleep and didn't wake up," he said.

"What? You mean Dad's dead?" I peered over Ray's shoulder at my father. He lay, and his eyes were closed.

"No. I mean he's asleep, and he hasn't woken up."

"Jesus Ray. It sounded like you were telling me that he died the same way you'd speak to a child."

"No, sorry. I mean, I think it's close. He makes a rattling sound when he breathes, and he twitches occasionally. But I think he can hear us."

Ray moved aside to let me pass him. I walked over and stood next to my father. I touched him. His cheeks were cold. So were his hands. I leaned in close. "I'm here, Dad."

He didn't respond. I'd seen that gaunt and strained appearance before. The same pre-death grimace stole my mother's beauty three years earlier. Cancer drained my mother of her life. Diabetes and pneumonia were sapping Dad of his. He was helpless within the shell which was once a robust body. His legs were nearly black from the lack of circulation and seeping bed sores. Dad's arms withered from atrophy. There was a time when his biceps flexed while using a giant wrench to repair a boiler or when jacking up the family station wagon to change the oil.

I watched my father, unable to accept his tortured providence. I had months to calculate his mortality, to estimate how much time he had left. Then again, who knew for sure? The doctors never did. And if they had determined a date and time for his demise, they did not divulge this to Ray, Cindy, and me. Ray sat down and folded his hands in his lap. I touched Dad's forearm and pursed my lips. The rattling noise Dad made when he breathed haunted me. Mom had made those sounds too.

"The doctor said he's hanging on." Ray leaned forward and rubbed his palms together. I saw him in my peripheral vision. I turned and faced him.

"Hanging on for what?" I could not imagine why Dad would want to suffer like this. Yet the answer was there all along. Dad wasn't afraid to die. His faith was absolute, and mom was waiting for him on the other side. That is what he believed. No, Dad did not want to leave us alone. He feared that he would disappoint us if he died.

"I'll be right back," I said. I walked out into the hall and sensed the relative quiet of the Palliative Care Unit. This was where patients were sent to die with some dignity. The nurses and doctors here were all specialists in end of life care. Priest and nuns at this Catholic hospital ministered to both patients and their families. With my back against the wall, I tried to hold back tears and maintain my composure.

An older nun, a pleasant-faced woman in her early sixties or so, saw me and walked over. She smiled, but this was a practiced expression which put people at ease and demonstrated confidence. One could only muster such fortitude from sincere conviction.

"Are you Gene's son?" she said. This was either a good guess on her part, or she had seen me walking in and out of the room earlier. "I'm Sister Teresa."

"Yes, I am. I'm Michael. Nice to meet you."

"I've been with your father most of the night. Is your brother Ray still here?"

"Oh sure. He's inside." I used my thumb to point to the door. As if she needed directions.

"How are you, dear?" She touched my forearm and looked me in the eye.

I took a deep breath and looked away. Then I turned my attention back to her.

"I need your help. I mean, Dad does. You need to do something my brother, sister, and I can't do."

"How can I be of help?" Sister Teresa clasped her hands together in front of her.

I looked at her. "Please tell my father that it is okay to die."

She tilted her head to the side and placed her hand on my shoulder.

"I mean, he's so stubborn. He wants to be here for us. I know my father. He thinks he's letting us down if he lets go. I want him to see my mother. She's probably in Heaven in her beautiful garden just like she had in the backyard of their home and is getting annoyed at him for taking so long." I laughed. Then I shut my eyes to hold back tears. Sister Teresa chuckled at my little joke.

"What was your mother's name?"

"Ann."

Sister Teresa walked past me and entered the room. I heard Ray greet her as I followed close behind. She pulled over a chair and sat next to Dad. At the end of the bed, Ray stood with his arms folded and his brow furrowed as if he were bracing himself against what he was about to see.

"Gene, it's okay. You can go to Ann now. She's waiting for you." She stroked his hair and spoke in a low voice. She stretched her lips in what looked like a smile, but I recognized as a steely expression worn by those who deal with misery daily.

"You've done a wonderful job, Gene. You and Ann have raised beautiful children, and they are all grown up now. They will be fine. You can go home to God now." Sister Teresa looked at me. I nodded in response. Words had escaped me, or perhaps I was too choked up to speak. I turned and walked into the corridor. The aroma of hospital food, human waste, and floor wax turned my stomach.

The people wandering by blurred into an indistinct, cacophonous throng where I zigzagged between obstacles toward the exit. I reached the automatic doors, and they opened. A rush of warm air worsened my sick stomach. I walked over to a nearby bench and placed my hand down first to guide me, and then I sat.

Inside, Sister Teresa had given permission to my father to die with dignity. I was the one whose bright idea it was for her to do this. Who was I to order anyone out of this world? I didn't want my father to leave me. I loved him so much, how could I think for one second that death was preferable to a few more precious moments of life?

For some reason, I remembered the family trips to the beach we took together. The hospital and the nursing home were on the same grounds near the Great South Bay. A breeze carried salty air that filled my nostrils and offered a small amount of relief. Dad loved the sea. He often told me that when he was a kid in Brooklyn, he would ride in his father's cabin cruiser out of Sheepshead Bay and dream of being a ship's captain when he grew up.

I recalled one Saturday during summer when I was about five or six years old. I wore my blue and white striped swimming trunks. Ray and I waded together into the surf at Jones Beach. Dad, wearing his baggy, light-blue bathing suit, patrolled the shoreline, ever-vigilant in case his boys were swallowed whole by the Atlantic. Ray and I body-surfed in the waves and sand filled our bathing suits. I remember running up to the water's edge as the sea reeled back. A wall of water climbed over my head, and a wave swooped down and dragged me under.

I looked up from beneath the surface. The roiling water clouded my vision. Sand, seaweed, foam, and sunlight mixed into a smeared canvass before me. In my confusion and fright, I saw a familiar pair of eyeglasses and light-blue trunks. Dad's giant hand reached underwater, and he grabbed me by the arm and pulled me out of the ocean. I had probably landed in just about a foot of water. If I stood up, I would have been out of danger. However, I was a kid. For me, this was as treacherous as a day at the beach could get. Dad saved me with his powerful hands.

My grown-up hands were smaller than his. I had not the strength or stature of my father. At that moment, I wanted to do nothing more than to reach out to him in his bed and pull him back to life. If I could have rescued him from the dark shoals of the afterlife he crept toward in those final hours, I would have done so. Instead, I ran away and instructed a nun to give him permission to die.

I stood and reached into my pocket for my cell phone. Cindy had texted me saying that she was on the way. Ray would be getting jittery without me around. Like Dad would have done, I straightened up, filled my chest with air, and marched back into the lobby. The folks darting around the hallway dimmed into the background as I focused on the far side of the hall where my father's room was. I paused at the door. Once more, I took a deep breath. My father waited for me, and I knew he could hear my voice. It was time for me to let him go.

Chapter 28

May 7th, 2009, 3:00 PM

Ray went home to his wife, Linda, and their kids. As much as he wanted to stay, I could sense that he did not want to witness Dad dying. Mandy had gone to work but promised to return to the hospital if anything had changed. Cindy arrived soon after Ray had left. I was relieved when I saw her enter the room. I did not want to be alone with Dad. The fear of being the only one with him during his final moments gripped me up until then.

My eyes were red and swollen from tears. I wanted to be tough, not show emotion, but I could not help it. Each time I felt the urge to cry a nurse came in to do this or that. It was awkward. The medical staff in that unit were accustomed to witnessing bedside vigils and the grief families experienced while watching their loved ones perish. But I did not want to shed tears in front of anyone who was not family. Thankfully, Dad had the room to himself. I sat in the chair next to his bed and let my mind wander. Dad continued with his sonorous breathing.

Ron and Larissa had been texting me through the night, asking how Dad was doing. They weren't together. Larissa had asked for a separation after our encounter. Ron had been aware of her plan to have me impregnate her. He went along with it because he wanted to keep her, and to do that he had to abide by her wish to be a mother. In the end, their differences were considerable. Ron and I were finished as partners as well. Ron transferred to a different precinct, and we had not seen each other since. The only reason we stayed in touch was that he called me to keep current with my father's condition. I suspected that after my father passed away, we would have no desire to remain friends, if that were at all possible considering I had fooled around with his wife. Mandy had found out what had happened and had a ho-hum reaction. As I suspected, she and Ron had been having a flirting relationship that had just about became a reality. Mandy confessed that she had feelings for Ron and that they had kissed once, but it had never gone further. Since I did not have a leg to stand on, I let it go. Mandy and I lived together, but our lives went on separately. I left a rose on the kitchen counter with a small love note a few days after she learned of my tryst with Larissa. She kissed me and said thank you. That was it. I wished she would have become enraged and stormed out of the house with her clothes in a suitcase, but she did not.

My daughter, Judith, was on a red-eye from Florida. I had called the night before and told her what was happening, and she had said she would hop on the first plane to New York. I insisted that she stay home, but she wanted to be there with her grandfather and me.

Shame. That was the overwhelming sentiment I experienced as I recounted the past few months of my life. My father spent fifty-three years with the same woman. He dedicated himself to aiding her during her lengthy illness and comforting her in her final hours. And there I was, the father of a daughter out of wedlock with a sham of a marriage to a woman whom I had cheated on and who had cheated on me. I had betrayed my best friend and partner. All my life I had venerated my father. I had idolized him for his courage and for his service. He was a devout Catholic, a man of profound faith. While he had flaws, few could say that he was anything less than an honest, devoted family man.

There was not a single characteristic of his that I had inherited. Yet he still loved me. Each day that I visited him in the nursing home he would tell me another story from his youth or about the war, as if he was passing along a legacy. He shared with me details that he never conveyed to anyone else. There were conversations he had with his mother, orders from his sergeants that came with bullets whizzing past their heads, and moments alone with his dad retold from his childhood.

I thought of my grandfather, Alphonse, and his nefarious life. He ran a numbers racket, smuggled whiskey and gin during Prohibition and was a loan shark who broke the arms and legs of deadbeats. Yet my father survived the war and led an honest life despite his upbringing. His faith was born on a stretcher as he was hoisted over a shallow grave, ready to be tossed in to keep him and the others who had been killed in action from stinking in the Italian sun. And what did I do with the example he had set? What sort of model did I make for my daughter? My heart sank.

Dad had told me that each Christmas he would sit in his room, away from Mom and the rest of us, and cry for his father. On December 15th, 1937, my father learned that his dad had passed away in the hospital. At the age of twelve, he had lost his hero. No doubt my father loved his dad profoundly and admired him.

My grandmother had told me how Alphonse had been struck down by illness. I had asked her one Christmas Eve when she was visiting us how my grandfather had died. Such a feared and strong man was no match for diseases, I had thought. I knew that Dad was saddened each holiday because he had lost his father just before the holiday. Grandma sat on the couch in our living room and patted the cushion next to her, motioning for me to sit. I climbed up to listen to her. She looked down the hall towards my parent's bedroom. The door was closed. Dad was in there alone. My mother was in the kitchen, cooking dinner. Finally, my grandmother told me how Alphonse had passed away.

Grandma said that diabetes had reduced Alphonse to a withered man. His legs became gangrenous and were amputated. She told me that on the day he died she had walked home from the hospital. She turned the corner on their block and saw my father sitting on their front stoop. It was almost three o'clock in the afternoon. The sun was low in the sky, and Dad wanted to play with his buddies. He had put on his coat and hat and had ventured outside, even though my grandmother told him to wait inside the house. After a half hour or so of sitting on the stoop with his knees up and his arms folded, shivering in the cold, he saw his mother down the block. She had her head down and held her purse in both hands. Dad watched her approach quickly. He got up and stood on the sidewalk. He shielded his eyes from the sun with his right hand and waved to her with his other. She saw him and stopped. Her shoulders sagged, and she placed her hand over her mouth. Then she straightened herself and continued towards him. Dad ran to greet her.

"Hi mom! When is Dad coming home?" My father halted in front of her. His mom wiped her eyes with a handkerchief and sniffled.

"Eugene, your father will not be coming home."

"Is he coming home soon? He's going to miss Christmas!" Dad shoved his hands into his coat pockets and breathed hard. He sensed something was troubling his mother. She placed her hand on his shoulder.

"Eugene, something terrible has happened."

"What mom?" His voice quavered.

"Your father died today." She knelt and hugged him. She cried softly, her cheek to his. She kissed the top of his head. Dad held her tight and wept. Finally, he broke away from her.

"No! It's not true. Daddy is tough. He's strong, and everyone is afraid of him. He's not dead. I don't believe you!" My father turned and ran down the block toward the florist.

"Eugene! Come back here. Come back now!" she called after him. My father reached the corner, and he stopped. He looked back. His mom waved to him, beckoning him to return.

The sound of a car door closing startled him. He looked toward the street and saw a big, black sedan parked at the curb. Mr. Molfetta gestured to him.

"Eugene come here. Why are you running so fast? Your mother, she is calling you." He leaned forward with his hand out. Dad eyed Mr. Molfetta. His mind swirled with images of him and his father visiting Mr. Molfetta and his wife on Sundays. Tears fell from his eyes. He panted hard, sucking in air through an open mouth.

"Eugene, I will walk you back to your mother. Come to me," said Mr. Molfetta. Dad did not move.

"Eugene come to me. What is wrong? Why do you cry?"

Dad balled his fists. "My father died!"

He turned and ran back down the block towards his mother and kept yelling.

"My father died. My father died!" my dad hollered until he met up with his mother. She caught him in her arms.

"Come inside, Eugene. Come inside. You're making a scene. Your dad would not like that," she said. She held his hand. Together they climbed the steps to the front door and entered their home.

Grandma said that Dad did not want any presents for Christmas, and that she did not want to celebrate the holiday herself. Every Christmas for the rest of Dad's life was bittersweet.

The door behind me opened, and I turned around, expecting to see a doctor or a nurse. Cindy walked in and stood beside me. She placed her arm around me and rested her cheek on my shoulder. Then she let go of me. Cindy looked down at Dad. I did as well. His breathing had slowed considerably. Dad's mouth opened, his false teeth had been taken out by the nurses, and his lips curled inward.

"Oh, my God. Something's happening!" Cindy wailed. She placed her hand over her mouth. Dad's breathing stopped. After a few seconds, he took another breath. I could hear the death rattle in his lungs.

"I'm getting a nurse," Cindy said. Then she turned and left the room.

"Cindy wait." I turned toward the door. She either ignored me or did not listen. I watched her make a right turn in the direction of the nurses' desk. She was gone for at least two minutes. In the period, Dad's breathing became more tortured. With each exhale, he groaned. I held his hand and leaned close to him. I wiped my eyes with a tissue I took from a box on the night table, and then I kissed his forehead.

"It's okay, Dad. You can go now. Mom is waiting for you." I hoped that he could hear me. I had read that one's sense of hearing is the last to go before death.

"Do something. He's dying," Cindy said. She had returned. I looked back at her. Cindy's cheeks were red, tears flowed down her face, and her voice cracked. A young nurse, a girl with blond hair pulled back, entered. I had not seen her before, but her eyes displayed empathy. I stepped aside to allow her to pass. She checked my father's IV line and eyed the heart monitor overhead.

"I'll see what the doctor prescribed for him that will make him more comfortable," she said. She smiled in a polite, reassuring way.

"He's dying, Cindy. You must tell him it's okay. He's hanging on for us," I said.

Cindy snatched a tissue from the box and blew her nose.

"I can't. I'm not ready."

"Cindy," I said. I put my hand on her shoulder.

"I have to go outside. Jeffrey wants to know how his grandfather is. He wanted to be here, but I told him to go to work." Cindy sobbed. Her breathing quickened, and she removed her cell phone from the back pocket of her jeans. Then she took a deep breath and closed her eyes. Cindy leaned over and kissed Dad's cheek.

"I love you, Dad. You were the best father. Mommy is waiting for you in Heaven." Her voice warbled. She straightened herself and then faltered. I placed my arm around her.

At that moment, Dad's breathing paused. His eyes closed, and his lips moved a little.

"Dad! Oh no, Dad. I love you, I'll always be your little girl." Cindy broke down and hugged me. I could not help but let my tears flow.

"Goodbye, Dad. You're my hero," I said. My voice cracked, and I sniffed hard. Cindy and I stood for a few moments, consoling each other. Finally, the nurse returned. This time, a young woman followed her. She was the doctor. She wore green scrubs, her light brown hair was in a ponytail, and she had a stethoscope draped around her neck. Cindy and I both stepped away and went to the foot of the bed to allow the doctor to examine our father. I looked away. Dad appeared small then. He had loomed so large in my life from when I was a child to the moment of his last breath that I could not imagine him struck down by death. He survived combat—nearly buried alive—and now he was gone. I wondered if he believed he deserved to die with dignity, with his children at his side in a hospital when his buddies met their fates in combat as teenagers.

"I'm so sorry," the doctor said. She clasped her hands in front of her. "Your father is gone. I can arrange to have the chaplain come by, and you're both welcome to stay here for a while. I'm sure you'll want to have family come to see him," she said.

My cell phone vibrated in my pocket, a text from Ray. There were others from Mandy, Ron, and of course, Larissa.

"Excuse me, doctor. I have to call my brother." I nodded to her and left the room. As I walked out, I watched Cindy typing on her phone. I was sure it was to her son, Jeffrey.

My thoughts became a blur as I wandered the halls and found the way to the parking lot. The sky was clear, and the weather was mild. I walked about fifty feet or so from the entrance for privacy. I called Ray first.

"What's happening?" Ray breathed fast. I knew he was driving to the hospital.

"Ray, he's gone."

"What? Oh no. Come on, Mike. I'm almost there. He's really gone?"

"Yeah Ray. Just a few minutes ago he went quietly." I wiped my eyes with a crumpled tissue that I pulled from my pocket. Ray did not speak, but I heard him sobbing.

"Oh, God. I wanted to be there," Ray said. His voice was strained. "Is he still in the room? Can I see him?"

"Yes, the doctor said she is giving us time for the family to get here before, you know, they take him to the morgue."

"Don't say that. Don't say *the morgue* like it's a coffee shop or a library. I know you're a cop and you're used to saying that, but I don't want to imagine Dad stuffed into a refrigerator." Ray's voice was harsh, scolding me.

"I'm sorry. Look, let's not argue. We have to get through this together," I said. I paced back and forth on the sidewalk. A man walking past me a few yards away stared in my direction as if I were making a spectacle of myself. I turned my back to him.

"Forget it. I'm upset. I'm sorry for snapping at you. I can't believe he's dead. We all knew it was going to happen, but you never prepare yourself for when it does," said Ray. He wept aloud, sobbing uncontrollably.

"Don't apologize, Ray. You're my brother, and I love you. You're almost here, so don't drive fast. You got it? I'll be here and so will Cindy. We'll say goodbye to him together. He's with Mom now." The words came out of my mouth, but unlike when my father spoke, there was no conviction backing them. I wanted to console Ray. One of my biggest regrets was not having the same faith in God that my father did. It was another aspect of my life that I deemed not to measure up to him.

"I love you too, Mike. Let me hang up. I'll see you in a few."

"Sure thing. Just be careful," I said.

"Hey, would it be wrong if I pulled into the 7-Eleven and got a cup of coffee to calm down? I want to call Linda and tell her what's going on. She'll have to break it to the kids."

"It would be wrong if you didn't buy both Cindy and me coffee," I said with a chuckle.

"Okay. I'll be there soon," he said. Then he hung up.

While talking to Ray, my text messages were piling up. I called Mandy.

"Hi Mike." She sounded like she was answering the call on any ordinary day.

"Hi hon. Dad passed away a few minutes ago,"

She took a deep breath.

"Aw, I'm sorry, Mike. I loved your father. Are Ray and Cindy there?"

"Cindy is. Ray will be here in a few minutes." I did my best to hold my weeping in check. I felt the world was watching me, so I headed for the privacy of my car at the far end of the lot.

"All right, I'll shower and get ready. I'll see you in about an hour, hour and a half," she said. She could not sound anymore nonchalant.

"Don't bother. I won't be here that long. Ray and I have to go to the funeral home and get things rolling." I used the key fob to unlock my doors, and I climbed in behind the wheel. After shutting the door, I turned on the engine, the air conditioning and news radio turned low. The voices in the background offered me some comfort.

"Oh, okay. Then I won't come by. Where's the funeral home?" Mandy sounded peeved, but I did not care.

"The same place where my mother was laid out," I said.

"The place on Park Avenue?"

"That's it," I said. I did not want to be so short with her, but I could not understand why she was not more upset.

"Okay then. I'll see you soon. Send me a text when you get there. I'll call Ron," she said.

"I will call Ron." I snapped at her. "Mandy, I'm sorry. I'm just a bit emotional, that's all." I pursed my lips together.

"It's okay, Mike. It's okay. I'm your wife. I'm here for you. Go do what you must. I'll meet you at the funeral home."

"Sure, thanks. I'll let you know when we get there." I lowered my seat back and placed the phone on speaker. We did not speak for what seemed like a solid minute.

"You'd better get going. I'm going to get in the shower," she said.

"Yes, you do that," I said, choking back tears.

"Mike?"

"Yeah, Mandy?"

"I really am sorry about your dad. He treated me like I was one of his own. I'll miss him."

"Thank you," I said. Then she hung up.

I tossed my cell onto the passenger seat and opened the window. The fresh air wafted in and offered gentle relief from my anguish. I picked up the smartphone again and read Ron's messages pleading for an update. I typed in a reply.

My dad passed away a few minutes ago. Then I hit send.

Without thinking, I called Larissa. She answered on the first ring.

"Mike," she said, nearly out of breath.

"He's gone," I said. This time I allowed myself to cry.

"Oh, I am so sorry. I felt it. I could tell that he passed away. Oh, Mike, Mike," Larissa cried. We both sobbed for a few moments, then Larissa spoke.

"Where are you? At the hospital?"

"Yes, I'm with Cindy. Ray is almost here."

"And Mandy?" Larissa's voice quavered.

"She's going to meet us at the funeral home on Park Avenue, where my mom was," I said.

"Do you want me to meet you there? I'm running to my car now." Larissa sounded like she was indeed sprinting.

"Yes, yes I do want you there. It would mean the world, but slow down, don't get killed." I smiled. I don't know why, but I did.

"Okay, I'll go slow, but I'll be there for you," she said.

"You already are, Larissa. You have been for a while."

"That's sweet, Mike. You're a good friend."

"Larissa, you are as well." I bit my lower lip.

"I love you, Mike. I'll see you soon," she said.

"I love you too." The call ended, and I slipped the phone into my front pocket. After I rolled the window back up, I lowered the air conditioning. The fan was too loud, and the sound annoyed me. For some time, I sat still, listening to sports radio. The broadcaster's words did not register with me and neither did the commercials and their accompanying jingles. My eyes fixed on the entrance to the parking lot. After a while, I saw Ray pull in. Cindy was all alone in the room with Dad, and I should go back inside. I shut off the engine, got out of the car, closed the door, and walked over to meet Ray. Dad's passing had an immediate effect. Suddenly I, Ray, and Cindy were the elders. We no longer had wise parents to call to help solve a problem or for advice on raising kids. We were the ones to set the example and pave the way. I was not sure what would happen with Mandy and me, but I was determined to make a better connection with Judith.

Ray saw me and waved. I raised my hand to acknowledge him. As I approached, I took my cell phone and unlocked the screen. I opened the messages and scanned the last one that I had sent to Ron. I read the words and their bleak, unmistakable meaning. Around me, families and friends of other patients meandered in and out of my hazy perspective. I breathed hard, each step was calculated, and I placed my hand over my racing heart. I considered the impact of what had just happened. I was a father, a husband, a police officer, a brother, and the son of a man about whom I had just begun to reminisce. My father died.

Epilogue

In the weeks since Dad passed away, much had happened. Ron and Larissa filed for divorce. Mandy asked for a separation, and then she moved into a new apartment with Ron. Larissa and I remained friends, but she surprised me when she announced that she was moving to Florida to live with her mom. I told her that I would miss her, but I assured her that I would see her more than she imagined.

My daughter, Judith, was my inspiration to improve myself. I had been such an absentee dad that it sounded like I was reciting a line from a familiar movie whenever I uttered those words. After the wake and the funeral, I told her all that had happened between Mandy, Larissa, and I. Also, I made sure to explain how ashamed of myself I was for my entire life. Judith told me that she was willing to give me the chance that I had requested to become a better father to her. My retirement date was coming up soon, and I wanted to sell the house, split everything with Mandy, and move to Florida to be closer to Judith. It was a happy accident that I would be close to Larissa.

Ray and Cindy planned the estate sale at Dad's house. For a week, we separated what we wanted to sell from what we wanted to keep. Clothing that belonged to our parents were sorted into three folded stacks: what we wished to sell, donate, or keep. The keep pile was considerably smaller than the rest, but Cindy insisted on preserving some of Mom and Dad's nicer clothes as keepsakes. Boxes of knick-knacks, furniture, and hundreds of books were priced for sale. As the three of us rummaged through the house, we joked that we might stumble across some hidden treasure that Dad or Mom might have squirreled away and forgotten about. Then I remembered something. My heart jumped as I recalled the item I wished to retrieve from somewhere within the walls of their home. I started my own search.

First, I combed through all the books in the cubby under the stairs. Then I used a flashlight to hunt along the crawlspace. I checked every closet and my father's armoire.

"What the hell are you looking for?" Ray asked. For three days, I tore the house apart, neglecting my duties in helping Cindy and Ray prepare for the yard sale. It was Saturday morning, an hour before we were open for business.

"I'll let you know when I find it," I said.

"There's no hidden treasure. We were joking," Ray said.

"I'm curious to know what it is that's got you so focused. Go ahead. Get whatever it is." Ray smiled and picked up a folding table. "Just don't run off with it. It belongs to all of us," he said. Then he went outside with a folding table in his hands. I went back upstairs with the flashlight and into the darkened crawlspace one more time. Ray and I had already cleared everything out, and I was wasting my time. I was hoping that there would be one more carton, an overlooked box that would contain the item I sought so desperately.

In disgust, I backed out and sat on my old bed. The comforter and linens were stripped from it, and there was just a mattress. I rested there, dripping with sweat, shoulders slumped and covered in cobwebs. Across the room, I eyed Ray's bookcase. On its shelves were some of his old college textbooks and some paperbacks. I got up and walked over quickly. I pulled the dozen or so volumes from the top shelf. It wasn't there. The second shelf yielded no results. I knelt and removed the remaining texts. My heart pounded, sweat dripped into my eyes. I wiped them with my hand. Then I saw it. It was the book that had intrigued me since I was a kid and that had launched me on a journey to investigate my father's military history for most of my adult life.

I walked back to my bed and held it in both hands. Mixed with my beads of sweat were tears. I used my tee shirt to wipe my face. I wanted to show Ray. Downstairs, I walked through the living room and paused by the storm door. Through the window, I saw Ray and Cindy working at the tables. Cars were lined up and down the street, and about fifteen or twenty people wandered around the driveway examining a lifetime of my parent's belongings. I took a deep breath and wiped my nose with my bare arm. Then I stepped outside.

"There you are. I thought you were taking a nap," Ray said.

I walked over to him. Three lawn chairs were set up behind a folding table next to where Ray stood by the garage. I placed the book down and sat.

"That's it? That's what you were on a mission to find, a book?" Ray stood next to me.

"Do you know what this is?" I asked.

Ray examined the cover. "Oh yeah. I remember that book. Wow, I can't believe he still had it. I thought he threw it out or something," Ray said.

"Why would he do that?" I crossed my legs and raised an eyebrow.

"I don't know. I'm just saying. He hadn't looked at it in years." Ray watched the crowd with his hands on his hips.

"Ray, can I have this? It means a lot." I touched the cover with my fingers.

"Of course, you were the one who was interested in all the history. Hell, you got the congressman to give Dad his Purple Heart. That belongs to you now. I'm sure Cindy won't mind." Ray turned his attention to a customer who approached.

"How much is this?" an old man asked. He held up a set of screwdrivers Dad had kept in his toolbox.

"You can have them for a dollar," Ray said.

"Nah," the man said. He dropped them like they were a pack of spoiled meat he had discovered in his freezer.

"What's this book? The Fighting 36th? Is that from World War II?" The old man reached for the hardcover, but I grabbed it first.

"I'm sorry. This is mine. We have other books on the table over there." I pointed down the driveway.

"Excuse *me*," he said as if I had insulted him.

"Were you in the army?" the man asked me. He had a patronizing tone, as though he were questioning my right to own such a book. I stared at him. He was probably in his late seventies. Perhaps a Korean War Veteran. Most likely, he had served in one of the branches of the armed services. I could make no such claim.

"Did you serve in the military?" the man persisted.

"The book belonged to our father," Ray said. "He was in the army during World War II. It's a special book." Ray walked around the table and drew the man's attention away from me.

"Our dad fought in Italy as part of the Italian Campaign. That book chronicles the history of the division he belonged to," Ray continued.

"That's very interesting. I'm sure he treasured it," the old man said. He looked back at me and nodded.

I watched Ray as he continued to engage the man, exalting him with tales he had heard my father tell us of his days in basic training when we were boys. It was odd listening to Ray, and I was impressed at his depth of knowledge about Dad's experiences during the war. For a while, I selfishly believed that Dad's story was my own. Somehow, due to my steep interest, I was the one qualified to provide the details of his service. I picked up the book and placed it on my lap.

I stared at the cover, which remained intimidating and unfamiliar. Bible black with the names of the dead recorded on the fading pages of history, it was a vivid relic. Now that I had recovered the book, I was reluctant to open it. Perhaps I was weary or maybe I needed more time to mourn my father's passing. My lifelong quest to understand the man I had loved and admired, yet had failed to measure up to, left me marked with dishonor. A part of me believed that my father would have told me that I did not have to be like him but to learn from his life. For some reason, I smiled. I would never see him again. Yet a bounty of treasure remained which I could touch, hold, and use to recall his enduring presence. I opened the book. Within the digest, there is a record of a battle on a bright afternoon in Italy where Gene had died and was born again in the heart of Velletri.

About the Author

Michael J. Kannengieser was born in 1963 in Amityville, Long Island. He was raised in the neighboring hamlet of Copiague. Michael became a member of the New York City Housing Authority Police Department on July 5th, 1989 which later merged in 1994 with the NYPD. After leaving the job in 1999, Michael worked at a private, performing arts college in their Information Technology Department. Michael departed in 2014 for employment in a large healthcare organization.

Michael has written two novels, "The Daddy Rock," and "Burning Blue," which were published by Decent Hill Publishing. "The Daddy Rock" is a police thriller about a cop who loses his wife and daughter to a drunk driver and then discovers that he has a daughter that he never knew he had from a previous relationship. "Burning Blue" is a horror novel about a cop who is shot in the line of duty and has a near-death experience. Instead of seeing the Pearly Gates, he sees Hell. Michael's latest book, "The Heart of Velletri," published by Dreaming Big Publications, is a departure from his previous police novels as the story centers around a man who reveres his father who is a World War II veteran and he is determined to discover the truth about his dad's military service.

Michael was the Managing editor for Fiction of the UK-based literary magazine, "The View from Here." The journal founded by UK author, Mike French, was an eclectic mix of fiction, essays, and interviews with interesting figures from the literary world. Michael's role was to comb through the multitudes of submissions for the finest short stories of up to ten-thousand words to be showcased in the magazine's "Front View for Fiction."

The Heart of Velletri

Michael lives on Long Island's north shore with his wife and two children. His dream is to continue writing and publishing novels that endure and entertain for years to come.

Made in the
USA
Columbia, SC